I0743830

awards for motley education

The Urd Saga, Book 1
(First Edition Published by Leap Books)

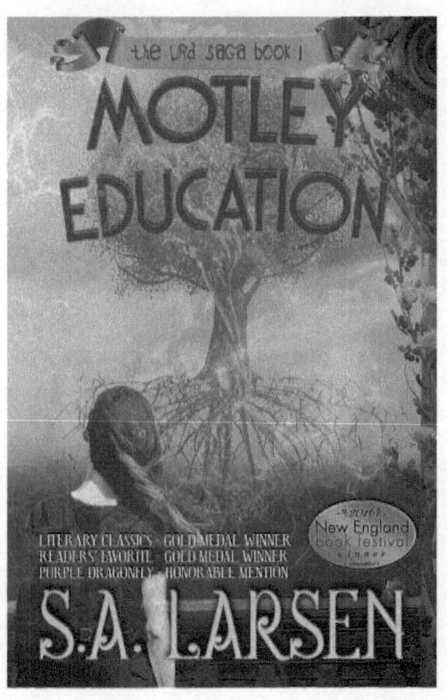

~ **First Place Winner** ~
2016 New England Book Festival for Best Children's
Fiction

~ **Gold Medal Winner** ~
2017 Readers' Favorite International Book Awards for
Children's Fantasy/Sci-Fi

~ **Gold Medal Winner** ~
2017 Literary Classics Book Awards for Juvenile/Grade
School Fantasy Fiction

~ Bronze Award Winner ~
2017 Feathered Quill Book Awards for Best Juvenile/YA
Fiction

~ Honorable Mention ~
2017 Purple Dragonfly Awards; Middle Grade ebook

PRAISE FOR MOTLEY EDUCATION

A Motley Education Book
The Urd Saga, Book 1

"A deftly crafted and consistently entertaining read from cover to cover! Indeed, *Motley Education* is certain to be an enduringly popular addition to elementary school and community library collections."

Midwest Book Reviews
Children's Bookwatch, May 2017

"A wonderful world full of dynamic characters, ever increasing intrigue, and imaginative worlds where amazing things happen! Motley Education is the perfect middle grade fantasy book to capture your attention and engage your imagination as you experience Norse mythology with Ebony and Fleishman. Quite engaging, which is perfect for the targeted age group, (and older readers as well!). I can't wait to see what comes next."

Readers' Favorite Reviews

"Full of thrilling twists and an intense battle between good and evil, this fast-paced tale, replete with magical beasts and lovable characters is a must read for young fans of paranormal fiction."

Literary Classics Reviews

"A great middle grade full of adventure. Fingers crossed for more!"

Casey Lyall
Author of the *Howard Wallace Series*

"My ten-year-old son read this book and LOVED it! He couldn't put it down! As a mother of boys, I'm always looking for good books that they love. This one is a winner!"

Kristin Smith
Amazon Bestselling Author of the *Catalyst Series*

"This middle grade fantasy is a perfect fall read! MOTLEY EDUCATION features a great friendship, wonderful world building, mythology and page turning adventure - I highly recommend it!"

Erin Cashman
Award-Winning Author of *The Exceptionals*

"This book is creepy, thrilling fun!"

Wendy MacKnight
Author of *It's A Mystery, Pig Face!*

"S.A. Larsen has created interesting characters, some good, some bad, which is as it should be, that are typical kids, except for their special powers. The author describes the scenes so vividly, it was almost like I was there. MOTLEY EDUCATION would make a nice addition to school classrooms and libraries (where students might wish they attended such a school as Motley Jr. High), as well as public libraries and your own. Recommended."

BJ Reviews

"I like a good mystery with a paranormal twist and this book does not disappoint! The characters are well-developed, the story is clever, and there are just enough surprises to make you gasp with delight. Middle grade readers looking for a fresh dose of magic will love this book!"

Lisa Schmid
Author of *Ollie Oxley and the Ghost*
"Author S.A. Larsen punctuates the tale with humor

and heart, creating a fantasy tale sure to entertain middle grade readers."

Cynthia Reeg
Author of *From the Grave Series*

"What an adventure full of humor, heart and horror! . . . incredibly imaginative and inventive. Kids in upper elementary will love this!"

Shari L. Schwarz
Author of *Treasure at Lure Lake*

"You spend much of the book biting your lip wondering who is good and who is bad. The ending is satisfying and sets up nicely for a series. Recommended for readers who like fast-paced adventure, mythology, or magic."

Kai Strand
Author of *King of Bad* and *The Weaver Tales*

DEAD

ALLEY

a
MOTLEY EDUCATION
book

The Urd Saga. Book 2

S.A. LARSEN

DEAD ALLEY

S.A. Larsen

Ellysian Press

www.ellysianpress.com

DEAD ALLEY
© Copyright S.A. Larsen 2023. All rights reserved.

Print ISBN: 13: 978-1-941637-83-8
First Edition

Editor: Maer Wilson, M Joseph Murphy
Cover Art:

Ebooks/Books are not transferable. They cannot be sold, shared, or given away, as this is an infringement on the copyright of this work.

All Rights Are Reserved. No part of this book may be used or reproduced in any manner whatsoever without written permission, except in the case of brief quotations embodied in critical articles and reviews.

This book is a work of fiction. The names, characters, places, and incidents are products of the writer's imagination or have been used fictitiously and are not to be construed as real. Any resemblance to persons, living or dead, actual events, locale or organizations is entirely coincidental.

~ special note ~

WELCOME TO THE WORLD OF YGGDRASIL!

Within these pages you will find a host of mythical creatures, enchanted lands, and gifted characters anxious to guide you through the magic of The Nine Worlds. But beware: all is not always as it seems. Dangers lurk in unsuspecting corners, and clues to mysteries will try to confuse you. Before you begin your journey, here are a few important things to keep in mind. Yggdrasil, also called the Tree of Life or the World Tree, has branches stretching beyond all of existence and roots that plunge to the depths of the cosmos. The Nine Worlds rest in its branches.

~ SPECIAL NOTE ~
For even more background, flip to the back of this book to discover intriguing Yggdrasil facts and mind-boggling whatnot. Plus, take the quiz to find out what Seven Discipline you are assigned to join!

For even more <u>fun information</u>, flip to the back of this book to discover intriguing Yggdrasil facts and mind-boggling whatnot. Plus, take the quiz to find out whether you're a Luminary or a Sensory.

~ Map of Yggdrasil ~

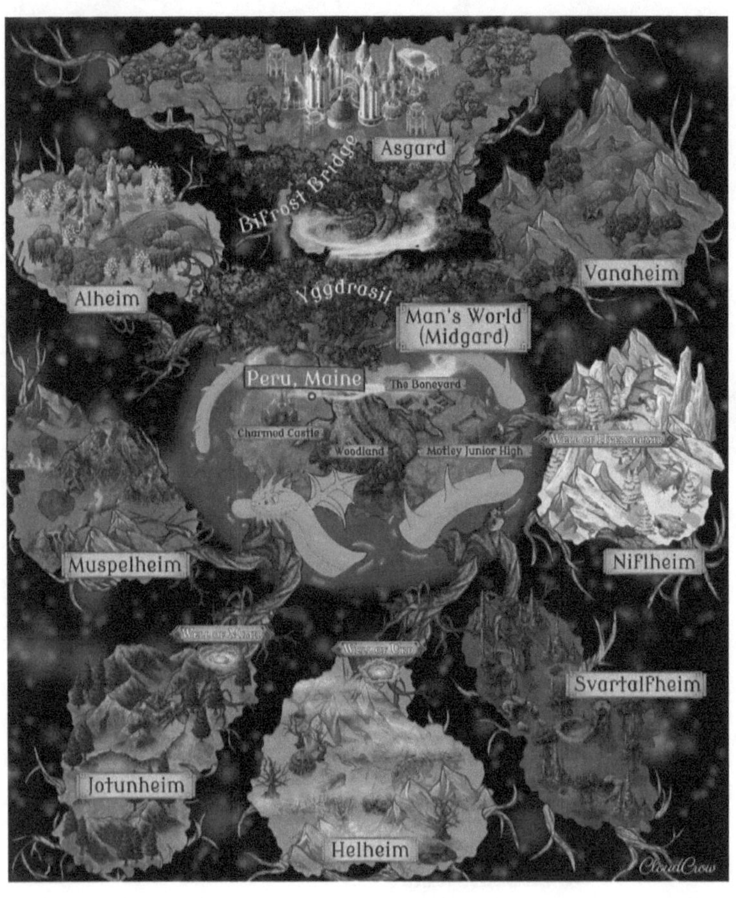

~Cast of Characters~

Main Characters

Ebony Charmed – Keeper of the Doors
Will Fleishman – Ebony's best friend & assistant
Lance McGyver – Live boy, but currently in spirit form
Rita Charmed – Ebony's mom
Ethan Charmed – Ebony's brother
Dan Charmed – Ebony's dad
Gladys & Gertrude – Ebony's twin aunts
Regina (Bat-Face) – Motley Headmistress
Seronious Bile – Dean of Njord Academy

Motley Students

Aiden Jones
Cain Erickson (Nickname: Erickson)
Cermet Hayes
Charity & Clare (Cheerio Twins)
Dakota Olson
Clint Dawson (Nickname: Dawson)
Dwayne
Glinda
Jacob
Jed
Magdalen Priest
Molly Warner
Quinn Olson

Njord Students

Aurelia
Marcus

etiquettes for spirit tracking

~ ETIQUETTES FOR THE ART OF SPIRIT TRACKING ~

1. One must never seek out a spirit not ready to move on.

2. One must never guide a spirit with your emotions.

3. One must never, ever make promises to the spirit world.

4. One must never attempt to help more than one spirit at a time.

5. One must never challenge or threaten a spirit.

6. One must give a hardy welcome to spirits when they make themselves known to you.

7. One must always thank spirits for talking with you.

8. One must always make sure to wear rubber shoes, when tapping into ghostly energy.

9. One must survey the surroundings for extraneous energy a spirit could connect with.

10. One must be diligent and courageous once you make the decision to aid a spirit.

R.I.P.

MOTLEY JUNIOR HIGH

FOR THE PSYCHICALLY AND CELESTIALLY GIFTED

Terms for Enrollment

Please read the following conditions set forth by the Council of Mentors through the Motley Code of Conduct. Your signature is needed to start the registration process.

As an enrollee at MJH, you attest to exhibiting skills from either our Sensory or Luminary group and agree to be classified as such.

Sensory students must exhibit psychic skills, such as bending metal or channeling spirits. Although, performing the two together is frowned upon. Spirits wound in metal can become testy and untangling them can be tough.

Luminary students must have an appreciation for the stars and life energy, and have an aptitude for crystals, charms, and potions. *Conjuring spells or energy to get rid of a sibling is strictly prohibited.

Note: Subgroups may be needed as students grow in skill and understanding, so nothing is etched in stone. Well, unless your name is found on a tombstone, which you'd have to take up with Keeper Coffer, our graveyard groundsmen. He's a bit hard of hearing so yell loudly.

Lastly, and most importantly, if you ever find yourself chased by a fire giant – which is totally absurd, but our legal team insists we add a disclaimer – don't hide. They have huge nostrils with which to sniff you out. It doesn't matter if you smell of perfume or poo, they will find you. Instead . . . RUN! But please avoid the boneyard out back of the school. Messing with the dead can cause all sorts of problems. See #1.

Enrollee: <u>Ebony Charmed</u>
Witnessed: <u>*Headmistress Regina*</u>

dedication

For Josh, Jake, & Kate . . .
my lights in the darkness.
And for Jesus & Mary . . .
Thank You.

chapter

one

The Mist

Out of the shadows stretched a crooked finger; shiny metal coiling around it to form a ring.

The ruby gemstone atop its center flared to life. Twig-like prongs sprouted from its sides and slinked along two bony knuckles to sheath a jagged fingernail in silver. The tip was so sharp that by the time you noticed it prick your skin, it would have sunk to half its length. And that night, it already glistened in red wetness.

The scent of moss hung heavily in the air. Stillness coated every surface, silence, for all lay bound by an ageless slumber. A woman paused at the threshold of a crypt. She scrunched up her nose, sniffing to the left and to the right. Ah, there it was – the lingering aroma of a location spell that had breached the ancient doorway.

A doorway meant to remain closed.

Dust and decay fell away as she descended the steps. Forgotten runes and sigils carved in the granite blazed with life. A breeze struck the mangled whispers and secrets hidden in her hair, horrors of Nature's disasters and Man's mistakes. She was the epitome of a hoarder. And she'd grown to enjoy it.

Pressing her leather sandals to the ground, boney twigs crunched in the crisp air. The goatskin pouch at her waist bounced against her hip; coins clanked from inside. Ragged ends of her drab gown clawed at the brittle grass until she stepped onto the dirt pathway. She pointed the sheath covering her finger and sliced it through the air, snipping a tail of mist. The mist stiffened.

"Sleep," blew breathily from her parched mouth. "Pay the debt owed me."

The tail of mist grew limp and coiled around her nail, its siphon of life. It contorted, surrendering its youth. At the flick of her finger, the mist slipped off, drifting downward to a patch of crippled twigs to lay still as though asleep.

She continued along the path and spotted what she'd been looking for. Dusty soil swirled beneath her sandals as she stopped. The wall of greenery wasn't nearly as alive as she'd remembered. With a whirl of her ringless hand, saggy leaves stretched their veins. Thin twigs thickened and slithered along each other, forming chunky knots. Lethargic rose petals inhaled and multiplied. She couldn't believe this place had remained in slumber with the boundary in such weak condition. But she was here. So no worries.

A murder of crows circled the sky above her. A few flitted down to stalk a hole in a rotten tree stump. Wings thrust up and out, each bullying the other for first dibs on their awaited prey. Two broke free and waddled to the woman's feet.

Life and all its curious wonders, she thought. *But curiosity can be dangerous.*

She bent over and plunged her metal nail through the torso of one bird, plucking it off the ground. The helpless creature whirled its wings in a flurry. Hoarse clicks and caws erupted from its beak. Silky, black feathers wafted against the breast of her gown. The woman patted her poor victim, her touch reducing the blackness of feathers to lifeless gray. Muscles hardened. Hollow bones filled. Eye sockets widened, and blackened pupils faded.

The crow craned its head back and gazed paralyzed into the face of its future.

"Live, my undead friend," the woman whispered.

She extracted her metal nail and released the crow as the second one wobbled to meet its friend. The undead crow pecked at the healthy one, its fate the same as the first. More crows heeded her call. Raising her arms, she splayed her fingers sending a subtle yet aggressive command. Undead crows took to the sky.

A grin caught her wrinkled lips. Basking in her accomplishment was premature, and she took pride in her work, despite her current appearance. It mattered not how others saw her. Or so she told herself. Duty called regardless of the darkness, for darkness was where she lived.

The ruby stone in her ring sunk into the facade of metal. Tension tugged the gears. Twiggy prongs retracted, returning to their resting place on either side of the stone. The woman gazed up at the night sky and hooded her head with her shawl. She summoned the energy around her. Her lips twitched with a smirk this time. Spirit trackers were never much good at covering their travels, at least not from her. Now, to follow this fresh trail to the girl with blue streaking her hair and the clumsy boy with a gifted lizard . . .

ChapteR

twO

Boneyard Training

he ghost of a toddler boy tip-toed between graves in the middle of the boneyard. Streams of fluffy fog ballooned outward with each of his steps, his thumb suckled in his mouth, his teddy bear pressed against his chest.

Ebony observed his movements from behind a weeping willow tree; Fleishman flanked her left, the cage housing his legless lizard Nigel swaying at his side.

"Description?" Fleishman whispered.

She finished jotting down notes in the journal Mentor Ursula Von Dufort had given her and leaned into Fleishman a little more, her touch sharing her ability to see ghosts. She should pay heed to the thickness of the boy's transparency or any dulling of his clothes. But all she could do was inhale the bubble bath scent lingering from his recently departed body and wonder what happened to him? Being a spirit tracker with skills that actually work was complicated.

"Type One, Independent Ghost Category, Subsection A," she answered.

"Meaning?"

She smiled at his thoroughness. "The boy is an average, harmless ghost looking to crossover."

"Maybe, or he could be an extra-celestial ready to drown us in slime," he said. "Again."

Point taken. Sure, the accidental sliming last week by a ghost turned nightmare had been a surprise. Who knew ghost vomit could be so powerful? And messy.

"I should check." Ebony flipped to her Hierarchy of Spirits & Ghosts chart.

A crow landed on a branch of the willow tree. It released a loud caw, which set off a shiver that crawled up Fleishman's arm and sent a vibration through Ebony. The fact that he was so easily spooked did not mingle well with their official job as spirit trackers, but he made do. His loyalty to her was endearing.

Another crow swept up to the branch and croaked at the first crow. Wings flapped. The birds paused; beaks tipped down at Ebony. If she didn't know better, she might think these birds were watching them. One crow lifted off the branch and batted at the other, croaks and caws mingling into a chorus, until the first crow soared into the sky trailed by the second.

Ebony broke touch with Fleishman to trace the birds' exit.

"What are you doing?" He flailed his hand out to grab her but missed as she hopped up on a stone bench nearby to see better. "Did you forget about the toddler ghost?"

"Of course not," she sighed.

The toddler dropped his teddy bear at his feet to plunge

his hand through a pile of fallen leaves. He tried to toss leaves at Ebony. She scrunched up her nose in a funny face, and he plucked his thumb from his mouth. A huge smile lit up his chubby face. His cuteness made her all warm inside.

Etiquette #2 from the Art of Spirit Tracking:
Never guide a spirit with your emotions.

She did her best to squelch her feelings for this tiny tot. It was hard, though. She refocused.

"The boy's form is clear with no foul odor attached, the pressure from his ghost weight on the ground is normal, and his inability to move corporal objects tells me he's still new." She set her voice to drone and continued. "He's still in ghost form because he hasn't crossed over for the first time. Once he does and his soul is refreshed, he'll be in spirit form, and no trouble to us."

The stunned expression on Fleishman's face was priceless.

"I mean, some returning spirits still go bad, but not as many," she said. "Did you know our souls get dirty while we're living?"

"You've been studying without me." Fleishman beamed.

She'd made him happy. That was good.

An otherworldly thread of energy, faint so most likely a reluctant spirit, brushed across her back.

Etiquette #1 in the Art of Spirit Tracking:
Never seek out a spirit not ready to move on.

According to the rules, she should ignore it.

A throaty howl echoed from the far field beyond the boneyard and up Ash Pathway to swirl around Ebony's new sensitivity to ghosts. That, on the other hand, she probably shouldn't ignore.

"Uh, Fleishman." Spotting wispy ghosts wandering by the tree line, she waved him closer and touched his arm. She referenced her chart and decided those ghosts were phantoms.

"Whoa," Fleishman began, "we've never seen that many Fades together before."

Cheese Whiz. "Fades, that's what I was going to say."

Tattered cloth fanned off the Fades, their hair smoky white. Darkness trailed them.

Ebony blinked to focus more clearly. No . . . not darkness, but shadows – their own shadows twisting and contorting as though struggling to break free. What would happen if they did?

"If you two are finished," Mentor Wizner interrupted.

She'd forgotten he was even there. Ebony dropped her journal into her satchel and jumped off the bench.

Fleishman hurried to fall into line. "Yes, Sir."

Ebony clenched onto her apprentice medium medallion dangling from her neck and followed. She looked at Mentor Wizner dressed in his drab brown robe and plain moccasins. They shared similar skills, which was probably the reason he'd been chosen to coach her in the art of spirit tracking for the past three weeks.

That was how long it'd been since her world had changed.

"Ignore the Fades. We'll deal with them during a future lesson," Wizner said. "For today, concentrate on the energy you are calling and make sure to stand your ground. It will aid in deflecting specters attracted to the area by the Fades."

"But you said specters can't pass onto hallow ground," Ebony said.

"That is true."

"And Fades can."

Wizner nodded.

"Then shouldn't we be worried about those Fades?" she asked.

"All depends on the stage of the Fade."

Mentors made no sense, sometimes. Fades, specters, extra-celestials, poltergeists, wraiths, and a bazillion different types of entities . . . she felt like slamming her head against a tombstone from info overload. But she had no time for being overwhelmed. She had her secret project with the Motley Mulisha – Fleishman and Lance – to work on. Then again, if she didn't learn to handle the different spirits more easily, she'd never make the connections to track Daenir, the dark elf who'd stolen Lance's body. If only Lance hadn't astral-projected his spirit from his body.

She inched in beside Fleishman, and he extended his hand for her to take. She didn't need to hold his hand to call on a Door to Yggdrasil. But being responsible for the doors was a lot to handle, and kind of lonely, so she slipped her hand into his. It made her feel better. She closed her eyes.

Warm energy swirled around her feet. Her skin tingled as it worked upward reaching her head. The ends of her hair lifted from her shoulders. A crack of electricity sparked the air. It was at this time that Fleishman usually flinched. He didn't, so she opened her eyes. His face tilted down at her. He flipped his long bangs in a silent "atta" girl. She still had lots to learn about being Keeper of the Doors and he as her official advisor, but they'd come a long way in a short time.

A familiar door materialized before them. The toddler boy clenched onto his teddy bear and slid a trusting glance up at Ebony. "Home," he said.

Ebony would like to tell him he was going home because . . . well, he was. Just to a different home. Was telling him half the truth still the truth?

Delia, their new light elf and fellow ghost guide from

Yggdrasil, stepped through the doorway to the Hall of Souls and pushed her metal goggles to crown her head. Her light blue hair tapped her shoulders and the fur collar of her leather vests. She smiled at Ebony and flashed a glance at Fleishman. His cheeks flushed bright red.

"*Kveðja*," Mentor Wizner interrupted the awkward exchange.

Delia crossed her right arm over her chest and rested her fist over her heart. Ebony mimicked her welcome signal.

Air swelled to the left of Delia as the familiar suction sound echoed off a nearby crypt. An over-sized desk appeared with a clear vision screen floating into place. Gears shifted, and steam released. The toddler stopped sucking his thumb. Two crows on the crypt steps flapped their wings; one waddled away. Pistons separated the desktop from its base, and a platform sprung up beneath the desk.

A neon sign blinked:

Spirit Applicant Check-In Counter

Entrance into the afterlife had become more organized since the boneyard reopened to guide souls to their next destination. The process was kind of like the line at the movie theater, minus the popcorn and the being dead part.

Dark vapor swirled around two figures behind the desk. One, skinny and sitting on a stool, tapped his boney fingers clickety-clack on a keyboard. A wheeze hummed from the cogs and metal of his middle knuckle. Brooding and much larger, the other figure bent at the waist, forcing streams of vapor to whisk out beneath his leather jacket. Some sputtered at his wrists like he'd burst a vein. Or maybe a gasket. A fluorescent glow ringed his green eyes as he stared at the boy. The tiny tot cowered behind Ebony's leg. She couldn't blame him. Fleishman had already backed behind a headstone, Nigel's cage hugged to his chest. Even with

Ebony's friendliness toward the odd and creepy, she wasn't fond of Goths, either.

"Asmund," the skinny Goth began, "must I tell you again to be gentler with children?"

"Sorry, Poe," Asmund said through his scruffy voice.

Poe softened the shadows of his face, appearing more human. He adjusted the collar of his dapper coat. "Nothing to be afraid, dear boy."

A hawk glided to land in one of the many Ash trees lining Ash Pathway. Wizner glanced from the bird to the school. A random gust swept over them. Parched leaves lost their grip on their branches and broke free littering the boneyard. Orange flower petals tumbled alongside them.

Mentor Wizner pressed a petal between his finger and thumb, questioning wrinkles creasing his forehead. "We should hurry."

"I agree." Delia's stare said something Ebony didn't understand.

Hurry? It was about time. Ebony bit the insides of her cheeks to keep the words she wanted to say stifled inside. They didn't want to wait? Good. Now they knew how she felt. Everyone from Mom and Bat-Face-slash-Headmistress Regina to the Council of Mentors had told her to wait, had forbidden her to look for Lance's body. But they'd been searching and hadn't found a clue to where Daenir had hidden it. Ebony was better equipped for the search. She'd quit playing hide and seek only a few years ago, where it had been years since the adults had played.

"Coin please," Poe said, his hand palm up in front of Ebony.

The boy opened his palm to reveal a bracteate.

Thank Asgard, Ebony thought; although she still wasn't sure how a departed soul got a coin. Before Poe could accept the shiny piece of metal, Asmund snatched it up. The coin brightened, and Asmund rolled it over one knuckle and then another. With each flip, it dimmed until his shadows completely absorbed it. He belched.

Ebony smirked. Despite his Goth status, Asmund might grow on her after all.

She crouched to the boy's level, brushing against her favorite gravestone, the one etched with Amphylis Margaret Moate – *a life devoted to the rearing of children*. Well, the last word was camouflaged in bird poop so technically she couldn't see it.

Amphylis peeked her ghostly head above the matted grass, presumably to see if it was over. The boneyard residents hid with their bones when a ghost sought her out; most of them, anyway. She wasn't sure why. Ebony shook her head at Amphylis, who sank back beneath the surface.

Pretending to brush a blond curl from the boy's forehead, Ebony wrapped her arms around his tiny outline – the one she could see; feeling it wasn't as easy. She wished Dad were there to see her succeed. But he was still MIA someplace in Yggdrasil, last sighting Jotunheim. She didn't like to think about it. She missed him too much. And since he'd been gone, Mom had been preoccupied with adult stuff and wouldn't even give Ebony five minutes to talk about Dad. In Ebony's opinion, after finding out that Mom had been responsible for Ebony's medium skills not working properly all these years – her mother, Rita, had bound them – it was Ebony who should be distant. But she was totally fine.

Crows glided over one of the boneyard's many fountains to land on the thick rim. One hopped off, feathers weathered and gray. The bird hobbled to peck a thick patch of shrubbery. Its flat bill splintered twigs, peppering the ground in shards. Ebony did everything to stay focused on the boy, but when the bird rammed its body into the shrub she gave up.

The orange petals were caught up in a breeze. They

spun above the ground, before dissolving into mist. Hooded shadows shaped like giant crows circled above the Fades by the back field. Dying leaves rolled over graves like tumbleweeds in the desert, pushed along as the wind exhaled. The hawk bristled its feathers from its tree branch.

Crows cawed out of sync. Two wobbled toward Ebony. Their wings dangled lopsided and shrieks croaked from their beaks. Their heads were cocked to one side. A third crow swooped down at Ebony's feet. Another landed next to it. The hooded shadows shifted direction, sailing closer.

Poe stood. Delia crouched low. A chill frosted the air, and the Fades in the field shrank back to let the tree line consume them.

Black feathers dropped from the sky.

Mentor Wizner shuffled forward as shrieking flared above them like fireworks. Ebony tossed her head back to see a hooded shadow flying straight for her.

Chapter

three

An Unfortunate Event

"Give me the boy!" Delia screamed.

The boy raised his chubby arms, stubby fingers wiggling at Delia. A gray crow stumbled into his path. Small ghost feet tripped, and tiny ghost knees, too new and pliable to catch the force, plunged through the earthy soil and sank; his legs folded up behind him. The crow opened its faded bill and struck the boy's hand. He squealed. His form drained of color.

Ebony kicked the bird away as Delia rushed toward her. More gray crows hopped off the fountain. Heads tilted oddly, deadness glazing their eyes – zombified like in the movie Ebony had watched during last Halloween's Spookyfest weekend.

A hooded shadow darted between the girls, slamming

them into tombstones and lifting the boy off the ground. Not a shadow, but some sort of creature.

"Impossible," Wizner's voice rasped.

The hawk soared into the air, chasing the whimpers of the boy. Dark figures peeled off the creature, shrieking in multiple voices.

"Don't listen to it!" Delia gripped Ebony's shoulder. "Hum a song in your head."

Ebony crumpled to the ground. She rammed her palms against her ears as the voices batted inside her head like the shrill of two draugrs fighting over the same corpse. "The ants go marching one by one, hurrah, hurrah," she sang.

Lame? Sure, but Aunt Gertrude and her little brother Ethan had sung it on the way to school this morning. It'd been stuck in her head all day.

"Get away!" Fleishman stumbled into Mentor Wizner to avoid a maniacal crow.

Trills streaked the dimming sky. More hooded creatures sailed along Ash Pathway, pausing to circle above Dead Alley – the abandoned area at the back of the boneyard where mounds of unwanted graves and their souls came to rest.

Poe leaped on top of the Check-In counter, lanky arms pointing at the creature. Each time he locked onto it the creature transformed. Images of natural disasters, violence, and rage splayed over its shadows.

Asmund pounded one vapor fist against the desk and lumbered off his stool.

Mentor Wizner and Delia chanted. They wrote symbols in the air, their movements in sync. A few crows stilled, the whites of their eyes brightening. The kidnapping creature jolted, and the toddler boy cried out.

Ebony screamed. She'd never been responsible for someone before, except her younger brother Ethan, but that was different. People believed in her. Even the kids at school had stopped treating her like a loser. She acted like their opinions didn't matter, but they did.

Pushing off a stone planter, she ran, tracing the creature's route in the sky. She'd promise anything for the boy not to be hurt. But that would go against:

Etiquette #3 of the Art of Spirit Tracking:
Never, ever make promises to the spirit world.

Etiquette was overrated.

"Stop!" she yelled. "I'll do what you want. I promise!"

"Ebony, don't!" Wizner and Delia said together.

The creature dove for Dead Alley. Wizner drew more symbols, and Poe shot streams of vapor that weaved into one. A shriek pierced the sky as it struck the creature. Asmund yanked on Poe's stream, tugging the creature backward; the boy's withering legs waved behind.

Ebony couldn't let this happen, so she stilled and called on another door. Fleishman skidded in beside her.

"What are you doing?" he asked. "Talk to me. I'm your advisor."

True, but he would want to weigh their options. There was no time for that.

Fleishman's voice faded as she searched for a door with her mind. The skin at her wrist tingled. A glow seeped to the surface of her rune tattoo – the one the door to the Hall of Souls had marked her with before her first journey into Yggdrasil. It hadn't flared like this since Nidhogg got sucked back to Yggdrasil through the portal in the gym.

"Ebony!" Fleishman broke through her trance.

A doorway pieced together in front of her. "Asmund!" she yelled, ignoring Fleishman. "Drag the creature here!"

She tugged on the doorknob. The seal popped, swinging the door wide. Odd that the opening was so blurry. The hooded creature squirmed in Asmund's grip.

"Wait!" Fleishman screamed as Ebony lunged forward and plunged her fingers beneath the blur up to her knuckles.

Thick tentacles of a sea serpent flailed out the doorframe; beads of water leaking out of the seal. Horrified, Ebony dodged the sting of suction-cupped claws. As she did, she brushed her glowing tattoo against the scaly skin. The serpent shrilled and flung her aside. She banged her head on the ground.

"Delia." Ebony heard herself whisper through the throbbing in her head.

But Delia was already racing past Ebony. "I've got the door!" She rammed her body against the thick wood, but her feet slipped on wet grass. "Eb-Ebony!" she stammered.

Ebony brushed tangles from her face and pushed off the ground to stand.

"I need help," Delia pled.

The water seal bloated. Beads of water thickened to streams, and the doorframe moaned. Ebony slid in next to Delia as the two girls gripped the door. They pushed with all their might, shoving it toward its seal.

"Just a little more," mumbled Delia.

With a few more grunts, they slammed the door shut. Delia hugged the doorframe, while Ebony rested her forehead against the door.

"That was close," Ebony panted, and Delia nodded in agreement.

A pain-filled cried echoed into the air from the boy.

"I have to find another way to save him!" At Ebony's words, the watery door splintered, breaking apart and forcing the girls to stumble backward. The pieces faded until gone.

The Goths continued their own attacks. Poe shot a stream of vapor into the air like a steel arrow, and Asmund caught it. He tethered it to the creature. The dark blob of chaos reeled but refused to release the boy. Delia extracted two handles strapped to the back of her fur-trimmed vest. At the flick of her wrists, metal whips lashed out and latched onto one shredded end of the creature's hood. It shrilled, shattering a nearby tombstone as it bounced off the gutter of a crypt.

The toddler slipped from its grip.

As the creature's hood melted away, its head was exposed. Framed by an exoskeleton, it was shaped like a man's face. The creature coiled in on itself, the numerous voices it emitted begging for mercy.

Asmund gripped hold of it. Whitish smoke billowed from the shrinking creature as he crumpled it in his fist, until the last swirls of vapor absorbed into his palm. A single orange petal slipped between two of his fingers and wafted to the ground. The bulky Goth crushed it beneath his feet. His stomach grumbled, and he rubbed it before pounding on his chest to release the wettest burp Ebony had ever heard.

The other hooded creatures still circling over Dead Alley recoiled. All the ground crows took flight, seemingly back to normal. Clouds parted, giving all their escape.

Delia jerked her wrists, retracting the whips, and bent over the boy. Bluish spots coated his ghostly skin. Soft lavender tinted his parted lips. His silhouette blinked like an iridescent bulb, the light dimming with each flash. Delia lowered her ear over the boy's mouth. She scooped him into her arms and trekked up Ash Pathway.

"What's wrong with him?" Ebony asked, her heart already telling her what was happening.

"It could be an infection or a reaction," Wizner answered instead.

Ebony's heart told her it was something worse. She walked alongside the small group staring down at her knees covered in white and black skull tights. She'd failed the toddler ghost.

Delia vanished across the threshold of the door to the Hall of Souls without a word. The door resealed. A strobe of light pulsated from Ebony's tattoo before it faded.

The Goths slid behind their desk. Other than a glance at Mentor Wizner, which communicated a silent message, it was as if nothing had happened. In a cloud of vapor, they vanished, literally *poofed* into nothingness, desk and all without a thank you or see ya later.

Amphylis floated up from her gravestone. "Thank heavens, Miss Ebony."

Old man Pottle, a crotchety goat of a ghost, hobbled out from behind an ash tree with Tanner, his farmhand, trailing him. He shuffled the deck of cards in his hands, probably to play poker. Other boneyard residents followed.

"She looks well considering," Amphylis said. "Do you not agree, Mr. Pottle?"

"Not sure if I does not or does, Ma'am Phylis, but I tell you . . ." He paused, a blank haze pooling over his russet eyes. Tanner reminded him what he was saying.

"Dang it! That's right," the old man said. "She's a catch for us spirit folk, that she is."

"She sure is," chimed in Victoria Givens, whose naïve church girl giggle would make even Ebony's tolerant twin aunts agree it should be a sin. "Isn't that right, Hargrave?"

"I would have to say . . ." Hargraves Synx, law apprentice when he was alive, expectedly began a lengthy explanation and discussion with George Yates, a newspaper reporter extraordinaire for the Biddeford Daily Journal from 1890 to 1932.

"Is it over?" Fleishman asked, oblivious to the ghostly conversation around him.

Ebony had a feeling it was far from over, especially with the glower Mentor Wizner stabbed her with. She also figured this would complicate finding Lance's body.

"You violated an etiquette." Wizner crossed his arms over his chest.

Ebony lowered her head. Even though it was wrong to break the etiquette, she'd done it to help someone. Did that make it less wrong? Were there degrees of wrongness?

Wizner began, "You are too spontaneous, not thinking before you act. Trust my better—"

"Older," Ebony said.

He exhaled. "Yes, older judgement. And for that matter, Fleishman, too."

It was safer to trust in herself. That she could control.

"Your effort to call on a door was valiant but misguided," Wizner said. "But no more door calling until you can control the ability. Plus, you have no idea how many doors are out there."

She hadn't thought of that. How many were there?

Wizner shuffled toward a side exit, and the kids followed. They passed Amphylis, who batted at orange petals with her eternally clean handkerchief.

"The graveyard's connection to Niflheim and Muspelheim makes it prime real estate," Wizner said. "And with it reopened to spirits, it's no surprise trouble found its way here."

"Looks like we have another mystery to figure out," Ebony said to Fleishman.

"No." Wizner stopped dead in his tracks. "This is not your concern."

"What do you mean?" she asked. "The boneyard is my responsibility. Does this have to do with why you don't want Lance here until he projects back into his body?"

Since Daenir had made Lance incorporeal, the secret Motley Mulisha had made a project of creating a location beacon to find the boy's body. Wizner said reuniting him with it was the only way he could reenter the boneyard safely. It was too dangerous for him being away from his bones; not to mention he wasn't even dead. Lance had astral projected to help her, so putting him back together was priority one.

Wizner's silence said all she needed to hear. She looked at the boneyard ghosts. Did it have to do with them, too?

"What was that thing?" she asked.

Wizner softened his voice. "Poe and Asmund were capable of handling tonight's unfortunate event. They've had to many times since the Vanir gods gave up Asgard to the Aesir gods and moved to Vanaheim for the sake of peace."

She firmed her glare. "That didn't answer my question."

Concern swept across Wizner's face, but he blinked, and it was gone. "A myth," was his final answer.

Chapter

FOUR

Ghostly Lessons

he woman swept a tree branch aside, anxious to tie off the loose end of this odd girl and her friend with the lizard. But she was stunned still by the sight of . . . It couldn't be, but it was. The ghost of the boy Lance whose body Daenir had asked her to dispose of. But she knew she'd find use for it, so she spelled it to a secret place.

He sat outside the perimeter of the cemetery, fingers pointing stiff as he stabbed at a small rock perched on a wooden bench. A smile tugged back her aged lips. Drawing on nearby energy to move a physical object took strength and practice. This boy needed both. His attempt was dreadful. But she could read in his ghostly form what she hadn't been able to from his physical body.

His energy held an increasing level of boldness and strength, where most ethereal energy once separated from the body, diminished. She clenched her goatskin pouch of coins – bracteates belonging to souls she'd collected. Having his bracteate would make this a lot easier. But technically he wasn't dead.

Gazing at him more deeply, she sensed a gamut of painful emotions. Trauma had visited this boy. That gave her pause . . . for a moment before she refocused. It wasn't her concern.

Could he be useful? Possibly, but he wasn't anywhere ready to reenter his body. As least, not for the new purposes birthing in her mind. Yes, a little time befriending this boy would be worth the detour, for detours sometimes yielded great finds. She was in no hurry.

"*Vertu hér*," rasped from her mouth as she drew sigils in the air.

The ground beneath her shook. Shoots of half-dead grass lengthened and stretched for the sky. Soil rolled away, splicing a chasm in between; pebbles and rocks crumbled to dust. Roots wormed out the opening, and thick vines coiled around a solid chunk of earth. The mound rose. Twigs wriggled aside to reveal the facial features of a girl.

"*Leyfi henni.*" The woman flicked her fingers to the side.

Roots and vines weakened, falling away from the girl's slender figure. Dingy garbs hung off her body. Clumps of soil clung to her hair making the color hard to see. Her chalky skin held a bluish tint with lines of darker blue disappearing beneath the wrist and neck of her clothing.

The woman blew out a long breath. Dirt and grime dissolved in cloudy plumbs off the girl. Her exposed skin deepened to a fair olive color and her hair was stark black.

"*Vaknaðu*," whispered the woman.

And the girl awakened, opening her eyes. Dilated pupils

shrank as her hazel irises grew. The yellow coating the whites of her eyes faded.

"You called?" the girl asked.

"Yes, Eve," the woman said and waved her hand over the girl, whose clothing transformed to jeans and a cropped T-shirt. "I need your help."

Abigail raised an eyebrow. "Will it buy me extra time out?"

"Perhaps," the woman answered. "Now, join me in a little game."

"What are we playing?" Abigail asked.

The woman faced Lance. "Friendship."

The woman sensed Lance's footsteps before she heard his voice.

"Hello?" the boy said.

She and Abigail turned his way.

"Yes!" cried the boy. "You can see me. I've only seen two other ghosts nearby, but they weren't interested in talking."

The woman had to swallow. Even without his body, his energy was robust, so much of what she yearned for and would make this all worthwhile.

"I'm Lance," he said.

"It's nice to meet you. I'm Elli." She gestured to her side. "This is my friend, Abigail."

The boy stuffed his hands in his pockets.

"You must be new," Elli said.

"You could say that," Lance answered.

"You haven't changed clothes since you died?" His expression at the mention of his death was precious. She knew it would be.

"Uh, change clothes? We can do that?" he questioned.

"Of course," she said. "Abigail and I can teach you."

"You've been around for a while, then," he said.

"You could say that," she repeated his words, and he laughed. This was too easy. Time to toss in some inner chaos. She stepped toward the cemetery.

"Wait," he said. "I shouldn't go in there."

"Why?" Abigail asked.

He sighed. "One of my friends is a medium. Her teacher said it's not safe."

"There's nothing like the living telling you how to be dead," Elli tsked.

By the bobbing of the boy's head, she knew he was considering her argument.

"I'll tell you what," she began, "we'll go to my special hidden place in the cemetery, and Abigail and I will teach you skills. But you may not want to share them with your friend, whose opinions might hinder what you learn."

He swept his hand through his dark hair, which hardly moved. "You're right."

Of course she was. "Follow me."

Chapter

five

A Pact of Spit

Charmed Castle shone in the glow of lanterns lining the long driveway. Ethan's bike leaned against a tall lantern near the front of the garage. Aunt Gertrude's 1976 Pacer sparkled in its metallic green paint next to Mom's black sedan. Most of the damage to the foyer caused a few weeks ago by that oversized, mangy mutt Fenrir had been repaired. But the carport archway where Dad parked his car had yet to be replaced.

Ebony's heart fluttered. Her nose tingled as it filled with mucus. Still no word from Dad, but Mom assured her all was fine. That didn't feel right.

The garage door opened with a familiar screech. Ethan raced across the driveway to his bike. *Vroom-vroom* noises rumbled from his mouth, which, a few weeks ago would have bugged her. Tonight, they sounded like home.

Stiff blades of grass swished against the sides of Ebony's combat boots as she rounded the house to the back deck. Entering through the kitchen might help her avoid her twin aunts. They loved questioning her about her training sessions.

"Thought we were meeting at the graveyard once you ditched Wizner?"

Ebony spun on her heels. "Lance!"

"Oops. Did I scare you?" He chuckled. "That's right. I'm a ghost. It's what I do."

Ebony sighed, feeling guilty being alive, which was all kinds of confusing. "You didn't scare me."

He sighed. "Seems I'm no good at ghosting, either."

"No, no. You scared me," sped so fast off her lips her brain hadn't kicked in yet.

This time Lance belly-laughed. "Calm down, E. I'm messing with you."

Ebony felt her cheeks warm. She gazed into Lance's soulful eyes, knowing the stakes could be much higher for him than simply being without his body forever. He wore the same oversized sneakers as always, but the sleeveless T-shirt showing off his biceps was new.

"Did you change your clothes?" she asked, and he grinned. "How?"

"By looking at clothing and imagining it in my head," he said.

"You'd better not look at a bikini then," she said, and they laughed. Laughing was good and something she hadn't done much of lately. "You're smart to figure that out."

"Oh, I . . ." his voice faded.

"You?"

"I saw another ghost do it and I copied."

Ebony frowned. "In the boneyard?"

He hesitated. "Around there."

"Not inside," she said. "Because you know what Wizner said."

"Thought we weren't listening to Wizner."

True, only after the earlier events that night, taking Wizner's advice seemed wiser. This myth liked ghosts. Or disliked them depending on the way you looked at it, and Lance was in ghost form.

"I should get used to this ghost thing," he said. "You guys are in school all day and I'm . . ."

Alone, Ebony thought. Her heart squeezed.

"Bored," he finished and sat on a step. "Are you okay?"

"Rough training session with Wizner." It wasn't a lie. Just lacked a few details.

"What'd you do, extinguish a fire giant?"

She wished. At least that she'd understand. She should tell him about Wizner's myth. He had a right to know that he was in more danger. But what good would it do telling him about things she didn't understand? She'd wait until she had answers.

"I take it we haven't found another way to find my body?" he said.

She stared at him. "We'll put you back together. I promise." She'd already broken *Etiquette #3* once that night. What would another one matter? She spit in her palm and held out her hand. "Motley Mulisha members stick together. Swear."

His face softened as he stood. "Making a spit pact with a girl feels weird."

Lance saw her as a girl? Most boys saw her as just Ebony. "I've been practicing physical touch with ghosts. Try to shake my hand."

"I've been doing the same thing. You know," he wiggled his fingers, "to scare the living."

"But you're alive," she said.

Silence crept between them. Being without his body

freed the teal of his aura to shine brighter, but also gave spotlight to the speckles of scarlet floating inside. Was cool Lance more scared than he'd let on?

Lance hovered his ghost fingers over Ebony's opened hand. She anticipated the touch like with the toddler – his essence brushing against her skin or maybe it was her skin brushing against his essence; she wasn't sure. She inhaled as a light caress swept across her palm. Lance slammed his palm over hers, trying to slap her five, and she giggled.

"What?" he asked.

She flexed her hand. "I could kind of feel you."

He laughed, too, and then his expression got serious. "Any word about your dad?"

Ebony shook her head. She knew Lance blamed himself for what happened when her dad had tried to help him. A thought struck her. What about Lance's father? He never mentioned his family. She knew nothing about him except that he was one of the boys taken from the boneyard last summer. No family had welcomed him home like the families of the other kids; at least no family she knew of. Someone should have checked on him. Maybe they had.

"Have you," she hesitated, "seen your family since you've been back?"

He shrugged. "I can't."

How dumb could she be? "I'm sorry. Of course, you'd feel sad seeing them."

"I don't remember them. Actually," he said more to himself than to her, "I don't know where I live."

He didn't remember? Old man Pottle forgot things earlier, too.

She had a suspicion that learning the workings of the spirit world would have to come sooner than later because Lance being without his body was doing more to him than leaving him in ghost form. Maybe there was more to Daenir's plan to create a new world than they'd thought.

Time to start digging for information.

"I'll ask my mom," she said. "With her working at Motley while my dad's gone, she has access to student records, right? She can at least tell me your parents' names and an address."

The red of worry in his aura didn't vanish, but it dulled a little.

"Go back to Fleishman's dad's barn and do homework or something," she said.

"I don't get why you share your homework with me."

"To keep you from falling behind and repeating sixth grade."

He smiled. "Is spooking Fleishman considered homework?"

"More like a training exercise, I'd say." They laughed.

"Off to read my brains out," he said. "I'll do more exploring later, so don't worry if I pop in and out."

"As long as you answer me if I try to contact you." Falling into deep concentration was another Wizner lesson she'd yet to master; she had connected with Lance a few times, though.

"Sure thing." He walked away but turned back. "Don't get into trouble because of me."

"Me? Trouble?" She clenched her satchel. "Never." And with that, the knot in her stomach constricted. Not because she was unsure of her words, but because this time there was no question they were a lie.

SIX

Discovery

rees grew denser the deeper into the forest Elli traveled.

Her game with Lance had been more delightful than expected. He would become what she needed. All he had to do was ask Abigail how Elli had saved her soul. Granted that had come at a price for sweet, innocent Abigail. Nothing in life . . . or in death was free.

She raised an eyebrow at an oddly cluttered area of forest. Scattered with so much debris, it looked like two rock giants had collided leaving pieces of themselves behind. A hole in the ground came into view. The remains of the girl and boy's underground cabin Daenir had mentioned.

Appropriate for the girl reaper's favorite place to be

below ground. She did specialize in the dead. To think her holier-than-thou guardians called her an average spirit tracker – a mere Seidr. She collected the dead to guide them and collecting for the Afterlife meant you were a reaper. And in this case, much more than that.

Most Seidrs communicated with, discerned the destiny of, and guided ghosts to the next stage of their journey. But this girl had been protected by the three high Norns. And that could only mean one thing. She would become a practitioner of magick trusted to alter destiny – a rare Seidr.

This must have surprised Daenir – a typical reaction of dark elves. Stuck-up, snobby skinny twigs. Probably the reason he never completed his plan. It mattered not to her.

A crow pushed by a nearby bush. She bent down, offering her undead friend her hand. The bird hobbled up her arm to perch on her shoulder. The bird dipped its beak at her, marbleized eyes not as blank as before. Elli basked in the knowledge that it knew its creator. They all would know, like the old days in Jötunheim.

Leaves rustled to the sound of giggles. Banter that equated to friendship – another element of humanity she'd never comprehend. Through the trees she saw them: the girl with colorful hair and Lance. Her magick expanded, feeling and sensing. She rubbed the finite hairs at her chin.

A smirk filled the wrinkled folds of her face. Her skin smoothed to the agelessness of her former self. Pastel pink flushed her cheeks. An ocean of infinite blues deepened her eyes. Lashes batted, fueled by youth. Roses bloomed in tiny braids to crown her head and flow throughout her hair.

Beauty beholden by creation, and beauty dies only to be reborn as Nature intended, accordingly written in the scrolls before time and space were born. *As beauty is soft it can deceive and mask the threat that lies beneath, the hope and light cannot be freed, for darkness itself she'll never leave.*

"And it shall be again," she blew into the forest breeze, sending shivers through the trees. At the touch of her breath, leaves stretched their blades flat, veins extending beyond the outer edges, transforming into jagged claws, an invisible lifeline reaching across each center. One leaf drifted to land in her palm. She swept her hand over it, composing a message of symbols and sigils.

Elli dangled her fingers above Nature's parchment. Corners curved inward, rolling to meet in the middle. The leaf whirled in her palm, fading with each rotation, until only a phantom shadow remained.

Her ears opened to the girl making a promise to the boy Lance. This would make it easier to snag the boy. Elli *tsked* the girl. Surely, she knew making promises to the dead – and almost dead in Lance's case – was not worth the risk?

Lance ambled to the woodlot, and the girl vanished inside her house. Divide and conquer worked best. Elli sank behind a tree to watch the boy. He paused and combed his fingers through his hair. Looking toward the house, he leaned away and chose a path in the direction of the graveyard behind the school through the woods.

She followed him.

Trial by Cheese Doodles

ebony pulled the sliding door shut and scanned the reflection in the glass of the rooms behind her. Both family room and kitchen were empty. Good. She headed to the pantry to tug out a bag of Cheese Doodles. What she needed was a snack.

She passed a canister of ointment and reed bags of powder set on the island. Leafed herbs sprouted from three narrow vases; a dried ginger root leaned against one. A handful of stout, mini candles filled a teal glass bowl, while incense, matches, and a variety of copper and tin bowls stacked up beside her aunts' grimoire. They were up to something, but they usually were.

"Gertrude," Aung Gladys' voice echoed from the hallway, "you're going to drop those."

Canning jars hugged against Gertrude's cable-knit sweater. Loose threads at the ends of her knee-length skirt clung to her signature striped black and white tights. Aunt Gladys looked like a bird ready for flight with the baggy sleeves of her blouse hanging over the books she balanced under both arms.

Ebony eyed the grimoire.

"Being sneaky." The jars clanked as Aunt Gertrude set them down. "I like it."

"Do not encourage misbehavior, sister," Aunt Gladys said.

"Oh, keep your meditation cards in a stack." Gertrude dropped a velvet bag on the counter and lightly pinched Ebony's cheeks. "I'm cheering on our great-niece's tenacity."

A tender frown from Aunt Gladys stifled Ebony's nervous giggle.

"Ethan, we're waiting." Aunt Gertrude directed her voice toward the foyer.

"Had to park my bike." Ethan skipped into the kitchen and hopped up next to Aunt Gladys. "I'm ready."

"Not before you wash your hands," Aunt Gladys said.

Aunt Gertrude extracted a stone from the velvet bag and held it in her closed hand. With her free hand palm up, she bowed her head and mumbled.

"Now, sister." Gladys slapped her opened palm. "Rita instructed us not to use our skills for everyday chores when it comes to the children."

"Remind me to spike your tea tonight with some wilder seed to rid you of your responsible attitude, sister."

Aunt Gladys guided Ethan to the sink.

"What were you saying?" Ebony whispered.

"A word here, a word there," Aunt Gertrude paused, "to wipe away my mystical fingerprint on the soap I hid from her."

Mystical fingerprints. That was a thing? Huh. Ebony

popped her snack into her mouth. "What are you teaching Ethan?"

"Luminary history, tales, and facts," Aunt Gertrude said.

"Not just any facts," Gladys added.

"That would be a waste of time." Aunt Gertrude twisted the cover off the canister. "Good point, sister."

"Of course, it is."

"What is?" Aunt Gertrude asked.

"My point."

"Which was?"

Aunt Gladys' face blanked. "Mandarin root! I don't remember."

The two sisters cackled, and Ebony rubbed her temples, impressed that Ethan could learn anything from these two. She chomped on another Cheese Doodle.

"Yes, yes," Aunt Gertrude said. "We're teaching him about being a Luminary."

"About the moon, stars, and natural energy." Aunt Gladys tapped the stone still in Gertrude's hand. "He's too young for casting."

"Undoubtedly," Aunt Gertrude agreed and winked at Ebony.

Or maybe not. She loved her aunt.

Aunt Gertrude handed Ebony the stone, and Ebony rubbed the marking etched on top – a rune stone. She remembered wanting to play with these when she was little, but her aunts said they weren't toys.

Aunt Gertrude continued, "You must remember—"

"That the grimoire says what we need—" Aunt Gladys opened the cupboard under the sink.

"At the time we utilize it," Aunt Gertrude said.

It was eerie when her aunts finished each other's thoughts. But this sounded important, so Ebony banked it in her brain.

"Out of hand soap?" Aunt Gertrude snickered.

"You knew." Aunt Gladys trudged Ethan toward the half bathroom. "That woman will never grow up."

Ebony sat on one of the island stools. "I hope not."

"I've always known you take after me." Aunt Gertie pointed for Ebony to set the stone next to the canister of ointment and the clear jar of garlic cloves. She ducked to peek out the window. "With dusk rolling in, the moon isn't bright yet, but it's visible. We should be good. The Fehu rune can represent prosperity and blessing. Never hurts to add a blessing to any act we do."

Ebony remembered this rune from Mentor Blu's Language & Runes study. She reached for a Cheese Doodle and bumped the corner of the grimoire with her arm. Tingles scurried along her rune tattoo, and she jerked her arm back.

"Something wrong, dear?"

Ebony rubbed her wrist. "No." Maybe.

"You know, the grimoire is for you, too," Gertrude said.

"I'm a sensory, psychic stuff. Only luminaries have grimoires."

"Gobbledygook," Gertrude insisted. "It's yours to use as long as you have a good reason and ask permission."

A silent movie of reuniting Lance with his body and curing the toddler ghost raced across her mind. "Can I use it?"

"For what purpose?"

Moldy cheese. She couldn't say it was to look for Lance's body. "Uh, homework."

"That would be cheating." Her aunt chuckled.

True, but if Wizner would have told her about his myth and let her search for Lance's body, she wouldn't need to use it.

"Did you know that sensory and luminary members share similar gifts, merely different methods of executing them?" Gertrude asked.

No, she didn't know that.

"Sensories don't need external aids like herbs and spells." Gertrude sliced the peeling off one side of the root. "They physically gather energy needed to perform an act, but that doesn't make them any less connected to their family's grimoire. Our grimoire is a compilation of our family's history, magick, relationships, and travels. It's a living, breathing genome of our lineage, and your psychic and natural energy is part of that." She winked at the open pages of the grimoire. "Isn't that right?"

Was she talking to the book? Ebony pushed off the rungs of the barstool to peek at the grimoire.

"I'm glad you agree," Gertrude said to the book. To Ebony, "The grimoire likes you."

"It talked to you?" Ebony asked.

"It's more a feeling," her aunt said. "Like how you sense what others feel."

Ebony plopped down on her stool. Other than seeing auras – colorful, life energy every person had – she hadn't bothered paying attention to this skill. When did she have time?

"Don't worry. You'll learn to recognize and use life energy around you." Gertrude lowered the knife blade. "Tapping into it should feel natural and light. That's how you'll know you should use it."

Once again, her aunt lost her.

"You are also connected to the grimoire because you are a Seeker."

"Thanks for reminding me that my former defective sensory skills got me labeled a Seeker," Ebony said through a mouthful of soggy crumbs.

Gertrude rounded the island. "Seekers are rare, child. It's the title that will house all your skills as a spirit tracker, empath, and a Seidr."

"Those are the same things."

"To some." Gertrude let out a sigh. "But not to you. A true Siedr is a practitioner of magick also, not only a guide to the spirit world, and, in time, will learn to discern destiny and be trusted to alter its course."

Like the 3Ms, her name for the ghost girls who'd been with her for years. She'd recently learned they weren't little girls after all. They were high Norns Yggdrasil had sent to watch over her. Her aunt had to be kidding. "I'm lacking in the skills department."

"Nonsense," Gertrude said. "Your medium skills are developing, and your other Seidr skills will come in time, more likened to the goddess Freyja. She's Seidr's foremost practitioner."

She compared Ebony to a goddess? And just when Ebony started to believe her. "This is more trouble than it's worth."

"That's because you're in junior high," Aunt Gertrude said. "What kids make fun of you for during your school years will become your greatest assets in adulthood."

"Weird because helping to defeat Nidhogg has made me kind of normal at school," Ebony said. "Whatever normal means."

"That's because you're defined. Everyone witnessed your skills, so they understand you, can label you, which makes you less scary."

"I was scary before?"

"Intimidating, there's a difference. People fear things they don't understand or things that don't fit into a perfect box. Usually, it makes them envious of that person."

Ebony tapped the Cheese Doodle in her hand. "That makes no sense. If someone is different, who cares?"

Her aunt smiled. "You're a good little herb, Ebony. If it makes it any easier for you, think of this part of maturing as a trial by fire."

Ebony held up her snack. "I'd rather do a trial by Cheese

Doodles covered in melted cheddar."

"In everything there is always something new to learn. You simply must look for it." As Gertrude sliced the last of the peeling off the root, her hand nudged the canister of ointment, sloshing some onto the countertop and her sweater. "Oh, for all the wisdom in the nine realms . . . Would you wipe that up for me?" She set down the ginger root and vanished under the archway without letting Ebony answer.

Chapter

eight

Book Chatter

om's voice echoed from the newly renovated foyer. Ethan raced past the kitchen archway to greet her and yammer on about his lesson with the aunts. "That sounds exciting, Ethan." Mom lingered under the archway to kick off her high-heeled shoes as Ethan marched past with a big paper bag stapled at the top.

Guess Chinese food was for dinner.

Mom glanced up. "Ebony, how was your training session?"

Ebony wanted to tell her the truth, that some freakish myth infected a ghost and that she was scared. But she went with what she thought Mom would rather hear.

"Good," she said.

"That's great," Mom said.

Ethan heaved the paper bag on top of the island. Aunt Gladys murmured how exciting it was to eat takeout food. Ethan emphatically agreed and followed Aunt Gladys into the dining room carrying the last two white cartons of Chinese food.

"Could you set the table?" Mom handed Ebony a pile of dinner plates.

"Sure," Ebony said. "But—"

"And get the silverware out, too." Her mother backed into the foyer. "I need to change out of these clothes."

Ebony trailed her. "Can I—"

"Don't forget paper towels."

"Mom!"

"What?"

"Do you know Lance's parents?"

Mom hesitated. "Why?"

"I don't know," Ebony said, her voice sounding small. "Maybe they could—"

"I told you the school would help Lance." Mom took a deep breath. "Concentrate on learning your skills, please."

A few weeks ago, Mom had been responsible for keeping Ebony's skills from her. Now she wanted her to focus on them. It was hard keeping up with adults sometimes.

What if her mother hadn't kept the truth from Ebony? Would Ebony be stronger in her sensory skills? Would she have been able to fix things earlier before they'd gotten out of hand with Daenir and Lance lost his body? Before this boy ghost got sick. Ebony felt her insides twitch.

Maybe she would have been able to keep Dad from being swept away by that fire giant.

"I know how crazy things have been since that serpent paid us a visit." Mom tucked a dark tangle behind Ebony's ear. "And how the Motley school system's way of teaching has changed because of it. And I know, or always knew,

41

there were dangers out there bigger than us, and now my daughter is smack dab in the middle of it all."

Yup, right in the middle of bad stuff happening to the boneyard – normally Ebony's safe place. But now she was responsible for it, which was different. And scary. She didn't know what to do, and her mother wouldn't listen.

"I'm sorry. It's so hard . . . " Mom stopped herself, but Ebony knew she was avoiding the white elephant in the room – Dad being gone.

It was as if talking about it would jinx him coming back. It couldn't, could it? Jinxes weren't like hexes, right?

Mom gripped hold of the banister, the gentleness gone. "The Council of Mentors has exhausted many avenues searching for Daenir and Lance's body. This is new territory and since the truth about Yggdrasil's existence came out there's more going on than you know."

Ebony stood still as her mother vanished upstairs.

"Your mother has been under enormous stress, but she does care," Aunt Gertrude said and followed Mom upstairs.

It sure didn't feel that way.

Ebony trudged into the kitchen to clean up Aunt Gertrude's spilled ointment but stumbled to a stop. The ointment was gone. The ends of her hair caught in the hood of her sweatshirt as she looked for a ghost, spirit, or even a real person.

No one was there. Except for the grimoire.

If the book could feel-talk to Aunt Gertrude, making a spill vanish wasn't out of the question.

Touching a grimoire without an invitation violated

Motley code and family rules; Gertie said permission and a purpose was needed. Purpose she had, just not an acceptable one to her aunts, her mother, the Council of Mentors, and probably other entities she'd yet to learn about. Then again, the book was open. What more invitation did she need? She'd seen her aunts work with the book before. It couldn't be too hard. They always asked a question first.

"Where is Daenir and Lance's body?" she whispered.

Nothing happened.

"Okay," she said. "What about how do I help the toddler ghost?"

Crackling nipped at the air. Ebony pivoted slowly, trying to see the sounds. As she did, the cover slammed shut, and the edges of the pages frayed.

She lunged forward. No! She hadn't meant to ask more than one question. The second one fell out of her mouth.

Threads thickened to twine. They snaked over the cover, securing the pages from sneaky eyes. A knot sank deep in her belly. She was sorry and rubbed her palm along the cover. A sting raced across her tattoo. Had the book shocked her?

Pushing up her sleeve revealed a bluish glow at one end of her rune tattoo. Up to that point, her tattoo had only lit up when the door to the Hall of Souls was near. Ebony reached for the twine. The glow from her tattoo brightened, and the twine stretched out of her reach. Delia had said the tattoo would be there to help her; she'd assumed it was with the doors.

Ebony swept her wrist over the grimoire. The twine quivered and dodged the light, which smoldered like a campfire ember near the end of a flame. The closer she moved her wrist the more the twine reacted until it disintegrated. Her thumb bleached to pale lavender as she inspected the glow. The ember dimmed.

The cover sprang open. Pages slapped together. The grimoire settled on a page of intricate lines and symbols. *The grimoire says what we need at the time we utilize it*, her aunts had said.

Guess it had something to say.

The scent of history, magick, and a little mayhem swirled off the pages. Sketches of constellations, vials of herbs, and mountain ranges led to cool enchantments, but Ebony couldn't be sure of her interpretation seeing how the readings were written in runes. She turned the page.

The image of a lighthouse caught her eyes first. Six granite pillars stood off to the left, sea water raging against the coastline. Her brow knitted, and she peered closer. Objects of different sizes were scattered in-between and around the pillars; a larger one was in the center.

The inky sides of the lighthouse grew fuzzy, and Ebony stepped back. The lines warped until each tugged off the parchment. She gasped.

Brick and mortar rose to erect the structure like a holograph in virtual reality. Symbols she recognized as runes and words of a foreign language coiled the base and up the grouted sides, gaining size as they did.

A three-dimensional circle broke free and floated to the six pillars. Three interlocking triangles and a spiny letter F adorned its facade. Images of prehistoric man, native huts, and animals shifted to horse-drawn wagons, cars, and skyscrapers that appeared like a movie reel darkened by shadows. Storms, fires, and other natural disasters, too, and within them stood a beautiful woman.

As fast as the images appeared, they distorted, bubbling as though heated from beneath. Each rippled, ironing out wrinkles to lay flat.

Ebony traced squiggly lines and boxes in the air with her finger. "This looks like a map," she whispered. Of what, she didn't know, except for a symbol that resembled a ladder. It was familiar, only she didn't know why.

The woman faded into what looked like the letter P. It was a rune, too, but Ebony had no idea what it meant.

Silvery sparks tumbled across the map to whirl around the pillars and the lighthouse. The different-sized images came into focus – people, lying flat or on their side or in a ball. But she still couldn't make out the one in the center.

This was worse than eating burnt cheese curds because she had zero idea what it meant. Asking Fleishman wasn't an option because she'd have to tell him how she got the information, and he'd be disappointed that she sneaked.

Salty air welled up, and the rush of ocean water rang in her ears. Her head felt light, seasick. Ebony leaned against the kitchen island, forearms landing on the open pages. The far end of her tattoo ignited. The glow crested the words, making them readable.

Ebony pulled back to gawk at her wrist. "No way."

She swept the light of her tattoo along the words, and the text translated – *A Protection Ritual for the Living, Unblemished, and Independent Spirit.*

Protection from what?

The list of ingredients read: stones of black tourmaline or agate, crystals, aniseed, cloves, bay leaves, sea salt along with specific runes. There were options to use these as sachets – little cloth bags to pin to your clothes – or talismans, like blessing crystals or Ebony's apprentice medium medallion.

And right there was the reason one sought protection . . . *a ghost distanced from their bones too long without moving on will turn to pure chaos.*

Her head snapped up. The boneyard residents hide with their bones. But distanced for too long? Did this include Lance? He was away from his bones. Did he have a time limit to add to whatever danger Wizner's myth posed before something horrible happened to him or before she and Fleishman would need this protection from him? Should she encourage him to move on despite not being dead? Could he do that?

Could this be the reason Daenir wanted Lance's body? But how could one boy's body cause that much chaos or matter that much unless . . . Maybe she and Fleishman had gone about this all wrong. Instead of concentrating on finding Daenir, should they look for a connection with Lance?

Her shoulders drooped. The thought of Lance being involved spread guilt up and down her spine. If he was, that didn't mean he was aware of it. Maybe someone had kept things from Lance all his life like her mother had with her? Her heart was all squishy again.

Ebony tried to turn the page, but the pages stiffened, glued together. She swayed her tattoo glow over the grimoire, and the book proved as stubborn as Aunt Gertrude had said. She resorted to pounding her fists against the book.

Words shifted, and runes scrambled, forming more elaborate symbols. Ebony dug out a pencil from her satchel to sketch each as best she could.

Taking a snapshot with a cell phone would be easier. *Cell phones are for seventh graders,* Mom's words rang in her ears.

The free-moving runes circled the images of people, converging into one final image.

Ebony's heart plunged to the floor, nicking her kneecaps along the way and making her legs tremble.

It was Wizner's myth.

A caption blazed across the page. Charcoal mist swirled and deepened to *Glundroða safnari.* By the time she thought of decoding the words with her rune tattoo, the mist evaporated.

"Whatcha doing?"

Ebony whirled round so fast she almost wiped out. "Ethan!"

First instinct was to get rid of him. Calling him Gamer would work, but after he'd helped her understand parts of Yggdrasil through his video game, she'd promised not to call him that anymore.

"I, ah . . ." She fanned the pages, but the book had a mind of its own, pages smacking her hands as though annoyed with her, tiny fists of wordage fighting against her.

Ethan puckered his lips to blow out a solid stream of whistled air. "You're playing with auntie's grimoire?"

The kid was smart, so lying was useless at this point. "I'm not. The book started flipping pages, and sure I was curious."

"They're gonna know you touched it," he said. "But I can help."

See, smart with a ting of smart-Alec. "I guess since you're here . . ."

Ethan pressed his hands together in a prayer. "Play Eons of Chaos with me."

"Later," Ebony said through a groan. "I stopped calling you Gamer. You owe me."

Ethan grumbled but conceded, tugging a handful of crystals from his pockets.

"Do you always carry crystals with you?" she asked.

"I am a luminary," Ethan said with so much pride Ebony had to smile.

He rubbed a white crystal over the open book and arranged it alongside blue, brown, and red crystals in a circle with the ends pointing inward. With palms down over the pages, he moved his fingers in different directions. The crystals vibrated, and a breeze swept over them. Ethan tugged his hands to his chest as pages turned and calmed.

"Hey, that's the page it was on," Ebony said. Who knew little brothers could be so useful? "How'd you do that?"

Ethan giggled. "I wiped your girly germs off it."

"Har-har." Ebony played dumb, but this must be that mystical fingerprint her aunt mentioned.

"I did," he said, his chubby face staring up at her. She wondered when she'd lost the chubby in her face.

"How about we play that video game after dinner?" she suggested.

"Really?" His face lit up.

"I have something else I need your help with."

Ethan crossed his arms. "It's gonna cost you."

"I figured that."

nine

Tactics

lli gazed at the eighteenth-century renovated barn. Clapboard siding made from repurposed material dressed the outside of the building. A valiant yet poor attempt to stop the signs of aging. In contrast, the oversized metal door latch appeared weathered, but probably hadn't seen more than a few winters. Just more facades, like almost everything else in this world. Nature held genetic markers, and she and Nature practically held hands.

The boy Lance walked up the stone path to the barn door. Elli sank back into the shadows and watched him shift onto the outer rim of his sneakers. He jammed his hands in the front pockets of his jeans. A nice boy, as boys went, especially because he held a vital ingredient to her newly-forming plan. It pleased her that she'd found such a special hiding place for his body. One couldn't be too careful in Yggdrasil, in the game of tactics and strategy, where gods and goddesses played the roles of kings and queens shuffling pawns around the chessboard of worlds.

Lance rubbed his ghostly hands together and reached for the latch of the door. He hesitated.

Elli grinned, knowing he would try but fail to lift the latch. She found the tenacity of ghosts attempting to do what they could in life amusing. Instead, they should embrace what they could do in death. Of course, this boy was an exception.

She'd chatted about the strange behavior of new ghosts and spirits with Hela, Queen of the Underworld. That bag of bones had a humorous take on the inhabitants of Midgard – Man's World.

"The second they're free from their flesh suits," she'd said, "they try to sliver back in. Pitiful gluttons for punishment, which, of course, is convenient for me."

She was one to talk, only owning half a flesh suit herself. Hela had cackled, jostling her words between the side of her throat with flesh and the side exposing the bone.

Elli absentmindedly brushed her hand against her pouch of bracteates. It was hard not to pity them. She paused. But pity was not Elli's job. No, she wasn't a banshee, a wailing weeper, or a solemn light elf. That would be funny, though.

The boy abandoned the latch and leaned into the planked boards of the wall. His body seeped through the wooden fibers, cells and energy dispersing. With the blink of her eye, she joined him inside.

Another boy shuffled between two over-sized, swayback chairs and a large wood stove at the farthest end of the barn. Books were laid out on the floor, each opened to mark his academic find. Ah . . . the boy with the strange lizard. She longed for his curious mind, but this was a discovery mission. Caution was key for deceiving and luring pawns into the destructive path of a rook or a knight.

The redheaded boy pawed through a small heap of firewood.

"Fleishman," Lance said and leaped in front of him, making faces.

The boy with the lizard, clueless to Lance's presence, tossed a splintered log on top of the smoking kindling. Lance held his hands in front of the fire. Elli almost broke into a sweat from watching this boy's efforts to fan the fire. She decided to show him mercy and flicked two fingers in the air, setting the log aflame.

"I did it!" Lance cried and gawked at his palms.

Pawns weren't the only ones who could deceive.

"Sorry it's taken so long to start this fire, Nigel." Fleishman secured the amphibian in his cage and the strap over his shoulder. The lizard thrashed his tale against the bars. "What's wrong?"

The legless lizard's eyes flamed a deep violet and focused in Elli's direction. She cloaked the space around her in dampness and grime, what one would expect in a dark corner of a barn. She stared at Fleishman and his problematic lizard.

"Lance is here, isn't he," Fleishman said to Nigel. To the air, "Nice, Lance. Pick on the guy without ghost sight. I set out some research books for you. Have fun."

"Yeah, fun," Lance muttered and tried to kick a table leg, but his foot swept through it.

Binding this boy's body had severely affected his ghost abilities, but that wouldn't be for long.

She seeped backward through the wall as Lance apologized to Fleishman. But his voice couldn't reach the ginger-headed boy's ears.

That Creepy Building on the Hill

Morning chatter surrounded Ebony as she pushed through the entrance of the school. Bodies with backpacks clogged the front hall. The pungent smell of wood oil mingled with the clean of body soap.

Constable Ramsey had shined the floors again, and some students had taken showers. Must have been the eighth-grade boys; most of the underclassman boys were still confused about proper hygiene.

Ebony scanned the students for Fleishman, excited to tell him about the grimoire's message. Instead, she crossed gazes with Cain Erickson – still a sixth-grade soccer star and her nemesis, only his posture was off. And all the color drained from his face.

Good. He should be out of sync after what he'd done.

Her heart squeezed in her chest. She hadn't seen him in three weeks due to his school suspension for trying to use his lame school project to take over Bifrost – the bridge to Asgard. He'd violated the Motley Code of Conduct. It wasn't a mere violation to her. Images floated at the outskirts of her memory – a grungy giant, serpents flying above the bridge, and her father telling her she had to go and that he'd be all right. If it wasn't for Erickson and his Councilor dad, her father would be here.

Almost as if he'd heard her disgust, Erickson looked away.

As she shook her head, annoyed that he was allowed back in school at all, a sting prickled the inside of her wrist. Uneven, red lines streaked her skin. She hadn't noticed how hard she'd been scratching. The itch had kept her up half the night. She'd have to ask Aunt Gertrude for some healing salve.

Ebony gazed at the foyer's mural. The Bifrost bridge she'd stood on battling dark elves and frost giants with her father stretched into the sky. She tapped the wall with her finger.

He'd been right there in this exact spot. With her. And Fleishman. Ebony exhaled. And Lance.

The planets and the airships were the same, even the fire giant cresting a mountain range. But parts of the mural had changed. Or evolved.

More detail lined the planked metal floor of the bridge. Violet strobes arched over the top in a makeshift covering she'd barely noticed when she'd been there. Creatures she recognized as the *Risastór Dýr* – oversized animals, saddled to pair with the gods and light elves in battle – lined in rows. Off in the distance, behind one of the majestic moons of Yggdrasil, slithered a large serpent. Her breath caught in her throat. She wondered where she fit into this painting, into this whole Yggdrasil equation.

"Beautiful artwork," a male voice said.

A tall man gazing at the mural stood next to her; his hands laced behind his back. The dark navy fabric of his suit partially covered his silver wristwatch.

Before she could respond – not sure she should; you know, stranger danger and all – her name squealed into the air by a group of seventh grade cheerleaders. A fanfare of perky waves came with it. Dakota Olson passed her with no notice, but his cousin Quinn tugged his earbuds out his ears to give her a shy smile. Three eighth-grade girls nudged in front of Quinn, glowering at her until they vanished into Ravens Dining Hall. Not everyone liked Ebony's new-found celebrity status.

Neither did she. She'd wanted to be normal, not Bearer of the Doors and noticed all the time.

Ebony sidled past Cermet Hayes, sneaking behind his squad of psychic scientists for quick camouflage but crashed into Motley's quarterback Jacob Andrews and a trio of football players. They parted like the Red Sea, and their big lug heads wobbled atop their string cheese necks as one said, "Hey, it's that girl, Edith."

"It's Evie." His friend elbowed him.

The third, Dwayne, swung his fist in a two-for-one punch. "Her name is Ebony, like the color."

Bravo, Cheeseheads. Ebony scratched her wrist again and bumped her toes into the heels in front of her.

Ghouls stalling punishment over the iced spike pit of Lake Vänern walked faster than these kids; at least she imagined it that way. What was the holdup?

Ebony rose on her toes, her view wedged between the shoulders of two football players. Mentors stationed at the opening to Raven's ushered students inside.

An assembly in the morning?

"Hey, serpent slayer."

"Clint," Ebony startled.

"Look, my close friends use my last name," he said. "And I'd say after what we went through with the whole serpent thing, we're close friends now. So, it's Dawson."

"Oh," she said. "Okay, Dawson." Her stomach fluttered. That was because Dawson was the only eighth grade boy to speak to her, and the only eighth grade boy all the girls wanted to speak to them. She wasn't sure why. He was just a boy. Yeah, a farm boy with all that natural bone structure, but everybody would catch up, right? Since when did she notice bone structure?

"You all right?" Dawson lowered his face closer to hers.

She should answer; ask him to push this group out of the way.

"Move it, people." Or she could wait for Charity, one of the Cheerio Twins, to do it instead. "I found your friend, the kid with the—"

"His name is Fleishman." Ebony shifted with students into disjointed lines.

"Does she know?" Clare, Charity's twin, asked.

"Shush," Charity huffed. "I haven't asked her yet."

"Ask me what?" Ebony said.

Clare faced her. "We know your mom works here now that your dad's on sabbatical."

Was that what everyone called Dad getting sucked through some mystical door with a fire giant?

"Your dad must have told her what's going on with Motley and that creepy building on the hill," Clare finished.

Ebony barely listened, weirded out that the most popular seventh grade girls were talking to her, and a little peeved that she was sweating out her armpits because they mentioned Dad. What did they know about Dad? Nothing.

Her body jolted sideways, swept into the dining hall with the rest of the herd.

"Honestly, why are we moving into the dining hall," she asked nobody, but everybody.

"I think it has to do with the new school." Cermet cleared his throat.

"Yeah, I saw someone putting up a new Njord Academy sign the other day," said a football player as his line moved ahead.

"No way," a kid cutting line said. "That place is abandoned."

Ebony inhaled, her exhale catching her words. It couldn't be abandoned. Lance was a student there. Wasn't he? Studying astral projection? That was what he'd said. He wouldn't lie.

Would he?

Quantum Study Mentor Fitzgerald Denarious pointed Ebony's line to a table near the right side of the hall. A reserved sign was set in the middle of one table. Emblem-crested, sweater-wearing kids about her age occupied those seats, including a girl with perfectly straight blond hair and a glare that could shatter the ice off a frost giant.

"Who are they?" Jacob asked.

Ebony had no idea.

"Take a seat," a mentor near the faculty banquet table up front yelled. "Any seat will do."

"My dad told me he's never seen anyone go in or out of that place," the line cutter said. "And his grandfather was a kid the last time anyone had."

Jacob took a chair next to the Olson boys. "I heard that's because they're vampires."

"No such thing as vampires," Charity gripped the back of a chair.

"That's what you said about huge ravens and fire giants," Clare said, and got a dirty look from Charity.

They paused as a group of students filtered through their line to sit at a table where two seventh grade luminaries were in a chanting battle trying to levitate pencils; students bet on who would win. Everyone knew the use of psychic skills and casting were prohibited in the common areas of the school, but they didn't seem to care.

"Maybe they're criminals," Dwayne offered.

Lance wasn't a criminal.

"I bet they're mental patients." Jacob wiggled his eyebrows.

Or a mental patient, either.

"I heard they're gifted like us," Quinn said.

That was better.

"Be serious," Charity said. "Motley mentors met with Njord elders this morning."

Wait, a meeting? Ebony slid into a chair. Had Wizner told them about his myth?

"And with your mother, Ebony," Charity said, chin lifted all snooty.

Mom? Ebony's heart didn't only squeeze this time. It held its breath. And let out a hiccup.

After she and Fleishman defeated the serpent Nidhogg in the gym, Mom had apologized for keeping Ebony's abilities secret from her, and Ebony had forgiven her. But trusting her again? Way harder. Mom's apology showed Ebony that people could lie with good intentions. She trusted everyone less.

Was her mother doing it again?

"Weirder was seeing Keeper Coffer in person," Charity whispered.

That shook Ebony from her self-pity party.

Keeper Coffer, who dressed like the undertaker from some black and white silent film and never spoke? Had he seen Wizner's myth?

"That guy is real?" Dakota asked.

A football player snorted. "I thought the school made him up."

"No, I saw him, too." Cermet shifted in his seat and brushed into Clare.

"Gross." Clare shooed him away and looked at her sister. "Did he touch me?"

"Focus, Sis," Charity said.

Two mentors clapped their hands, and everyone quieted.

"That's better." Headmistress Regina tried to sweeten the boom in her voice; it didn't work. "Please look over the packet your mentors are passing out."

Muffled voices rose, and private discussions ensued.

"As most of you have speculated, the large brick building on the far side of town is a real school." Bat-Face raised her stubby arms at the man with salt and pepper hair standing next to her. "Please welcome Mr. Seronious Bile, Dean of Njord Academy."

Monetary Jack! This was the man who'd spoken to Ebony by the mural.

Student chatter rose, and a mentor hushed them.

"Dean Bile will also be serving as the interim Overseer of Motley," Bat-Face finished.

Wait, what? Someone's replacing Dad. Ebony's heart plummeted down her chest. She was pretty sure it splattered on the floor, breaking into a million pieces. *Did Mom know?* She searched for Fleishman through the maze of seated bodies and fidgety limbs.

"I'd like to thank your headmistress for giving some Njord students a tour of your beautiful school," Dean Bile said.

Half the heads of the student body turned to face the far table occupied by the Njord students.

"Let me start by saying," he continued, "prior to two and a half centuries ago, Njord Academy was a thriving, educational establishment for students much like yourselves, and run by some of my ancestors."

Bat-Face clasped one hand over the other with a loud slapping sound. She apologized.

"Due to circumstances at the time, the academy closed," he said. "But after a lot of hard work, the academy is ready to once again take its rightful place."

Rightful place. Erickson's Councilor father had said the same thing the night they showed up and Fenrir tore the foyer off Charmed Castle.

"We reopened our doors quietly last year as a trial run with only a handful of students enrolled; to ensure we could make a go of it again," the headmaster said.

Lance. Did the Njord students know him? Or maybe Mr. Bile? Was that why he stood beside her earlier?

"We are of a similar belief and creation system as Motley, but until the events of a few weeks ago remaining separate made sense to us," Dean Bile said.

Bat-Face clenched her hands. Did Njord's history bother her?

"However, with the true existence of Yggdrasil unveiled, we believe it necessary to evolve with such change." Dean Bile tipped his head at Bat-Face and she shifted her weight. Or did this man make her uncomfortable? "Thus, your headmistress and I have decided to resurrect the old Norse tradition of competition. For the next few weeks, all students will train in their given skill set. The end of training will culminate in the first, jointly-held Raidho-Tiwaz – the annual Ullr Games."

The hall erupted in gasps, simultaneously with the ringing of Dean Bile's cell phone.

"No need to jump the mystical hammer, kids." Bat-Face laughed at her joke. No one joined her.

Mentors worked to quiet the room. Bat-Face nodded at Seronious, and he tucked his phone into his pocket.

"Dean Bile must leave for another engagement, but let's thank him for joining us," Bat-Face addressed the dining hall.

A gaggle of groans, claps, and muffled *thank yous* filled the hall. Seronious Bile gave a snipped wave and was followed out the side entrance by the Njord students.

Bat-Face scurried to that entrance (a sight no one should have to witness) to peer out the window.

Spinning on her feet with surprising agility, she said, "Listen up. We have important work to do and little time to do it. As you are aware, the faculty has made changes to our school curriculum to mirror our new knowledge of Yggdrasil's existence. As of today, Motley is implementing sub-groups under our Sensory and Luminary titles called Runes of the Seven Disciplines. Schedule updates have been remotely saved to your jacks. Make sure to upload that information to your note screens. You will undergo a series of trails to determine which discipline best embraces your gifts."

"Trial?" Charity said. "Sounds like work."

"We are in school," Clare said, and her sister mimicked her.

Dwayne whispered, "Anyone feel like Motley is upping its game now that this other school is official?"

"The next two weeks will be spent educating you in the seven disciplines." Bat-Face clasped her hands in front of her. "Let's get ready for our friendly games."

"Friendly games?" Jacob pressed his chest into the table. "I don't think so."

"If I'm playing, I'm doing it to win," Dwayne said.

"We don't have to be mean," Clare said.

"Yes, we do." Charity crossed her arms. "They're not one of us."

Us? Did she mean us as her groupie friends or us as a school?

"That's right. Motley sticks together," Dwayne added.

"Speak for yourself." Charity glared at him.

Guess that answered Ebony's question.

"Oh," Bat-Face paused, "and Njord is hosting a joint-school dance this Friday so you can all meet before the games."

The auras in the room shifted from angry and confused to excited and energetic. Either way, the wave that crashed over Ebony was gross because school dances were . . . well, gross.

"A dance? Yes!" Charity twisted in her chair and gripped her sister's shoulders. "We should buy something new to wear."

Apparently, Charity had changed her opinion about Njord students.

Ebony caught sight of Glinda's red hair in the crowd. No one knew about Lance other than Glinda, Fleishman, Delia, and a few adults. Odd danger had invaded the boneyard, sickly crows had infected a ghost, the grimoire had fed her a cryptic message, and mentors met with Njord's elders from Lance's school.

It would have been less suspicious to shoot a message of fireworks in the sky saying Nothing Strange Is Going On.

Chapter Eleven

Scrambled Innards

The chill from the wall seeped through the back of Ebony's shirt. Fleishman slowly walked up to her.

"I'm sure Dean Bile showing up—"

Ebony raised her hand to stop him.

"You can't always refuse to hear me out."

She shook her head.

"No, you agree or no you disagree?" he asked.

"Both. No, I mean . . . This was supposed to be simple." She counted on her fingers. "Create a location beacon, find Lance's body, put him back together, and have a cheese celebration."

Ebony waited for Fleishman to give her a rundown of all that had happened and all they would need to change.

But he didn't. He stood there, his eyes soft on her. He knew she had more to get out.

"I've been thinking so much about helping Lance and now this little ghost boy," she paused. Guilt and hopelessness cinched around her chest. "My dad, he's over there. And now our mentors are meeting with a new school, and their dean is filling in as our Overseer." Her gaze dropped to her combat boots. "It's like they're moving on without my dad."

"Aw, Ebony," Fleishman said. "No one's forgetting about your dad."

"It feels like it," she said. "Even my mom won't talk about him."

"I know how to make you feel better." He toweled his face and mumbled through his fingers. "Can't believe I'm saying this, but we should go to Njord's dance on Friday night."

Ebony pushed off the wall. "No offense, but you have fewer moves in your dance arsenal than I do. I'm not wasting time at some dance when Lance . . ."

The idea she was thinking must have swept across her face because Fleishman smiled.

"Are you suggesting we attend this dance to dig for information?" she asked.

"Nope, you suggested it," he said, but his smile grew big.

"I'm proud of you." Ebony flung her arms around him.

"Ebony." He pointed to himself. "Not a hugger."

Instead of releasing him, she pushed him behind a nearby trashcan like a linebacker on a mission.

Rita Charmed stood outside the main office. Njord's Dean nodded his head of graying hair and took in whatever her mother offered to their conversation.

Mr. Seronious Bile. His name alone could make cheese curdle.

His students were gone, except for the girl with perfectly straight, blond hair. She pursed her lips at Ebony.

Her mother tipped her head back in laughter and shook Seronious' hand.

How could she be laughing like things were normal? Like Dad wasn't gone? Maybe her mother didn't want to discuss Ebony's father because she had better things to do. Like laugh with some creepy guy. A force wrapped around Ebony's ribcage. The pressure made it hard to breathe.

"Miss Charmed," a voice called.

Ebony jumped back, landing on Fleishman's toe, making him squeal. The headmistress tapped one clunky shoe against the wooden floor.

"Will Fleishman."

Nothing good ever came after an adult used your full name.

"Don't you have a study to be at?" Bat-Face asked.

"Yes." Fleishman stepped around her and backed down the hallway. "Going now." He disappeared up a spiral staircase.

Bat-Face took a step in the opposite direction and cleared her throat, which Ebony interpreted as *Follow me.* Ebony did, and she scratched her wrist, again. What was with this itch? Maybe it was a sign of rain or that she'd win money like when your palm itched.

"Now, Ebony," Bat-Face began, "how are things going for you since the gym incident?"

"Uh . . ." Was this a rhetorical question?

The woman raised a bushy eyebrow.

Guess not. "Um, okay."

"Finding it a challenge to keep up with your studies and training?"

"No."

"No hiccups or issues?"

The headmistress was not an Ebony fan, so why the concern?

"The spirit world is a vast place," Bat-Face said. "We may not be fully informed of how complex it is. You never know when a new or old spirit kind could pop up."

Did she know about Wizner's myth or was she testing to see what Ebony knew? Ebony wasn't sure what to say. She decided to do what Aunt Gertrude often said – *if you don't know the answer pass the buck.*

"I'm sure if anything like that happened Mentor Wizner would tell you."

Bat-Face's sunny demeanor turned to storm clouds. She inched closer, her big body looming over Ebony. "In the aftermath of the gym—" Her gaze bored into Ebony's face like Nidhogg's arrival had been her fault. "I don't expect any issues from you during Raidho-Tiwaz. The Ullr games were implemented to teach many great values. Remember, you're a Seeker."

Yeah . . . Even though Aunt Gertrude told her being a Seeker was rare and special, she still didn't believe that.

"We're proud of her Seeker status." Ebony's mother ambled toward them, pencil skirt restricting her knees and briefcase gripped in her hand.

We were? Her mother had never said that before.

"Is there a problem, Headmistress?"

Whoa . . . Was Mom sticking up for Ebony?

Bat-Face cleared embarrassment and a bit of intimidation from her throat. "Of course not, Rita. We were talking about your daughter's progress with Mentor Wizner."

"Wonderful," Mom said. "I'm sure you told Ebony how hopeful you are for what new Seidr skills she'll develop."

"Why, yes. Always a pleasure to have a Seeker in our midst." Bat-Face smiled, exposing her square teeth.

Mom edged her pointy high-heels up to Bat-Face's thick-soled shoes. "If I hear that you've said otherwise, you'll have me to deal with, regardless of whom was given the interim overseer position."

Ooh, Mom pulled Dad-rank. On top of that, it sounded like she had wanted to fill in for her father until he returned, like protecting it for him, but Seronious Bile got the position. Maybe Mom was on her side after all. It seemed Ebony wasn't supposed to feel bad about being named a Seeker anymore. She didn't want to, either.

Mom pressed her palm at the base of Ebony's back to guide her away from the headmistress.

"I need you to stay away from the cemetery for a while," Mom said.

"Why?" Ebony asked.

"Because your aunts could use help with your brother at home."

That was true, but Ebony knew from the bright crimson bursting anxiety in her mother's aura it wasn't the only reason. It had to be because of Wizner's myth.

"You can train at school with Mentor Wizner during your free period," Mom said.

That was the lamest idea ever.

"Promise you'll listen to me, Ebony."

Ebony would hang out with her brother, but no way would she abandon the boneyard. "Okay," she said. Granted that was half the truth, but it was still true, right?

twelve

Raw Bones

Ebony slipped under the archway and shivered; it always felt cooler in Mentor Ursula's study.

She paused at a poster listing the top ten spirit tracking etiquettes:

Etiquette #8 from the Art of Spirit Tracking:
If you tap into ghostly energy, make sure you're wearing
shoes with rubber soles.

Ebony tapped the tips of her combat boots together. Yup, she was prepared.

Cermet smiled as Ebony passed his pod, but Erickson's piercing stare made her stop.

Aw, he was in Planes & Mystical Beings study with her?

Being a channeler of spirits, it made sense. But it wasn't like he needed to find spirits; they found him. Only the cheese gods knew why any ghost would look for him on purpose when there were other channelers in the world. She sank into her pod.

Luminary students Dakota and Quinn Olson – classification Charmed – sat in the front row, while sensories of other skills like Molly Warner (a telekinetic) and Aiden Jones (a psychic shield) were closer to the back. Even Glinda was seated in a back pod and she was a closet clairvoyant.

Aside from Cermet, the only other student mediums there were the Cheerio Twins and eighth grader Magdalen Priest. Her family was rumored to be centuries old to the area and specialized in the exorcism of maleficent spirits and celestials. With the girl dressing in black and always wearing a silver cross around her neck, it was probably true.

Extraneous energy swelled near the front of the study. Some of it came from the assortment of antique furniture and items stored near three windows that overlooked the back sports fields and the archway to the boneyard. She wondered what life stories came with the child's rocking horse, xylophone, and CB radio. Most of the energy permeated off the elegant wardrobe and two chests that set to the left of the mentor's desk. Nothing came from the bureau on the right.

Ebony scraped her wrist on the edge of her pod to alleviate the itch that was back.

Mentor Ursula scurried into the study, books stacked under her arms: *Baneful Beasts*, *Tools of the Apprentice*, and *Apparitions*. Leaning over her desk, the woman released one book at a time, each thudding upon contact. Her long, bluish-gray hair swayed over both shoulders, and the bangles on her wrists clanked on her desktop.

"Lots of material to cover. Such little time," she said,

while freeing the portable note screen from her desk and jamming the jack into its side portal. "As I'm sure you've already noticed, this is a mixed study of luminary and sensory students. Combining for group learning and execution will benefit all."

Mentor Ursula dragged one trunk closer to the other. Almost everyone tipped forward in their pods, curious to see what was inside. But Ursula simply sat down on one trunk and tapped her note screen, causing all student note screens to bleep. Students groaned and plopped back into their seats.

"The pages I shared with you are to be studied until you can recite them in your sleep." She laughed at herself, which was much sweeter than when Bat-Face did it.

Ebony glanced over her note screen.

The Hierarchy and Stages of the Spirit World

Three Types:
    1. Independent – physical spirit beings with personalities
    2. Detached – inanimate objects such as old ships and airplanes, and animal manifestations
    3. Extraneous Phenomena – poltergeists, vortexes, extra-celestials, and the undefinable

Most of this looked familiar to Ebony from working with Wizner, but she glanced back at animal manifestations. Could this myth or the sickly crows fit into that?

"Let's focus on the Independent ranking, which is broken into five levels." Ursula held up a drawing of what looked to Ebony like the toddler ghost. "Level One is the Unblemished – newly departed souls, seeking guidance to their next destination. Vulnerable, they need the most protection because everything about them from their smell and energy auras is new. Their shades are duller than in life, but still intact."

"Shades?" Jed asked.

"We each have a shade. It's the part of our soul that emanates emotions, empathy, concern," Ursula said. "Many in the spirit world long for these."

Was that what Wizner's myth wanted? Ebony could still hear the toddler ghost's cries.

"Evil," Magdalen mumbled in a sinister voice, and Aiden chuckled.

"Level Two gives us what people refer to as Ghosts and Spirits. They are essentially the same as they existed in the living world, content with existing among us in this form. The difference is that Spirits have made peace with being deceased and have cleansed their souls by crossing through the Shroud – the curtain to the next life; they have chosen to return to our world for various reasons. Ghosts have not made peace with being of the non-living and have declined to crossover to clean their souls. Regardless, both must live close to their bones on hallowed ground."

Close to their bones, repeated in Ebony's head.

The air thickened, and the wardrobe jostled.

"There's an arm coming out of the wardrobe," Charity said.

Those without the ability to see spirits cowered in their pods.

"Oh, my." Ursula rushed to open the wardrobe's doors. "I'm terribly sorry."

An elderly lady wearing a string of pearls, a young woman with blond hair, and a little girl in a frilly dress ambled out of the wardrobe. The little girl skipped to the rocking horse.

"Stay calm, everyone," Ursula said. "Say hello to our guests, who have come to help us with a little exercise. I've been expecting them."

"But I can't see them," Dakota said.

As Mentor Ursula tapped the Motley emblem pinned to her blouse – inner-school communication system – the study door opened and with it brought Mentor Nesbitt in his long, tailored sports coat. A thick stream of smoke and the stench of rotting grass trailed him.

"A little sage burning," he said and snuffed out the smoke, tucking the remains into the leather harness attached to his thigh. Rune stones tumbled out of the velvet bag in his other hand.

Nesbitt set a stone in one corner of the room. Arms raised, fingers and hands forming invisible symbols much like Wizner had done in the boneyard. Greenish energy wafted between his fingers, trailing up his arms to connect with his aura. More astounding was that Ebony could see it.

That was new.

A chant slipped off his lips the faster he wrote. For each corner it was the same until he finished in the center of the room, drawing a line from ceiling to floor and from wall to wall.

"Would a luminary student like to tell me what he did?" Ursula asked.

Glinda spoke. "He warded off the room so nothing bad can get in."

So, Glinda was a luminary, not a sensory. According to Aunt Gertrude, that meant she used spells and runes to exercise her clairvoyant skill, which was different then a sensory clairvoyant using psychic skill. But the result was the same.

"Good, Glinda," Ursula said. "He also insured that the spirits here now can't leave until I break the ward." To the three spirits, "It's a precaution. You understand."

The young woman and elderly lady bowed their heads in response. A creak of the rocking horse was all the little girl had to offer.

Mentor Ursula thanked Mentor Nesbitt, who paused under the archway of the door and bent down.

"I'm placing more runes here along with a few crystals I've prepared ahead of time," he said. "Don't panic when I set the last one in place."

A collective gasp rounded the study.

"I can see the ghosts," Dakota said.

"Me, too." Color rushed to Quinn's cheeks.

"This spell should last about half an hour or until the barrier these runes and crystals are binding is disturbed." And with that Mentor Nesbitt exited the room.

Mentor Ursula tapped her note screen again, getting answering bleeps from the students' screens.

Etiquette #6 of the Art of Spirit Tracking:
Give a hearty welcome to spirits when they make
themselves known to you.

"Jed," Mentor Ursula faced him. "Would you give it a try?"

Jed shifted in his pod, but eventually slid out to stand. With one hand, he fiddled with the side seam of his jeans, while the other hung stiffly at his side. Ebony wasn't sure what skills Jed had, if any.

"Um . . . hi," he said. "Oh, and welcome." He slouched back into his pod.

Ursula clapped her hands and tapped her portal screen, making the next rule appear.

Etiquette #7 of the Art of Spirit Tracking:
Always thank spirits for talking with you.

Ursula turned to Cermet. "Would you do the honors?"

Cermet's face turned a ghoulish green, but he stood anyway. "On behalf of our class, I'd like to thank you for coming."

The little girl continued rocking and the elderly lady remained still. But the young woman jerked her head at Cermet. A pinpoint of black bloated from her chestnut irises, covering both eyes.

Cermet staggered backward, stumbling into his pod.

"*Aftur niður*," Mentor Ursula commanded.

Beige swept over the young woman's irises and her posture softened.

"Sometimes ghosts need a reminder of how to behave," Ursula said.

Ebony slid to the edge of her seat. No boneyard residents had ever acted like that.

Ursula pointed at the elderly lady. "Here we have level three of the Independent group – the fade stage. This level along with level four and five resemble the aging process of living people. With each level their symptoms worsen. Early stages show deterioration of energy, memory loss, slowed skills, and disinterest at times. The only way a spirit can drop to level three, four, or five is to have been separated from their bones."

The grimoire – *separated from their bones . . . turn to pure chaos*. Ebony thought about old man Pottle. "Can it be reversed?"

"Returning to their bones can restore them," Ursula said. "That's if they haven't been away from their bones too long."

"What's too long?" Ebony asked.

"It's different for every spirit," Ursula said.

Not helpful. "How?"

Mentor Ursula tapped on her portal screen, transferring the hierarchy to the white board up front. "It hinges on how much their spirit has been affected and how advanced their symptoms are. This young woman's energy has begun to flicker, putting her at a more advanced fade stage."

Ursula's voice dulled as Ebony focused on the white board.

Level Four – the phantom stage: like a fade, but more severe symptoms.

Level Five – the specter stage: a more erratic silhouette, with numerous abnormalities – changing forms, physical possession. They can be hostile, fidgety, and vicious.

"And if they lose their shade," Ebony heard Ursula say, "souls grow numb. Like zombies."

Panic plummeted down Ebony's throat to kerplunk in her stomach.

A groan rumbled from the young woman. Her cheeks narrowed, her lips moving in slow motion. Mentor Ursula inched forward like a hunter trying to calm a rabid lion.

One of the trunks shook. It rocked harder, lifting all sides and forcing the hinged box to jump. Magdalen, Quinn, and a few other students slipped from their pods.

The young woman twitched, and a separate silhouette pried itself from her figure. It flickered, an iridescent bulb shorting out. Wisps waved off its human likeness and denim overalls.

"A specter!" Magdalen said.

The specter growled, his movements frantic, stance

predatory. Yes, this was a man or at least he used to be.

The elderly lady popped in next to the child, cradling her in her arms.

The cover to the small trunk unsealed. Ghostly hands slinked over the edge of the opening. Two heads appeared, torsos, and then the rest of each body. Bones creaked. Joints cracked. Limbs bent awkwardly, while remnants of tendons and ligaments dangled helplessly. Bare feet pressed onto the floor. And by bare Ebony meant with no skin on them! These weren't ghosts or men, but both ethereal and solid skeletons.

The figures tilted their heads, hollow eyes red and jawbones curled in a gnarl.

Students stood, but Mentor Ursula waved them to stay put. Fists clenched at her sides, she inhaled. The room sparked with psychic energy, and one figure stopped. Unfortunately, the other got away. And smashed the lock of the closed trunk.

Hinges clanked as the cover burst open. Mist spilled over the edges in a blanket of sparkles. It pooled onto the floor.

Mentor Ursula raised her hands at the mist. "*Vertu kyrr.*"

One Cheerio twin pulled the other out of her pod and backed for the archway. "Let's get out of here."

"Do not break the barrier!" Mentor Ursula cried.

Glinda was somehow there, at the entrance. She blocked it and chanted in a low voice. Dakota helped keep the barrier intact by capturing one twin at the waist and the other by the arm.

The center of the pooling mist spurt sparkles into the air.

"We must contain this," Ursula said. "But don't worry. This is only an exercise."

This *still* was an exercise?! Ebony had a mind to conjure

a door to escape through but seeing how that hadn't worked out in the boneyard, she'd better not. She focused her mind on her second idea.

The puddle of mist let off another round of sparkles. Its center wobbled and rolled over itself before it began to rise. It swelled and slumped forward as if yanked at the top by a string.

"We must tell it to back down," Ursula said. "Repeat after me. *Aftur niður!*"

A few students mumbled, but most were stunned silent by fear.

Sparkles separated from the mist in streams, twisting and threading into a solid form – Feathers. Black and lifeless gray feathers.

Dread shot through Ebony's stomach. There was no way this looked like what it was. No. way.

A face slowly emerged through the mist and forming feathers. Eye sockets burrowed out, and a chin grew pronounced. Feathers thickened at both sides and the bottom of a torso taking shape.

Mentor Ursula had abandoned her short command and was yelling a long chant in some language Ebony had never heard before.

More of the mist congealed into feathers until a dark figure stood before them. It bent at the knees and soared off the floor, transforming as it did into the darkened, hooded entity of Wizner's myth.

Ebony almost threw up. She slapped her hand over her mouth just in case she did. She glanced at the other students. Some faces were blank, some were flushed with horror, while some had vanished beneath their pods. Her racing heartbeat pounded in her ears, dulling a heinous shrill from the skeletons as they sped for the specter. Their rattling bones echoed off the walls.

Watching a full-on skeleton run was the creepiest thing

Ebony had ever seen. She turned away because if this was real then what happened at the Boneyard was real, too. And even though she knew it had happened, she wanted to pretend it hadn't. Just like with Dad being gone, Lance's body being stolen, and all this possibly hurting him. Did she want the easy way out? Yes! She decided because she certainly didn't want to deal with Wizner's freaky feathered myth.

The specter wailed and raced to Glinda under the archway. Mentor Ursula slid in next to her, bellowing the chant at the specter. It frantically switched directions to flee toward the windows, but it wasn't fast enough.

One skeleton latched onto it; slivers of ghostly flesh flaked away. Boney fingers raked into the specter's wavering figure, and its ghost energy sputtered.

Ebony turned her face away. This hurt her heart.

Mentor Ursula left Glinda and began drawing symbols in the air all while never breaking her chant. Wizner's myth slowed, seeming stunned. It quickly recovered to snatch the elderly lady off the floor; the little girl ghost dangled in her arms.

Glass shook. Kids screamed and pointed at the windows. A shadow spread over the athletic fields, gaining weight and speed the nearer it drew.

Ebony rushed to a window and pounded on the lock. Coils released. The panes of glass sprung up in time for Hugin and Munin – Ebony's raven messengers from Yggdrasil – to soar into the study; they'd heard her cry for help.

Armored breastplates glistened under the florescent lighting. The ravens shifted as their hollow bones and feathers bloated bigger until they reached half their normally massive size. A handful of black crows flew in behind them. Frantic caws engulfed the room.

At sight of the healthy crows and over-sized ravens,

Wizner's myth dropped the elderly lady and little girl to swoop for the open window. One skeleton crouched and pushed off the floor, leaping into the air close behind the myth. Legs folded beneath. Arms flailed out, bones contorting into wings. Not just any wings, but those of a crow with graying feathers. The black crows shot through the air like arrows, chasing the myth and skeleton-now-crow out the window.

Hugin chattered while Munin pecked at the remaining skeleton. Bone fragments scattered. Dim light beamed off the specter and pulsed once, twice, and the specter vanished. Munin landed a huge chomp to the skeleton's left limb. It shrilled and backed away, one step and then more. Mentor Ursula shoved the trunk forward as it fell backward, capturing the skeleton. She slammed the cover shut and refastened the lock.

Other than a few kids panting, silence engulfed the room. Hugin and Munin busied themselves pruning their feathers like they'd woken from a nap.

"What was that hooded thing?" Ebony asked.

Ursula pushed off the floor to stand. "There are many things we've yet to learn about Yggdrasil. That would be one of them."

If Ebony hadn't seen the deep burgundy of concern thread through Ursula's aura, she might have believed her.

"I expected a few surprises during these first exercises," Ursula said. "The skeletons were Hrár Beins or as we call them Raw Bones – ghostly energy turned to pure chaos."

"What's that mean?" Clare asked.

Magdalen brushed off her legs. "They're empty shells, mindless."

"You mean zombies like draugrs?" Cermet said.

"Draugrs are flesh zombies," Ursula said. "Raw Bones have no ghostly self or soul left."

"What happened to the specter?" Ebony asked.

Ursula looked at the floor. "It died."

"Ghosts can't die." Charity stepped next to Clare.

"Oh, but they can," Mentor Ursula confirmed.

Chapter

Thirteen

Interlude

Elli ambled away from the school on a paved trail leading to the graveyard. It wasn't right she was having so much fun. Then again, what was that saying? *When in Midgard . . .*

She'd burst into an outright cackle when the trunk covers opened. To see chaos in action among humans so young had been a delightful treat; they made frightening them too easy. She hadn't expected her leaf message to be answered so swiftly and by a human no less. But Councilor Erickson despised Motley almost as much as she did her own enemies. Granted, he had his own personal agenda, which she'd offered to aid . . . for a price.

The melody humming from her mouth grew more fluent with every bump of her fingertips along the wrought iron fence. Her lips softened, the outline plumper. Age spots faded from her hands. Wrinkles smoothed out across her skin, and she breathed effortlessly for the first time in a long time.

It wasn't easy being the personification of old age, you know. All the aches and pains, and the crabby attitude. She would feel bad for mortals, comfort them at their end while waiting for a spirit-tracker or their reaper if they didn't need her to get old. Her existence was such a rip-off.

Yes, it was, but no mind. It wouldn't be much longer.

Two Mist Gypsies flanked the shadowy entrance to the forest. Both bowed in her direction.

"At least someone reveres me." She whirled her fingers once, releasing them from her presence. What she had to do would be easier done without distractions.

Entrance to Niflheim or Muspelheim - take your pick read the inscription on the sacred archway. She pressed forward to amble over the threshold, but a thick presence stopped her.

"Wards," she said.

A well-played move by the girl's mentor. He'd not only battled her Mist Gypsies the other night, but he'd also warded down the graveyard; well, as much as was within his power. He must have come back because the protective scents of holly and star anise were everywhere. They smelled awful. This might keep her Mist Gypsies from stealing shades and consuming souls here, but it wouldn't stop them from creating havoc. Unfortunately for him, no ward was strong enough to deter her.

Her touch lit an inscription of runes scrolling down the insides of the ancient gateway. *"Miðju miðstöðvar milli Yggdrasil og Midgard,"* she read in the native dwarf tongue. "The center of centers between Yggdrasil and Man's World." She pressed her ring, the one on her usually-crooked finger, into one of the runes. The glow washed-out. Pebbles ground beneath her sandals as she entered the graveyard.

Ash Pathway was longer and better groomed than she remembered. Clever of those Norns to have mountain ash, the most protective wood sacred to Yggdrasil, planted here; ironic the trees flourish among the dead.

A dainty snort vibrated her nose, the bulbous end reshaping smaller and more delicately refined. As much as she enjoyed this game of catch and release it wasn't strategic, and strategy was a must to achieve checkmate. It was time to up her game.

The crossroad to her home away from home had to be up ahead. It'd been a long time, but the tumbleweed of decaying monuments that had once shone brightly couldn't be moved by anyone, least of all mortals. And not after what she'd done to insure its future survival. Duplicating and transferring growth from Yggdrasil to her own private cove had been a brilliant move, if she did say so herself. An arsenal of Nature at its best and worst all her own. Surely nothing the gods would expect.

She held her palms up. Air stirred. Energy from the dead lifted, connecting with her. This had become her favorite part.

Streaks of blues and yellows whirled around her feet. They traveled up her body, transforming her tattered clothing into sparking gold material. The pouch at her hip glimmered into a diamond and pearl sash to hug her waistline. Coin bracteates from inside the pouch circled around her wrist to form a beautiful charm bracelet. She released the mangled whispers of Nature's disasters from her tresses. Graceful, caramel strands tumbled over her shoulders and down her back. Her neckline glimmered with bronze gems. Her angelic smile turned up with a devious edge that Odin himself would have to admire.

"Odin," she *pffted*. "Nothing but an old man with a swollen ego and authority complex." Though she spat the words, the sounds came out as a song, a sweet lullaby to any hearing ear. "It used to be this way." She let the memory sweep her away.

Sunlight painted the crest of a mountain range. Reflections of blues and tangerine flowed downward, highlighting clefts in the rocks. The land smelled of pine and spice. Trees so green and in every shade imaginable. Gold and more gold coated parts of nature as it could only do there. It was so beautiful.

"Heim," trembled from her, softer than a whisper.

A lone tear slid down one cheek. This was the reason she never allowed for memories. They did nothing but strip her anger and weaken her resolve. Her limbs tensed, her vengeance intact. She had pledged herself to this plan long ago. Atonement was necessary, even for immortals. The Vanir house she was born into shouldn't have traded her during the peace agreement. And the Aesir house should have found her more valuable.

Longing and despair slashed at her memory into the past. The chain of her bracelet disintegrated. The shiny bracteates dulled and clanked into her tattered coin pouch at her waist. Worn leather re-laced her feet into old sandals. Grime sprinkled the cotton that abraded her aged skin. All the discomfort from the cycle of life returned.

She leaned on a tombstone. Tired – tired of being something she was never meant to be, tired of carrying the judgment of an act she had no control over, and tired of chasing her dream of returning . . .

Twigs snapped up ahead. She refocused and watched branches wave beyond the brush. Could it be children? *The children?*

Straightening her crooked back, she parted her lips to give her nose more room to wiggle. No sweetness or sugary bits in the air. It wasn't children. Maybe a ghoul, then.

No, the reek of ghoul saliva wasn't there. Another

possibility would be one of Yggdrasil's ridiculous rodent messengers: mangy squirrel gossipers. But the ammonia stench that came with rodents couldn't be detected, either. (Ammonia stench equaled urine. Those pests liked to pee everywhere. They called it scenting. She called it disgusting.)

She dragged her hand over the top of a tombstone, and it wiped away clean. Seemed someone had swept up the dust mingled with fears and vermin she'd sprinkled atop tombstones and poisoned the craggy ground with. Her brow furrowed at the passing of another scent.

A spell. The use of sage signaled the makings of a spell. But only a powerful witch would risk casting here; too much energy of the dead to accidentally tap into.

She careened the corner at the crossroads of Wolf's Crossing and Bjorn Trail. Nature's greenery thickened. Branches knotted, and vines coiled, creating a dense wall of coverage. The ceiling of trees mushroomed above, blotting out the sky.

With one flick of her fingers, a thicket of overgrowth imploded. Splinters of twigs littered the air. Vines recoiled. Branches brushed aside, and leaves milled to dust.

There they were. Her old guard dogs crowded by unkept shrubs and croaking vines. All appeared undisturbed, except for three branches on a sycamore bush – one of her many traps.

No doubt about it. Someone had been here. This would not do. She pinched a crippled twig between her fingers; it withered in her hands.

Who dared enter Dead Alley?

Fourteen

Mission Location Bacon

old the provolone! Ghosts. Could. Die.

Poof. Gone.

Like forever.

Ebony shifted in line, unable to decide which salad to order. She should have a sandwich. With peanut butter. Not because it was full of protein she'd need later when ghostly things needed doing. But because it would stick to the roof of her mouth and distract her from thinking about the Raw Bones and Wizner's myth.

Once Ursula closed the window to her study, it looked as though nothing had happened. Maybe nothing had because not a soul, dead or alive, mentioned a word about noise, clicketing Raw Bones, or messenger ravens from Yggdrasil visiting Motley. Ebony wondered if Nesbitt's ward of the room also cloaked it to appear normal. Probably. Armed with a peanut butter and jelly sandwich and a chocolate milk, she sauntered to the lunch table where Fleishman sat with his unopened salad and dropped her lunch next to Nigel's cage.

"You'll never guess—"

"Raw Bones." Fleishman cut her off. "I heard."

Ebony sat down. "How?"

"Charity and Clare."

Figured. She popped the clear cover off his salad and picked up the extra fork he always brought for her. She should have gotten a salad.

"Wizner's myth showed up, too," she said.

He lifted one shoulder.

"And you don't think that's a big deal?"

"Of course, I do. It's just," he hesitated. "Headmistress Regina wouldn't let me take Nigel out of Mentor Lyn's room."

Ebony scratched her wrist. "You never carry him around school."

"But . . ." He patted Nigel through the bars of his cage. "He must have been scared."

She stabbed a cucumber with her fork. He wasn't serious?

He stared at her.

He was serious. "I know Nigel is your pet."

"Hey," Fleishman said. "Nigel is more than a pet."

She couldn't believe they were having this conversation. "What about vicious, iron-spiked, energy-zapping wormasarous?"

Fleishman eyed her.

"I meant warrior serpent. Better?"

The blue line on Nigel's back glowed a deep purple.

"He approves."

"Anything to make Nigel happy," she said.

His freckles bounced on his cheeks as he chewed. "Was the Raw Bone as freaky as last night?"

"Pretty much." She thought about it. "But not as much now that I have an explanation for the gray crows."

"Like I say, knowledge is power," he said.

"Exactly." She leaned in as two girls walked by their table. "That's why we need to know more about Wizner's myth."

He stopped chewing.

"You saw what it did to the toddler ghost," she said.

"I'm not sure what it did," he said.

"It came back." Her voice quivered. "And it paid a lot of attention to Dead Alley, which makes me want to search that place."

"That's only because the 3Ms told you to stay out of it," he said. "You know you like to do the opposite of what you're told to do."

Ebony sputtered her lips at him. "What's your excuse for staying out of Dead Alley?"

"I'm terrified of what's in there."

"That's shocking," she kidded. "So, I shouldn't be suspicious that my mom ordered us to train in the school with Wizner instead of in the boneyard?"

He hesitated, visibly taken back by this information. "Still, leave this to Wizner."

"We can't," she insisted.

"Why?"

Because I peeked in my aunts' grimoire and it showed me stuff! "Because," was all that came out.

"Because isn't an answer," he said.

She tossed her fork down. "During the exercise in Mentor Ursula's study, one of the gray crows pecked a ghost, which made it weak. And Lance is a ghost, according to Underworld standards, at least for now. And the ghost . . ."

"What?"

"It died," she whispered. "Ghosts can die."

He leaned forward, and she explained what happened to the specter. The idea of how final the specter's death was sliced a wound in Ebony's heart she was sure would never heal. Being responsible for ghosts in the boneyard was serious stuff.

"Of course!" Fleishman almost choked on the cherry tomato in his mouth. "Ghost energy is energy, and all energy can be made to disperse into another form. Explains that Raw Bone turning gray crow. And we know the possessing entities will weaken the spirits or hosts they attach themselves to. Plus, if a black hole exists and there's pure chaos," he paused, "and who knows—"

"Slow down," she rasped. "You're so far ahead of me I'm dizzy."

"Sorry," he said. "What happened to the other guest ghosts in the study room?"

"Hugin and Munin left to guide them back to their bones. I guess volunteering earned them a restart to their spirit journeys." At least something good came of all that.

Fleishman nodded his head. "The fact that this ghost died after being pecked . . ."

His last syllable faded, and he stared softly into Ebony's eyes. A tickle attacked the tip of her nose, but she let it be.

"Does that mean the toddler ghost won't get better?" she asked.

"I'm sure Delia is working on it," he said.

"We have to do something, too," she said. "There's no doubt now that the graying crows made the ghosts sick, that Wizner's myth is involved somehow, and that Lance is in danger, probably all the boneyard ghosts. The real question is who or what made the crows sick in the first place?"

Fleishman tapped her arm. "You're right. We'll figure this out, and it will be okay."

"Easy for you to say," she huffed. "You're not the misfit

seeker Yggdrasil put in charge of the boneyard."

"No, I'm the skittish sensory Yggdrasil put in charge of the seeker who's responsible for the boneyard," he said.

Ebony snorted. "Your job's worse."

"Nope," he said. "We're in this together."

She paused, wanting to agree but was unsure if that was true.

By the way his cheeks fell, she knew her silence bothered him, but he moved on. "We could ask your aunts about the myth."

"And let them know we're breaking rules looking for Lance's body and whatever this thing is?"

"Right," he nodded. "Follow the rules. What an awful thought."

Ebony ignored his atypical jab. "What if we should be looking for something else?"

"Instead of Daenir?" He raised his eyebrows.

"Maybe Daenir took Lance on purpose, and these Raw Bones slash crows, the sick boy ghost, the myth showing up, and that it's happening in the boneyard are no coincidence."

Fleishman stopped mid-bite, his thinking meeting hers. "A bigger connection between Daenir and Lance is possible. Do you think he has anything to do with this?"

"No." But she wasn't sure. "Do you?"

"We don't know much about Lance, really," Fleishman said.

They collected their half-eaten salad and Ebony's not-even-touched lunch and exited into the school's foyer, dumping their trash in the trashcans. Ebony should tell him about the myth image from the grimoire. But Fleishman received stressful information best when spoon-fed, otherwise it could get ugly with him flailing and pacing like a madman.

At the top of the staircase, she pulled him aside and tugged her grimoire scratching from her satchel. "You should see this."

"What is it?" He slid the paper out of her hand.

"A lead on Daenir or Lance's body, maybe both."

"These are the Old Norse language and maybe runes. Only . . ." He covered a few lines with his pinky. "They're more complicated. Like there are too many hashmarks."

"Can you read them?"

"Maybe." His eyes brightened.

"I think this part is a map." She pointed.

"This looks like your handwriting." His tone went flat.

"Um, yeah. I copied it down," she said.

"From what?"

"It doesn't matter."

"It always matters with you," he said.

"Hey." What was up with his tone?

"Where'd you get this?" Fleishman jabbed at her paper. She sighed. "You won't believe me."

"What did you do?"

It seemed he'd gained confidence since battling Nidhogg, which she'd like much better if he used it on someone else. She snatched the paper and waved her rune tattoo over it, thinking it might decode again.

"What are you doing?" Fleishman asked.

"Nothing," she huffed.

"Your skin is red." He looked at her wrist. "Did you get bit by a crow?"

The worry in his voice punched her in the gut. "No."

He pressed the back of his hand to her forehead. "You're not warm."

"And you're not a thermometer." She ducked under his arm and headed to Mentor Blu's Language and Runes study.

"What if you're sick?" he called after her.

"I'm not sick." Could she be sick? She turned and held out her hand. "Look at my paper."

Moving next to her, he tugged on the edges of the paper to straighten out the wrinkles. "Covering up some lines, these might mean to uncover or shed light on."

"That's the lighthouse the grimoire showed me!"

"I knew it." He shook his head. "Your aunts' grimoire?"

"It wasn't on purpose. The book was alone in the kitchen and flipped pages," she said and tapped her paper in his hand. "It showed me this stuff. Don't worry. Aunt Gertrude said the book was for me, too, even though I'm a sensory."

"So, you told them what the book did," he said.

"Not exactly."

He pursed his lips and glanced at the paper. "Is this a stick figure?"

"Yeah, a woman," Ebony said. "And behind her was all kinds of different bad weather. Oh, and there were these pillars and objects laying all around them. It was weird."

"Hmm . . . so maybe we're looking for a woman who survived natural disasters, and . . . I have no idea about the pillars. Maybe they're a landmark in Yggdrasil someplace?"

"Could be," Ebony agreed.

"I bet there's information in the history section of Motley's Public Library. Hey," he paused, "I've seen these three triangles before."

"Where?" Ebony asked.

"In Yggdrasil, on medals and jewelry," he answered. "I need to do more research."

Of course, he did. Ebony tossed mental confetti into the air. "Where should we go? I'll call on a door."

"Whoa." He held up his hands. "Wizner was right to tell you not to call on any more doors. And where in Yggdrasil would we travel?"

"Why does everything sound logical when you say it?" she exhaled. "Can I at least check on the boneyard after school?"

"It's too dangerous, Ebony."

She crossed her arms and pouted.

He dodged two students passing by and sighed. "We stay no longer than five minutes."

"Done," she said.

"And how about we visit Xander in the Archive this weekend to research. At least that's on local ground and not breaking any rules," he said.

"Can't wait to see how this fits into Mission Location Bacon."

"Remind me why we're calling it that," he said.

Ebony counted on her fingers. "One, it's a mission. Two, we're trying to create a location beacon and now more. And three, take the e from beacon and you have bacon, which rhymes with location."

"Your thought process scares me," Fleishman said.

"It sounds better." She shrugged. "Plus, you won't forget it because it annoys you."

"I retract my previous statement," he said. "Your entire brain terrifies me."

Ebony ambled down the hallway. "Then my job is done."

fifteen

Gone Girl

Pebbles skidded beneath Ebony's boots as she stopped to let Fleishman catch up.

She scanned the boneyard, which was brimming with ghostly activity from gossip circles to the Boneyard's officials discussing governing rules and the upcoming Boneyard elections on the ghostly plane. A crowd of ghosts gathered at the gambling pit where old man Pottle frequented. Ebony wasn't sure what he gambled away, though.

Giggles filled the air as ghosts danced around an angel statue keeping watch.

A sweet smile swept across Ebony's lips. She was the reason for their renewed happiness. Plus, she knew their category of ghost – Independent. It felt good, yet strange to see her medium skills as something positive after years of being ashamed of them.

Controlling her ability made her proud, but she was obligated to use it. Only, with danger near, she had no idea how to keep this place safe.

"Is running part of your training now?" Fleishman panted.

"You said I only had five minutes to check on the boneyard residents," she reminded him.

"Since when do you listen to me?"

Ebony laughed and laced her arm with his. "Come on. Everyone's over there."

The same hawk she'd seen before drifted above their heads. The bird released a hoarse screech and landed in a nearby tree.

"What's his problem?" Ebony asked.

"See the crows in the tree next to the one he landed in," Fleishman said. "He's probably deciding which one to pick off."

Gross.

"By the way, the bigger ones are ravens, not crows," he said like everyone knew that.

Three smaller birds (also known as crows) waddled down Ash Pathway, bumping into each other like they'd stepped off the Tilt-O-Whirl at the Oxford County fair. They stumbled onto a fork in the path that veered down Wolf's Crossing; the other path curved around the backside of the graveyard to Dead Alley.

Amphylis waved from a few rows away as the two neared. Tanner leaned against a tree, sprig of grass in his mouth. Hargraves nodded his head as he and Victoria returned to their conversation. George didn't acknowledge them, too busy reading the same newspaper publication he read every day. Pottle touched the brim of his forever dusty farmer's hat in acknowledgement. He plopped down on a concrete slab that covered a family of graves and fanned his deck of cards between his fingers in some Old Western parlor trick way.

"Pottle scares me," Fleishman whispered.

"What doesn't scare–" Ebony paused and tugged Fleishman past the last row of graves. "Fleish."

"I see it." His voice cracked.

Mottled half-moons cupped under old man Pottle's eyes, lightening his cheekbones to chalky white. Faint blue dots blotted his skin like teenage acne. Ebony scanned the other residents to find most looked drawn with a loss of color, but relatively normal.

Amphylis lumbered between him and a large ceramic planter. Her gray hair frizzed at the ends.

"Amphylis, are you okay?" Ebony asked.

"Why yes. Feeling a tad out-of-sorts is all. Presumably due to cold weather coming," she said.

"Surely it's nothing," George said, face angled at his newspaper.

It was not nothing, but Ebony didn't want to scare them.

"Tanner, pick up those cards," Amphylis said. "Must keep my graveyard clean."

"Yes, ma'am." Tanner shuffled the cards into an orderly deck.

A familiar increase in air pressure filled a rectangular area nearby. Wooden panels warped into a solid door. The door knocker drew into the shape of an elaborate tree. The seal popped, and Delia spilled over the threshold.

"Ebony, Fleishman," Delia said, "I have a message from the Watchers."

The boneyard ghosts gathered nearer as Delia whirled two fingers in the air. A large, rolled-up leaf appeared in her palm. She whispered a chant and blew over Nature's scroll, unrolling it to reveal sigils and runes etched on the inside. Delia held up the message to read.

"Since the cemetery reopened to the spirit world, supernatural elements from Yggdrasil have vanished at an alarming rate. We believe this is connected to the orange petals and the sickly crows. The petals are from the scarlet poppy fields in Vanaheim. Normally, they hold wonders. But these petals have been altered in color and potency to act as a poison. And although your defeat of Nidhogg protected the Well of Urd, security has been amped up around the other two wells."

The leaf withered and crumbled to dust.

A faint ache gripped Ebony's stomach. Wizner myth had to be part of this. But what was this?

"I'm here for another reason," Delia said. "The toddler ghost has gotten sicker."

"Oh, dear boy," Amphylis said.

Ebony's heart sank.

Old man Pottle mumbled and paced. Tanner tried to calm him, but the man only grew more agitated.

"What has been done for him?" Hargraves float-walked forward.

"We've treated him with plant extracts, medicinal herbs, therapeutic crystals and chants," Delia shared. "Even used the mystical salve from a fire dragon lily stem of the healing pond in Alfheim. The illness is not a physical ailment, but a complex spell ignited, we believe, by ingesting the mist from these poppies."

"Then shouldn't we be sick?" Ebony asked.

"The spell has an underworldly element to it, targeting the spirit world and crows. This is supported by Hela's claims that energy is wavering in the Underworld," Delia said. "Our fear is that this is only part of the spell."

"Meaning?" Fleishman adjusted his hand on Ebony's arm.

"The living might be next." Delia scanned the ghosts. She tipped her head at Ebony. "I must report back about this." And with that she and the door evaporated.

"Did you start the party without me?" Lance said, plopping down on a tree branch.

"Lance!" Ebony said, panicked because she didn't want him getting sick, too. But also, because he didn't know about Wizner's myth, the toddler ghost, or how the boneyard residents weren't feeling well. She needed to tell him, soon. But what was the sense in making him worry or scared? She'd tell him when they figured this out.

"Looks like changing clothes is getting easier for you," she said, hoping he couldn't see the residents' symptoms from where he sat.

"Yeah." He shrugged in his long-sleeved rugby shirt, a baseball cap covering his head.

Pottle leaped from his stone perch. His hand teased the gun at his hip, trigger finger jittery, and a hiss quivered off his thin lips. Tanner raised his hands in the air. The Adam's apple in his throat bobbed from his swallow. Pottle sucked in a breath, slurping saliva to the back of his mouth, and drew the gun from his holster.

"Cheat'n, eh." The old man's voice sounded strange, an echo through a hollow tube.

Fleishman stepped behind Ebony.

"No . . . no, sir," Tanner stuttered. "Aces high."

"I seez an ace, boy. How'd you thinkin' it high meanin' you win?" Pottle tossed his cards on the slab.

"They're dead." Fleishman's voice shook. "Does it matter if Pottle shoots him?"

Ebony grimaced. "And you're the brains of this operation?"

Lance snorted from his branch.

"Aces high means the ace has the most value in the deck, sir," Tanner said, his voice fading at the end.

Old man Pottle stilled and then holstered his gun. "I reck'n you're right."

Tanner helped the old man sit down.

"Poor Mr. Pottle," Amphylis tsked. "Seems his forgetfulness has worsened. He's been without his bones for so long."

"Without his bones?" Ebony asked.

"His bones aren't buried here." The woman released a labored sigh. "Not anymore."

"Anymore?" Fleishman asked.

"Although earthquakes are rare in these parts, there was quite the tremor some time ago," Amphylis said. "Part of Mr. Pottle's family crypt sank into the earth. His bones along with his daughter's bones were lost."

"That's terrible," Ebony said.

"After that his daughter's ghost could not be found." Amphylis glanced back at him.

"She ran away?" Fleishman asked.

"She was lost." Amphylis tapped the end of her nose with her handkerchief.

"Lost?" Fleishman asked before Ebony could.

"We don't know how," Hargraves said.

George glanced up from his newspaper. "She was gone."

"Gone," old man Pottle grunted.

"I don't remember seeing a Pottle crypt," Fleishman said. "Where was it?"

All went quiet.

"In Dead Alley," Hargraves whispered.

Amphylis shushed him. Ebony and Fleishman gazed down Ash Pathway to Bjorn Trail and the fork in the path that led to Dead Alley.

"A possible vortex or black hole for that energy," Fleishman whispered.

"Rumor was that the disturbance came from a quarrel between the gods," Hargrave said.

"No more, Mr. Hargrave," Amphylis said. "It cannot be discussed."

Ebony and Fleishman stared at each other. They may not be telepathic, but they were thinking the same thing.

Lance jumped down from the tree. Ebony tugged Fleishman away from the residents, hoping Lance would follow. She had to keep their sickly appearance from him. At least for now. He changed course to step up beside Ebony.

"I don't want to end up like that," he whispered, staring at Pottle.

Ebony's heart did that lumpy bounce in her chest. She scanned the ghosts before her. Each had a life (and death) story that belonged to them alone. She had never considered that before.

This place had been her escape, where she never worried about being Ebony. It felt heavy with responsibility she didn't want, but at the same time she couldn't let anything happen to it. Feeling overwhelmed didn't give her the right to ignore it, and she couldn't turn her back on Lance, even if he was involved. But she had no idea what to do, and no amount of training could prepare her for this in such a short time. She hadn't even grown hair on her legs, yet she was expected to care for souls and the Great Beyond.

"You won't, Lance." She ignored Fleishman's frown. "Come to Njord's dance with us to see if you recognize anything."

Fleishman didn't comment. Instead he leaned away, breaking connection with her ghost sight.

Was he mad because she invited Lance? It wasn't like she'd planned to. It just happened.

Wizner's words replayed in her head *You are too spontaneous, not thinking before you act. You must trust my better judgment and Fleishman's too.*

Fleishman headed to a boneyard exit. She quickened her pace and reached out to him, but thought better of it. *Trust*, she thought. She should have talked to him before offering. He was disappointed in her.

Dealing with the dead and living people was similar. Everyone had the same basic needs and wants out of life: to have friends, to be cared for, to be safe, and to belong. For the most part, that responsibility laid on more experienced people like the adults in Ebony's life. And now on Fleishman. She hadn't thought how he was handling this.

Was he having a hard time, too?

sixteen

Berserks

ebony trudged beside Fleishman through the sea of bobbing heads in the hallway. Neither had said a word since their boneyard visit the day before.

"I'm sorry I didn't talk to you before I invited Lance, Fleish."

"Finally." He shifted his backpack on his shoulder, stopped dead-center of the hallway. "I get your thinking behind it, but you could have asked what I thought. Why didn't you?"

She shrugged because she wasn't sure. She had no reason not to trust Fleishman, but she couldn't shake the fear that squeezed her heart when she thought of trusting.

He bit the corner of his mouth, squishing up one cheek

and examining her like she was a science anomaly he struggled to figure out.

A stinging itch shot through her rune tattoo. Gripping her sleeve to rough it over her wrist didn't give any relief. Neither did bunching up the fabric to air out her skin. It was blotchy, lumpy, and swollen.

"That looks worse," Fleishman said.

Chatter drifted in their direction.

"I . . ." Ebony sucked in a slushy breath and froze as her tattoo sparked blue.

"What is that?" Fleishman gawked at her wrist. "Why is it glowing without a door?"

Before she had time to answer – not like she was going to, though – he backed her to the hallway mentor station to wedge her body between it and the adjacent wall, using his body as a shield.

"This has happened before?" His voice dripped with *You didn't trust me, again.*

She exhaled anxiety. "With the grimoire."

"Ch . . . ch . . . charmed," Erickson's voice oozed over Fleishman's shoulder, "and Will, cuddling."

A few boys snorted. Even Jed. Ebony stabbed him with a glare. Had he forgotten how she'd helped him in the gym with Nidhogg? When Jed noticed, he dropped his head, finding his feet interesting.

Her heart pounded. Erickson deserved a verbal flogging, but losing her temper wasn't how the bearer of the doors should act. Being responsible was tough. It called for acting opposite to how you were feeling, which made it confusing, too.

Erickson edged up to them, his head held at a strange angle. His pupils expanded, erasing most of his green irises. Breath of salt and vinegar chips steamed the side of her face.

"Thurisaz," Erickson said, his body jerking. "Odin,"

came out in a croak. He drew a symbol in the air and at the same time intersected it with the fingers of his other hand. Two fingers folded into his palm, straightened digits separated to a V. He hiccupped, "Berserks."

Ebony had no clue what *thurisaz*-whatever meant and saying Odin . . . she'd bank that for later thought. But calling her berserks was way out of line.

His pupils shrank. Confusion wrinkled his forehead. He backed away. The pain in Ebony's wrist vanished and so had the glow.

"Where's your pet lizard, Will?" Erickson asked like he hadn't acted bizarre. "Maybe I can transform it like I did my school project."

"Stay away from Nigel."

Wow, Fleishman said that. Out loud. She liked him using his bolder confidence against Erickson. But Erickson was her Achilles heel, the person that got under her skin and made her feel badly about herself. She wasn't perfect, but she'd learned a lot recently and didn't need to feel that way about herself anymore.

"Your project failed," Ebony said.

Erickson's face beamed redder than the fire lava of Muspelheim. She kept going.

"You're the reason my father isn't here."

The red tint drained from his cheeks.

"Can't believe they let you back in school." That was mean, but she had so much going on inside, some of it had to come out or she'd burst.

Erickson recovered. "They know I'm needed here."

Ebony stepped back. What did that mean, and who were they? Before she could question him, he tugged his friends away, only not before Ebony noted a change in his expression. He looked sad, worried.

Erickson didn't do sad and certainly not worried. More like smug and arrogant.

"Are you okay?" Fleishman asked.

"Sure. Why?" she asked.

"I've never heard you talk like that before."

The bell chimed, and she raced to Mentor Nesbitt's study room, so she didn't have to answer.

Chapter

seventeen

Land of a Thousand Soul Eaters

entor Nesbitt clapped his hands. "There are numerous worlds in Yggdrasil such as Alfheim or Svartalfheim and ruins like the Gjallarbrua Bridge, the Forest of Ironwoods, or the mystifying and said-to-be-haunted Shifting Hollow to explore. But now we're moving on to Jotunheim, land of the giants."

Ebony shifted in her pod. Her butt hurt. This study period seemed to go on forever.

Mentor Nesbitt drew on the screen embedded in his desktop. Two vertical lines crossed two horizontal lines that formed a tic-tac-toe board blinked on the note screens attached to each student's pod.

"This is simplified, but it gives you a geographical idea of where one world is in relation to another." He pointed to one square. "Here we have Jotunheim, a vast land of dark forests, cold waters, and the sharpest mountain peaks in all of Yggdrasil. It's said to have some of the harshest terrain in all the Nine Worlds."

"And the biggest giants, right?" Dakota said.

"That's true nowadays, but it wasn't the case at the beginning," Nesbitt said. "To the Norse, the word giants, *jötnar* in their native tongue, was the name for a tribe of humanoid-spiritual beings whose power and strength equaled both tribes of gods – the Aesir and Vanir."

"You mean angels?" a girl asked.

"No," Nesbitt huffed a chuckle and leaned against the front of his desk. "Definitely not angels. The word giant referred to their superior abilities not their physical size. Ancient scrolls and folktales dubbed them with the title Mist Gypsies because gypsy means wanderer, which is what they did, and they could speckle into mist and vanish."

Wizner's myth.

"I know a few people I wish would speckle into mist and vanish," Caleb said, and a few kids laughed.

Nesbitt drew a circle and scribbled Innangard inside. On the outside he wrote Utangard, which Ebony recognized from the grimoire.

"Doesn't that root word mean fence?" Fleishman asked.

"Good eye, Will." Nesbitt beamed with delight. "Innangard means inside the fence and Utangard means outside the fence. Whatever lives inside is civilized and ordered, and whatever lives outside the fence – which is everything but Man and the gods – is uncivilized and chaos."

Did he say chaos? Mentor Ursula talked about pure chaos and the grimoire showed her . . . Hold. On.

"Psst . . . Fleish, do you still have my sketch?" Ebony asked.

Fleishman fought with the zipper of his backpack for a few seconds, before it slid open. He pulled the page out and handed it to her.

"Ah, Will."

Fleishman froze mid-pass.

"That must be information on this subject," Nesbitt said. "Go ahead. Share it with the class."

A silent plea marred Fleishman's face. Ebony hoped she didn't look as guilty as he did.

Nesbitt extended his hand and ambled down the aisle. Fleishman handed it over, and Ebony watched her precious scribblings disappear into Nesbitt's pocket.

"You may retrieve it after the Ullr Games."

After the games! Ebony wanted to scream. That note could save her friend. Nesbitt should have a Declaration written against him. Manual labor would be her verdict. Wash white boards or chip paint off the wooden shed outback. This was a crime. At least it felt like one.

"Mist Gypsies roamed the landscape of Yggdrasil, charged with keeping balance between what existed outside and inside the fence," Nesbitt continued. "They were the equal force of destruction that counter-balanced the constant creation force of the gods. Good cannot exist without evil. There is no day without night, no rain without drought, no cold without hot. Two equal opposites that give stability."

Nesbitt wrote *Glundroða safnari* on his screen. He dragged his stylist under both words and said, "Chaos collector."

Ebony slid to the edge of her pod.

"See," Nesbitt began, "if chaos takes over, Man would return to the beginning when only dark elves existed and held rule over chaos."

When only dark elves existed? Could this have been what Daenir wanted? Collect tons of chaos to release all at once? That made sense in the scariest of ways.

"What did they do to keep balance?" A seventh-grade girl asked.

Nesbitt tipped his chin up. "They made Nature's storms stronger, threatened extinction for some species. For humans they stripped some of their souls."

"Soul eaters?" Caleb joked.

"Yes," Nesbitt answered.

That was the most horrible thing Ebony had ever heard.

"But *sluagh* are Fae," Fleishman said.

"The foulest of the Fae," Nesbitt answered.

"Wait," Caleb said. "Fairies like Tinkerbell?"

"Nothing like Tinkerbell," Nesbitt said. "Fae are humanlike and appear in every form of mythology. Sluagh are the Fae's bad guys. Mist Gypsies are Yggdrasil's sluagh. After the peace treaty was forged between the Aesir and Vanir gods, Mist Gypsies were needed less and less. Around the same time, a lower nature goddess of the Vanir, who'd been accused of conspiring to kill the god Balder, was cast out to the land of the Jötnar to create more balance."

"So, a psychotic goddess was left to hang out with a bunch of soul eaters," Caleb said.

"Allegedly," Nesbitt corrected.

"And this doesn't bother anyone?" Charity squealed.

"No, because after that time Mist Gypsies dwindled in numbers, giving more visibility to the giants we see today. No one knows what happened to those Misty Gypsies, only that history shows they fell away and are only thought of as a myth now."

Ebony and Fleishman gawked at each other.

Ebony scooted out of the way as students left the study. "Mr. Nesbitt," she called.

He crossed his arms. "I hope you're not asking for your note back early."

"Uh, no." Ebony frowned. She'd forgotten about her scribbles until he mentioned them. "Do you have any maps?"

"Of Yggdrasil?" he asked.

The map the grimoire showed her had to be in Yggdrasil. "Sure."

As Nesbitt walked farther into the study room, Fleishman sidled up to her. "What are you doing?"

"Digging."

"You're not telling him you saw a chaos-collecting, soul-eating Mist Gypsy in the boneyard?" he asked.

"No," she scoffed. "He'd think I'm crazy."

"Not to mention seeing one is impossible," he said.

"Nothing is impossible, you've said." She continued, "Improbable, but not impossible."

"Throwing my words back at me," he said. "That's harsh."

Metal reels squealed, making the kids wince.

"Sorry about that." Mentor Nesbitt lifted a hefty pile of poster-sized papers from a wide drawer and heaved them onto a mechanical tabletop. "These are the maps I have. But honestly, who knows how accurate they are."

He thumbed through maps of all sizes. There were the Jotunheim foothills and ranges, and the Poppy Fields of Vanaheim, where Delia said the petals came from.

Ebony pointed to the poppy fields. "What are these?"

"Abundant fields in Vanaheim where the Vanir gods live," Nesbitt said. "Much of their healing antidotes come from the poppy fields."

"What about poisons?" Fleishman asked.

"They can be found in the fields, too," Nesbitt said. "Wisdom has taught me that most things are neither all beautiful and good, nor all ugly and evil."

As he slid one map onto the done pile, the corner of a smaller map showed itself beneath the disheveled stack. Ebony slid it out. Over half of the map was torn away, but numerous landmarks were noted in runes like the complicated ones from the grimoire.

"Where is this map to?" she asked and flipped it over. "There's no location key or name."

"From the faded parchment and print, and the tears, it appears to be one of the older maps, most likely left to me by my predecessor. Huh? These markings..." Nesbitt cleared his throat. "It's not important."

Uh, when someone said something wasn't important that usually meant it was. "What?"

"It's just," he hesitated, "part of this marking has also been used in historical writings with the Vanir to represent the section of our cemetery we don't use anymore."

Dead Alley?

Ebony peered closer. She saw the symbol of a crisscrossed ladder from the grimoire until Nesbitt covered parts of it, leaving what looked like a person with its arms raised in the letter Y.

"This is the *Algiz* rune," he said. "It's used for protection and securing the safe-keeping of something."

"You think something is hidden in this map?" Ebony asked.

"I'm not saying that." He traced his finger under a row of faint markings. "But these are of the ancient language associated with the Vanir, too. Something about gemstones and healing."

Ebony gripped Fleishman's forearm. Hadn't he mentioned Yggdrasil jewelry? And the boy ghost could use some healing.

If she'd been a wolf her shackles would be ramrod tall.

"Look at you, Ebony," Nesbitt said. "Your interest in this is wonderful. Want to borrow this map to see if you can unravel the mystery?"

"Really?" She investigated his face. He trusted her. Maybe believed she could find answers. An adult was giving her space to work out an answer for herself. This felt good. Nesbitt earned a lot of cheese doodle points in her eyes. She should buy him a bag.

He reached for an elastic band. "There's nothing that brings a teacher more joy than seeing a student hunger for knowledge."

Little did he know the knowledge Ebony hungered for might get them all in trouble.

"Things must be difficult for you, right now." He straightened the maps into a neater pile.

He wasn't going to make her talk about Dad or tell her to be easier on her mother, was he?

"It wouldn't hurt for you to give yourself a compliment occasionally," he said.

Huh?

"You are a talented young lady," he said. "You have a lot going for you."

Oh, he had no idea what she had going for her. Or coming after her. It wouldn't surprise her if the new attack on the boneyard flipped sideways and danced. Did people attract this stuff; you know, like a magnet? She pivoted for the door with Fleishman close behind.

"Oh, and to borrow implies returning the item, so make sure I get it back when you're finished with it," Nesbitt called after them, but they were gone.

Boneyard Brew

ebony tugged Fleishman behind a large tombstone.

"What are you—"

"Shh." She peeked around the stone. "Erickson's over there with Seronious Bile."

Fleishman leaned out from the other side of the stone. "What are they doing?"

"Talking," Ebony said. "Look, the Dean is leaving."

Waiting until Dean Bile was out of sight, Ebony shifted to crawl closer and snapped the dry twigs of a vine dangling over the tombstone. Amputated foliage dropped to the ground. Everything quieted. Except Erickson, who spun on his feet.

"Who's there?"

Ebony shared a sigh with Fleishman, and they stood.

"Oh, it's you two," Erickson said while stuffing something into his backpack. "What are you sneaking around following me?"

"You mean like you're sneaking around meeting Dean Bile?" Ebony said.

She scurried toward him and shoved her hand into his open pack. He yanked on the bag, but she'd gripped hold of what he'd tried to hide. A scarf, soft to the touch. No, the fabric was a stole worn by all Motley Council members. This must belong to his father.

"Are you trying to channel a spirit, maybe one of *them* you mentioned earlier, to talk to your dad?" Ebony asked. "Because if you are, you'd better—"

Ebony flinched as Erickson jerked the stole from her hand.

"You think you know everything." He hung his head, fingers brushing against the fabric.

For the first time, Ebony saw her nemesis as a scared little boy, helpless and . . . sad. Pretty much how she felt when she thought about her father. There might be more to Erickson than she thought. Like feelings. Aw, now she felt bad.

"Erickson," she said.

"Forget it." He turned and ran up Ash Pathway.

Fleishman inched next to her, his attention matching hers watching Erickson grow smaller the farther he ran until he vanished out the exit. "We should check on the residents and leave, too."

"And peek inside Dead Alley," she said.

"We're not doing that."

"Why not?" Her voice faded behind a small crypt: *The descendants of Trenton Hayes – nobody knows the real story.*

She paused at the ornate fountain that marked the center of Ash Pathway and tipped her chin up at the abandoned eighteenth-century chapel.

Stonework etched in runes and glyphs framed the double wooden doors. Carvings of a dynamic compass showing the four cardinal points set as the facade's backdrop. Stone shingles blanketed the roof, while atop the corner points sat the statue of a gargoyle, each with its own mysterious expression.

"Those things are creepier than the sick crows," Fleishman said, catching up.

"Creepier than that." Ebony pointed to Nigel in his cage.

The line on Nigel's back glowed blue. "Despite your insults, he likes you."

"Of course, he does." She signed the peace symbol to Nigel. "We get each other."

A quiet moment passed between them. "Do you miss using sign language?"

"A little," she answered. But not as much as she missed the 3Ms – Mayhem's funny pranks and Meandering scolding her for them. And using Mischief's card game cheats back against her to win at Texas Hold'em or War. Ebony knew gaining full use of her medium skills was a trade-off for not needing them daily. Their time with her had always been temporary. Yggdrasil needed them, which made sense with them being the high Norns – weavers of the Past, Present, and Future. But she could use their help right then.

"We've never paid attention to the runes and symbols all over the boneyard," she said. "I wonder if they mean anything?"

Fleishman sighed. "With all that's happened, I'm sure they do."

Amphylis dusted the opposite side of the fountain. Her steps lagged like Ethan's video game when the internet connection was poor, and her skin looked paler. Tanner joined her with old man Pottle trudging behind. His outline frayed at the ends, and his skin lacked that signature ruddiness of a farmer from long ago. Ebony touched Fleishman so he could see them.

"How do you feel, Amphylis?" Fleishman asked.

"A tad under the weather."

Victoria yawned, "Sleepy."

"And dizzy," Tanner said.

Three crows land on the fountain. Obnoxious caws batted at each other like they were arguing. More crows, magpies, and ravens hovered overhead; some settled on tree branches or the chapel. No sight of the hawk that had been hanging around, though.

As Hargraves and Victoria strolled by Amphylis, one crow pecked at Victoria's ghostly hand. She screeched. The other birds released their discord in loud croaks and caws. A group of Independent ghosts scurried away, and Hargrave took Victoria's hand in his. Amphylis rushed over.

"Is she okay?" Ebony asked.

"I believe so," Hargraves answered.

The crow hopped from the tree branch onto the chapel roof. Black feathers faded to gray as it stalled, swaying from one leg to the other like a clock pendulum.

"That's it." Ebony released Fleishman and climbed the iron bars gating the chapel entrance.

"Don't touch it," Fleishman said.

"Someone has to figure out these crows." She stretched her arm higher.

Fleishman ambled closer. "You're going to fall."

"I'm afraid Master Fleishman is correct, Miss Ebony," Amphylis said.

Two crows plopped onto the roof. Ebony waved the back of her hand at one to make it fly away, but her jerky movement shifted her boots between the iron grating. She grappled for the bars. The crows soared into the air, their joint caw sounding like a command. Ebony wrapped her legs around two of the bars. Fleishman lunged forward, his arms held high, but he didn't know where to support her with her butt dangling in the air.

"A little help," she said.

Amphylis waddled nearer, and Tanner secured his straw hat on his head as he jogged to the chapel.

"Fleishman! Now," she yelled.

"I, um . . ." He adjusted the angle of his arms and readjusted until he lowered one elbow closer to his body to cradle her in his arms. She was too high up on the bars. "Let go."

"No way," she said. "You'll never catch me."

"Forget it." Pinching the fabric of her skirt with two fingers, Fleishman tried holding her weight that way, but he must have thought twice because that inched up her skirt.

"What are you doing?" she yelled.

"Sorry!" He looked away to avoid seeing her unmentionables and angled his shoulders under her bottom to steady her. "Okay, now let go."

"And what? Balance my butt on your shoulders?" she asked. "No thanks."

In more fluent moves than Ebony thought him capable, Fleishman lowered one shoulder and twisted his chest flush with her back while thrusting his arms in front of him and catching her under her armpits. The only sound was her combat boots slamming against the hard chapel steps.

"Don't ever join fire and rescue, Fleish," Ebony said.

"Nonsense, Master Fleishman did marvelously." Amphylis fanned herself with her handkerchief, and Tanner slapped his knee, which Ebony took for meaning good job in farmhand language.

Fleishman's forearms tensed under Ebony's armpits, and he dragged her backward.

"What are you . . . doing?" She tried scooting her feet

under her to push her back off his chest to stand, but he hauled her over a row of poorly marked graves toward Nigel's cage.

"There are ghosts everywhere," he whispered.

His brain often got in the way of their new reality. "We're in the boneyard."

"But normally it's the regulars," he panted. "They're all out right now."

Ebony roved her eyes over the ghosts as Fleishman continued towing her away from the chapel. They were all out. Some cowered by stones or crypts, while others ducked beneath the surface. Most looked like they had when they'd died, but a few faces had adopted that same chalky complexion she'd seen on Amphylis.

Fleishman changed course to avoid stepping on a grave and its occupant peeking above ground. He passed the Pitts Family crypt – *Four generations living up'tah camp. Pitts here, Pitts there, Pitts almost everywhere* – and Miss Prim and Miss Proper sitting on the steps. Of course, that wasn't their real names. But their ugly hooped gowns and tarnished tiaras screamed of old money, so the names felt right, and they didn't seem to mind being called either. Both died of consumption forever ago, and forever ago was the story they told.

A few ghosts dodged Fleishman's trail, except for Roger Sputtenickel, whose forehead met the back of Ebony's combat boots up close and personal. She mouthed an apology as Fleishman slowed.

Murky shadows seeped out of cracked markers and stone to whirl around Roger. Amphylis sunk backward. Victoria clung to Hargrave, and Tanner tugged old man Pottle behind a statue of an angel with a broken wing. George turned the page of his newspaper.

More blackness sprouted near Roger. Vines of charcoal billowed upward, short and long pieces breaking off. He swatted at casted shades nearest his face. Muddy russet infected the peaceful yellow of his aura, and the edges crumbled away, leaving them jagged as though gnawed off by teeth. Static ignited. Loose debris whirled and clung to his cheeks, his neck, the hairs of his eyebrows. A booming honk thrust out poor Roger's mouth, a cough so fierce he practically hacked up one of his dead lungs. Fingers of mist clawed at his decrepit clothes.

Something black and solid jutted out of the ground.

Chapter

nineteen

Inked

"It's fog. It's just fog." Fleishman repeated over and over.

"It's not fog," Ebony corrected.

"Let's pretend it is."

"You don't pretend," Ebony said.

"I can start." Fleishman insisted.

Images of their last battle with creepy fog billowing out of a crypt raced across Ebony's memory.

Black stems protruded from the ground like hairs growing too fast. Some clawed for the treetops; others withered back below the cold earth only to resurface again. Ravens and magpies took to the sky. Crows settled on the ground nearest Roger. He sputtered and wiped black feathers off his tongue with the sleeve of his officer's coat.

"What in tarnation . . ." He coughed up more feathers.

"The feathers are real." Fleishman picked up one that had fallen from Roger's mouth. "Shorter in length with a blunt end . . . This is a crow feather."

"Is that good or bad?" Ebony asked.

"Not sure," he answered. "Crows are messengers to some. You know, like the Egyptians, Native Americans—"

"Get to the important part!" she yelled.

"They can be sages, tricksters, and omens of change."

Crows closest to Roger pecked the ground, movements stiffening.

"Like Chaos," Fleishman continued.

Ebony's eyes widened as she thought about what Nesbitt had said about chaos.

"Or even a message of death," Fleishman finished.

"You're a downer, you know," Ebony said. "Plus, everyone's dead here."

"We're not."

Stressed metal vibrated the boneyard, and Ebony bent her knees to steady herself.

"The feathers from Roger's mouth are turning gray." Fleishman pointed.

Roger gasped. Feathery threads waved off his lips. His elbows bent at weird angles from his palms slamming against the ground. A force pressed into him from beneath and shook his ghostly frame. Pain widened his mouth in a silent scream.

Ghosts retreated to their graves, and the chapel shuddered. Reddish light seeped between the seal of its doors. Hinges clanked, and wood moaned. A shadow swept over a copse of trees. Ebony wondered if Erickson was back, but instead she found the hawk landing atop a tall Birch; it released a hoarse screech, and a copper tile slid off the roof and stabbed the earth below.

"I take it back. I don't wish it was fog," Fleishman whimpered.

Air bloated, heavy and thick. Ebony's ears clogged with pressure. More black crows joined the cacophony of birds in the neighboring trees.

A guttural voice batted at them from behind the chapel doors. Flat grave markers vibrated, and loose pebbles shimmied at their feet. Ebony gawked at Fleishman.

A volcano of black and gray feathers erupted from beneath Roger, heaving him from his grave like the cork of an overly-fizzing soda bottle. The force sent Ebony and Fleishman tumbling over Nigel's cage. Fleishman crawled after Nigel whose cage door had unlatched.

"Are you okay?" Lance asked, jogging toward her.

Ebony pushed off the ground to stand. Where had he come from? Had he been watching them, or had he just arrived? Ooh, she didn't like feeling unsure of Lance's friendship.

He brushed his ghost fingers through her hair. Though she couldn't feel any touch, she imagined it soft. Lance cared. How could she think he was involved with Daenir?

"What's wrong with Roger?" he asked.

Roger rolled over an unmarked grave and wrenched his hands around his throat – the international sign for choking that Ebony had learned in Health Discipline study. They slid in next to Roger. Lance dangled his fingers over Roger's mouth, trying to pinch the feathers. His pupils dilated; brow folded in a million creases.

"Come on!" Lance groaned, his voice sounding too deep for a young boy. Fat veins muddied the whites of his eyes, and he froze in place.

"Lance," Ebony said. She heard Fleishman calling her over the booms echoing from the crypt. "Lance!" she bellowed and swung her arm, plunging her fist through his torso. What was wrong with him? She tried again, and this time the pressure of hitting something solid folded her wrist back. Lance stumbled backward. Her knuckles had grazed his chest.

Fleishman struggled to scoop Nigel off the ground and rushed toward them.

Roger croaked louder; his brown eyes wider. Ebony still didn't understand how ghostly physics worked, but the feathers needed to come out. She reached for him.

Wood splintered from one side of the chapel. Another copper tile spilled to the ground.

Chatter from the gathering crows thickened, and autumn leaves shivered. Ebony's tattoo warmed. The skin tingled, a thousand needles prickling her marking. She flipped her wrist over. Flecks of light leaked out the band of her sleeve and spilled into her palm.

"Your arm." Fleishman dropped down beside her, Nigel's cage clunking next to him.

She tugged the cotton to bare her wrist. The same end of her tattoo had the familiar ember as earlier, only the other end lit with an ember, too; both pulsated like florescent bulbs.

The bluish gleam spilled from each ember. Both raced for the center of her tattoo like gasoline lit by a match. The separate glows met and splintered off in a new line that wrapped around Ebony's wrist. A bulb-shaped letter P jutted out its center; a second shaped like the letter F intersected that.

Ebony recognized them from the grimoire. "My rune grew."

"Yes." Worry threaded Fleishman's voice. "But with what?"

Two crows tousled, nearby, captivating their fellow birds.

A brutal honk spat from Roger's mouth. The ground quaked, and a stone bench tipped over. Glass shattered, showering down from two round windows at the top of the chapel. Fleishman fell sideways on Nigel's cage, and Ebony and Lance fell over Roger's body. Chunks of wood exploded from the side wall.

Blackness thrust out the demolished wall of the chapel. One huge paw stomped on the ground. Razor-sharp claws pierced a slab of splintered wood and clung tightly. Fenrir's massive head poked through the rubble. His almond-shaped eyes were as green as Ebony remembered, but they were haunted where they hadn't been before.

Ebony," the gigantic wolf strained, his teeth bared. Tone muscle stressed as he tugged backward. "No!" Fenrir bellowed over his shoulder in the opposite direction of Ebony.

Was he being pulled backward? Maybe the chain he dragged from his back paw had caught on something.

"I must tell . . . her." Soupy saliva shivered down his fierce canines and dripped to his paws.

Ebony inched forward.

"Where are you going?" Fleishman asked.

"To hear him out."

"After what he did to your house?" Fleishman shuddered. "We can't trust him!"

Trust. Did a person need to mislead you several times before they became untrustworthy or could it be a feeling that told you? Because Ebony had a pang in her stomach, but it felt different than when she'd kept information from others.

"You," the wolf grunted. "His body . . ."

"My body?" Lance's ghost face dimmed.

The wolf's muscles strained. "Hall . . . of Slain, something's wrong."

It all happened at once: Roger choked up a messy wad of feathers, a steamy gust blew out the dilapidated chapel, and Fenrir was yanked backward so hard he vanished. But not before he barked, "Folket Fr—"

"*Folket Fra Nord!*" shouted from Roger's mouth and not in his own voice.

"Look!" Fleishman screamed, and a feather wiggled

free between Roger's lips, away from the light of Ebony's new tattoo. "It doesn't like your light. Use it!"

Use it? She brushed her fingertips over her tattoo. When Ebony had ensured that Gillingr – part of the Queen of the Underworld's crown and hollow of her ship – was returned, Hela had said it would always be there if Ebony needed it. The door to the Hall of Souls could work the same way. It hadn't simply marked her with a rune, but it had given her a gift she hadn't begun to explore.

Ebony wondered if that applied to most things in life.

She swept her wrist over Roger's stomach. He let out a roaring burp and up came the rest of the feathers spurting from his mouth.

Crows lifted into the sky.

"I don't recall pheasant tasting so dry." Roger brushed off his officer's trousers; the clasps on his Army coat clanked.

Ebony fell back against Fleishman's legs and rubbed her wrist. Miss Prim and Miss Proper ducked out from their crypt and ambled closer.

"How'd that happened?" Fleishman traced her newest tattoo, and Ebony sighed, which made him sigh. "Tell me. You have to trust people again."

"No, I don't." The conviction in her voice surprised her. She hadn't realized how strongly she felt about it. What if she never learned to trust again? She'd said no, but did she mean it? It felt lonely if she did. She was more confused than ever.

"How am I supposed to do my job when you only share what you want with me?"

A wall of frustration shot up between them. Ebony's chest tightened. He was right. She hadn't been thinking about how this affected him. She was afraid. Of what? She wasn't sure.

"My wrist started itching the night the grimoire spoke

to me." Her voice sounded small. "But why mark me with this?"

Fleishman pushed to stand. "We'll figure it out."

Ebony turned to Lance. He hadn't spoken in a while. "Lance?"

"I had a premonition," he said.

"Of what?" she asked.

"Us, right here. But the scene blurred and changed." His gaze shifted between Ebony and Fleishman. "You were running from something. When you split up to run in different directions," he paused to swallow, "I saw what was chasing you. A creature with huge muscles and hair on its shoulders, back, and bottom of the calves. The legs were strong and solid muscle. It carried a spear, and on the head balanced a dressing made of horns, bones, fur, and . . ."

Ebony hugged her knees. "What was it?"

"Not what." Lance swallowed again. "Who."

"Okay," Fleishman said. "Who?"

"It was me."

# Chapter twenty

Ink Splotch

low grumble vibrated through Elli's chest.

This was not good. She felt a growl readying to burst from her mouth. It wasn't bad enough this meddlesome pair interrupted her search for the caster who'd created spells in the graveyard. Now that mangy mutt Fenrir had shown, playing both sides of the fence. So predictable. It wouldn't be long before these two pieced information together.

It seemed this strange girl with colors streaking her hair would be far more trouble than anticipated. Ebony Charmed was a free-thinker, risktaker, and caregiver. Worst of all she had a courageous heart. Those were the dangerous ones. She also had access to a powerful grimoire; that much Elli had known. But no frivolous magical collection of spells, potions, or other had ever left that bind mark on a being, let alone a measly human. And in this girl's possession, it could wreak havoc with the ultimate goal.

The powers that be of Yggdrasil had taken a liking to her. This would not do. The peaceful division among the Aesir and Vanir gods must end. She tapped the elegant ring on her finger, the one past two bony knuckles; the mechanics of the gears fired up. A distraction was needed.

And glancing around the graveyard with its pitiful residents gave her the perfect idea to accomplish that. It would simply take a little time.

twenty-one

Dancing Pages

GIF. And Ebony was glad it was almost over.

Bat-Face hadn't been kidding when she'd said the next two weeks would be preparing for the Ullr games. Students had spent the last three days memorizing everything from Yggdrasil geography, creatures, and races to the rune alphabet until Ebony thought she'd vomit. Not to mention Wizner bringing spirits into his study for her training. This had left zero time to work on Mission Location Bacon.

"Ready?" Ebony's mother asked.

Ebony glanced at Njord Academy with its shadow casting three-times its real size and limbs of brick and mortar stretching from three annexes. On the building's facade, plantation shutters lined both sides of dark windows while fabric awnings dressed the tops. A sharp breeze slapped the fabric of two windows against the glass, pining it there and giving the windows a piercing gaze. Ebony released a stuttered sigh. At least the main walkway looked innocent enough. But so much had happened lately that Ebony wouldn't be surprised if it came to life and rolled up like a huge tongue.

"Yup," Ebony answered. "But tonight, you're Rita Charmed, not my mother."

"I understand." Her mother strode up the school's walkway. "Have a good time."

Fleishman leaned into Ebony, but said to Lance, "That was weird."

Lance eyed him. "Not any weirder than you using the word weird."

"What's weird is that I might be okay with her here," Ebony chuckled.

Round tables draped in brown cloth lined one side of the large room. Colorful strobes flickered in contrast to the dim lighting. Music jammed from an elevated platform that housed the DJ and his musical gear.

Ebony spotted the Cheerio Twins chatting at Olympic speed with some Njord girls. Clint and a few Motley eighth-grade boys leaned against a long table stacked with drinks. No one was dancing yet, so Ebony decided to get a drink, not that there was a chance in all of Yggdrasil she'd dance, anyway. Sugary mist dowsed her finger as she cracked open a small soda can.

"Lance, do you recognize anything?" she asked.

The bomber jacket he wore reached his earlobes as he shrugged, and he frowned beneath his baseball cap. "Not really."

His voice felt heavier, more lethargic than she'd heard. She chalked it up to him being depressed. Who wouldn't be, in his position?

Fleishman sidestepped Ebony to let a group of boys up to the table. A boy with spiked hair smiled at Ebony. The voice inside her head yelled for her to say something, but all she had was a smile in return, her voice silenced by his big blue eyes.

"You're that Ebony girl from Motley," the boy said. "The one with the huge lizard."

Ebony tried to swallow, but it seemed she'd forgotten how. "The lizard is only big when it becomes a serpent, and it belongs to him."

Fleishman raised his hand awkwardly.

"Cool." The boy nodded. "I'm Marcus."

"Should have known you'd be meeting kids from the dark side." A boy with shady hair and bangs tipped blond elbowed Marcus.

Dark side?

"Remember what happened last time you did that?" The boy turned to Ebony, not giving his friend a chance to answer. "We were snooping around Motley's cemetery and—"

"Hey," Marcus said and exchanged a stern look with the boy.

"It's fine." The boy pushed Marcus away. "The next thing we knew the other kids disappeared."

"You were in the boneyard with those kids last summer," Ebony said.

"Yup," the blond boy answered like he'd won something.

Now was the time. She had to mention Lance. But what if she didn't like their answer? She'd better ask before she talked herself out of it.

"Then you know Lance," blurted off her lips.

The boys looked at each other. "Who?"

Ebony stopped her inhale. What was she to say to that? Lance's shoulders drooped, and he clenched his hands at his sides. She stepped closer to them. They had to know him. She'd prove it.

"He's a student here, studying astral projection," she said.

Neither boy said a word.

She raised on her toes, one arm shooting in the air. "He's about this tall with brown hair."

Fleishman cleared his throat and shared what happened in the gym with Nidhogg.

Do you know these guys? Ebony mouthed to Lance.

The muscles at his jawline flinched, anger thick in his clenched teeth. If he'd been a student here and at the boneyard that night, why didn't he know them?

"Oh, we heard about bizarre stuff happening at Motley," one boy snorted.

Bizarre stuff? All right, it was bizarre, but no one should say that except a Motley student. Could Nidhogg in the gym have been a set up to get them all here, to give Njord the opportunity to go public?

"You never know what could happen at the Ullr Games," the boy said.

That sounded like a threat, and by the way Dawson and his eighth-grade friends closed in, they agreed.

"Cut it out," Marcus said, turning from the boy. To Ebony, "Ignore him."

Pink glitter and neon nail polish crashed into their tiny meet and greet as a group of Njord girls edged up behind the boys. Strong perfume assaulted Ebony's nostrils. The only reason she held back her gag was because she came eye to eye with the girl who'd stared at her when she visited Motley with Seronious Bile. But this time, the girl smiled.

This school was confusing.

"Hey, Amber," Marcus said to the girl and turned his attention to his friends, giving Ebony and Fleishman a chance to slip away.

"They know more than they're saying," Ebony said.

Fleishman swept his bangs across his forehead. "Yeah."

"Lance, what do—" Her chest squeezed. "He's gone, again."

Fleishman touched her shoulder to scan the dance floor. "He was here a second ago."

"Maybe he's looking for answers," she said and vanished through an adjacent doorway, whispering Lance's name with Fleishman scurrying after her.

The scent of aged wood and ancient history welcomed them into a wide hallway. Stone sea serpents lined one wall. Statues of winged horses carrying warriors stood at the entrance to a large foyer. Ebony stubbed the tip of her boot as she slowed her pace.

"Valkyries." Fleishman said, staring at the horse statues.

"They're all named Valerie?" Ebony said.

"No, Valkyries," he said. "Female warriors on flying horseback."

"Uh . . . if you say so."

"Tough girls like Wonder Woman or Storm from the X-Men," he clarified.

"Ah . . ." Ebony nodded.

"They choose from the dead warriors after battle."

"Personally, I'd rather my warriors be alive, but that's me," she said.

"The Valkyries award them entrance into Valhalla."

"Which is?" she asked.

"The Hall of the," he paused, "Slain."

Ebony stilled. "That's what Fenrir said. We should go there."

"You can't call on any doors, remember," he said.

"I'm not supposed to," she corrected.

"And you're not going to," he said. "We'll visit the Archive tomorrow."

"Everything is always tomorrow." She trudged down the hallway. "What if there's no tomorrow for the boneyard? Or Lance?"

"Where are you going?" he asked.

"To find Lance. I'm picking up strange vibes here." She spun to face him. "Don't tell me we need more facts, either."

"Facts give us answers."

"Some answers. Relying on facts alone leaves no room to believe or the imagination that something might be bigger than what we know." She clamped her hands on her hips. "Wizner labeled that thing in the boneyard a myth. Nesbitt called those bazillion-year-old giant humanoid-spirits a myth and gave them a name, Mist Gypsies. Lance had a weird premonition, and we've got sick boneyard residents, graying crows, poisonous poppy petals, and these Njord kids are a mystery."

He raised one corner of his mouth. "You might have a point."

The imaginary reel in Ebony's head flashed: *#One4Ebony*.

"Mist Gypsies collect and eat souls, which is gross by-the-way. More facts," she finished.

"Your last fact is technically an opinion," he corrected.

Goat cheese. *#NegativeOne4Ebony*

Ebony stopped at a group of paintings on the opposite wall. "'*The Bewitching Forest by Brísingamen, of the goddess Freyja.*' Aunt Gertrude talked about Freyja the other day."

"She's the goddess in charge of the Valkyries," he said.

"For all the cheese . . ." Gertrude hadn't compared Ebony to any old goddess, but a tough one.

Fleishman tapped his finger against his chin. "If I was a betting guy—"

"Which you're not."

"No," he paused, "but I'd say Njord Academy is of the

Vanir god lineage. Look around. The Valkyries, the statues, the Bewitching Forest, and Freyja are all associated with them."

"What about Brísingamen?" she asked. "Did he paint this?"

Before he could answer, a loud bang echoed from the other end of the hall. The two tracked the sound into a wing that opened to a large area of stonework, open-beam rafters, and books cased in elegantly carved bookshelves. A sharp draft whirled at them.

"Did the air conditioning turn on?" Ebony asked.

Fleishman pointed next to the dual wooden staircases that curved around the side walls. "I don't think that's air conditioning."

They stood paralyzed as books and loose pages spun around the room.

From a shadowy corner, Elli watched the two misfits back around chairs to exit the room. Too bad she cloaked the true cause of the chaos; because if they could see it, they wouldn't leave. Their beloved friend Lance was coming into his own and his own would suit Elli perfectly.

Lance flipped book after book; his simmering growl deepened. It was a beautiful thing watching him take on some of his true strength that would be his once he reunited with his body. He hadn't even realized he'd moved objects with such ease in his current ghostly state.

"Are you doing this?" the boy Fleishman looked to Ebony.

"Of course not." She fiddled with her hands, her

expression – a little shock, a bit insecure – priceless. Unfortunately, Elli also noted brave curiosity. That strength could throw a wrench into the bigger plan. She'd need to curb it.

A glass cabinet housing some of Njord's most important history set aglow in between two bookshelves. A delicious grin fluttered across Elli's aged lips. Raising both arms, she drew intersecting symbols in the air. The cabinet glass shattered, and an alarm blared.

"Oh no!" the boy Fleishman rasped. "We have to pick this up."

"There's no time," Ebony said.

"I've got it," a voice said. "Go."

Amber slipped out from a quaint study nook.

"Why would you help us?" Ebony asked.

"I'm not. I'm helping myself." Amber nodded her head at two baby boars that weren't there before. "I'm on Dean Bile's watch list but catching these little guys should get me off. They've been clawing up furniture all over the school for a week."

Amber chased the boars out of the room and disappeared into an adjacent hallway, while Ebony and Fleishman hurried to rejoin the dance.

Elli stepped up next to Lance.

"Did I do this?" he panted, noticing the damaged.

"You must learn control," Elli said. "That is all." It was more than that, but he didn't need that information.

"I don't know," he said. "I . . . I got to go." And with that he vanished.

Elli tapped one crooked finger to her lips. She couldn't have that boy doubting her. He was too important to everything.

The door to the foyer sealed as Ebony backed into it. Mom was in the kitchen, talking to her aunts, so she slid off her boots and ambled upstairs to her bedroom. It had been a long night.

Pitter-patter drifted from her brother's half-opened door. She pushed it wider to find Ethan playing a game. He nudged his headphones off one ear and spun his gaming chair to face her. He dropped his head to look at his hands.

"You're home."

She leaned against his doorframe. The deep red in his aura and its slow movement said he held lots of confusion inside. He also was scared. Ebony sighed out, "I live here."

"But," Ethan tipped his head up, "you haven't been home much, lately."

"I know," Ebony said. It didn't feel right without her father. "I'm sorry."

Ethan set his controller down and after a long pause said, "I miss Dad."

She sat on his bed. "Me, too."

"What if he doesn't come home?" Ethan's voice sounded younger.

Ebony patted the spot next to her on his bed. He stood, his chair rolling backward, and sat beside her. She draped her arm over his shoulder. It felt oddly okay; she hadn't hugged him in a long time.

"Dad will be back."

"How do you know?" he asked.

"Because . . ." She hadn't realized until that moment, but she believed whatever kept her father away was vital to what was going on at the boneyard and with Njord. She trusted him to come home when it was time. Strange because she wasn't in a trusting mood, lately, but she'd trusted Dad even though he'd gone along with her mother to keep her skills from her. Maybe she should try harder with Mom. "Because he's Dad. He would have never risked fighting on Bifrost if he thought we couldn't handle things at home."

Ethan bobbled his head back and forth, seeming to accept her explanation. He held up his controller. "You owe me a game."

"I do." She picked up a spare controller. "But I'm not good."

"I know." He shrugged. "I'll help you."

It amazed her that the kid who stuffed green beans up his nose and snorted them at her like darts could also be sweet. She settled in to play and looked at his wall.

"That poster's new."

"Ooh, yeah. It's a berserker," he said. "Auntie Gertrude bought it for me."

Not surprising.

"Isn't he great!" Ethan flipped through skins for his character on his computer screen. "Look at him. Totally bad, but good at the same time."

"Looks like he needs a shower." She thumbed her controller.

"Berserkers don't shower," he said. "They're warriors, tough and mean. And they get mad, wicked mad. They rage in the game. It's awesome."

"So, they're monsters," she said.

"Yes and no. They're normal people, but they get so angry they forget," he said like that made sense. "But if they find someone who's good and true, they can remember who they were before they turned, and their anger can be used to help people. If I have one on my team, I can use it for good or bad against my enemy." He twisted to click his controller. "Watch this."

Music cued in as an animated video clip played.

A room of stone and mortar appeared. At its center gathered a group of people, all wearing red robes except one dressed in white – the medicine man or shaman. The huddle broke at one end to let a tall man amble to the center, the fur pelt draped across his shoulders swaying down to his ankles. Wooden beads tapped his bare chest, and the bangles around his wrists clanked.

A chant echoed off the rocky walls.

The shaman swept the end of his robe from his feet and stepped forward. Another followed, carrying a bowl in his hands. The shaman dipped his fingers into the bowl of wet soot and drew black sigils on the pelt-wearing man's face, arms, and exposed thighs and calves. The soot sunk into the man's skin, vanishing.

"Hreidmar Svavarsson, son of our people," the shaman said, "I bless you by the strength of the fiercest winds, the cunning mind of the wolf, the vengeance of Nature, and the longevity of the nine realms. Do you accept the challenge to be our guardian, our watcher, our protector, and Man's corrector when evil breaches the boundaries?"

"I do," Hreidmar said.

"Those who come after you will uphold your cause. You will carry on through your ancestors." The shaman placed a crown of bones, fur, and horns on the man's head. "You will be fueled by anger no man can match and no god will want to face. Only the true heart can match your fury." He strung a necklace of charmed crystals around Hreidmar's neck. "It is done."

At that, the man dropped to his knees and howled, pain stretching across his face. His limbs tensed. The odor of burning flesh swirled in the air. The sigils resurfaced as brands seared into his skin from the inside out.

The red robes widened their circle around him, and he

tipped onto his side, writhing and shivering. Bones cracked. His muscles swelled. The breadth of his back widened. Stubble thickened across his ruddy cheeks. And all went still.

Hreidmar rolled to his knees. He tipped his chin up, emerald eyes sparkling, and reached out his hand to accept the axe the shaman offered him. His eyes lightened to brilliant yellow then to blazing scarlet.

The scene faded, and a phrase scrolled across the screen. Ethan paused it.

"So that's a berserker," she said.

"Yup, the first one," Ethan answered. "And those are the guys that made him."

Words of greenish mist swept across his frozen screen. "The People of the North."

twenty-two

The Archive

bony strolled down the long, underground corridor. The clomp of her boots bounced off the cold concrete that fully enveloped the secret tunnel; the echo of her steps lingered behind her.

She swept by runes and sigils etched into the walls; each positioned at the exact distance from the next. In contrast, those fixed into the floor looked less ornate, like they'd been tossed into the air and lay where they landed.

Passing a plated door of oak, she slowed her pace and read *"School Supplies"* on a sign dangling from the doorknob. She'd seen her share of doors and doorknobs, lately, but that didn't stop the need to examine each even if they appeared normal. Rumors had it that passageways had been dug throughout the school's foundation. She wondered whether this room or one of the other doors along this tunnel led to the area beneath the gymnasium where Erickson had met with his father before that fire giant had swept her dad away. She shook that idea from her head and continued forward to where no other students could enter.

The metal knob cooled her palm as she tugged on the wooden door. Brackets creaked, sounding strained. The seal popped with a release of air. A sense of safety washed over her, and the pungent scent of eucalyptus filled her sinuses. She slipped into the cavernous foyer of the Archive.

She and Fleishman had been granted special access to the Archive since their victory over Nidhogg. It gave them a place to avoid the new attention focused on them and an escape from the whole Yggdrasil thing. But really, there was no escaping what they'd witnessed lately.

From the reference station, Xander Willington, Jr. – sophisticated doer of all things Motley and official Archivist of the Three: past, present, and future – nodded at her; he was Man's counterpart to the high Norns of Yggdrasil. His black, pin-striped suit fit his thin frame, the dark color popping off his pale skin; a burgundy handkerchief peeked out from his breast pocket. If she didn't know better, she'd think he and Poe the Goth were related.

Ebony slung her satchel over the back of a chair and waved at Nigel in his cage. "S'up, wormasarous?"

Nigel's back brightened with a bluish glow in his usual response.

"I'll never know why he likes it when you talk to him like that," Fleishman said.

"It's our thing." Ebony slid into her seat. "What's all this?"

"Reference books," he said. "These scrolls are Xander's written testimony of when we brought the kids back from Yggdrasil and the battle with Nidhogg."

Yup, her name was right there.

"I was hoping to find a connection between Daenir and Lance's body, the crows and these Mist Gypsies, or the boy ghost's illness. Instead, I found something strange. One of the returning kids said they heard underground grumbling in the boneyard before they were taken."

"Giant's stomp," she suggested.

"That's what I thought, but feeling it coming from underground? That doesn't add up." He tugged a piece of paper from beneath a scroll. "I sketched what I could remember from your note. It's a little off."

"Looks accurate to me," she said.

"Let's start with these three triangles . . ." He glanced up from the table. "Xander, do you know anything about Yggdrasil medals or jewelry and medicines or cures?"

"Do I know anything," Xander scoffed. "This way, please."

Xander ambled under an archway of carved stone and another. Ebony recognized images as Aztec and Egyptian from the water tunnels beneath the Hall of Souls where Lynheim retrieved Gillingr from a giant.

The skinny archivist climbed a wooden ladder that clung to a universal railing system connecting the entire Archive. Stretching his lanky arms above his head, he shifted a metal chest and candelabra until he gripped two books, leather bound and reeking of secrets. As he tugged them free, Ebony heard a congestion of teeny squeals. A light thud landed on her combat boots.

"Bookworms," Xander muttered. "I thought I collected all you nosey little stinkers."

Ebony gently pinched it off her foot. Pinkish at the front, it blended to deep red at its tail, in total about the size of her pinky. It resembled a miniature Nigel, only with legs and oversized eyes.

Xander handed Fleishman the books, while opening his

palm to Ebony. "Give it here and go about your business."

Ebony hesitated. "You'll be nice?"

"Of course," he said as Ebony handed over her new pink friend. "Bookworms are invaluable to archiving our history. They are the first transcribers, you know." And with that he was off.

Back at the table, the twine binding both books strained as Fleishman and Ebony flipped pages. Like the grimoire, the scent of dried leaves and age permeated the books.

A plump sun, shedding its rays, hung above words and symbols on one page in Fleishman's book. Faded letters listed a chant to transform metal into energy or a substance of more value. Two serpents revolved around a huge eye decorated another spell. Leaves embroidered in gold and tangerine seemed to wave off tree branches that sprawled over the edge, creeping, crawling.

"That tree looks familiar," Ebony said.

"Says it's from the Bewitching Forest."

"Isn't that—"

"From the painting at Njord, yeah." For once, Fleishman cut her off. "Says the forest originated from Brísingamen, the torc of the goddess Freyja." He tapped her page with his finger. "A torc is a necklace, so look in your book for that."

"Note to self – Brísingamen is not a painter." She nodded and fanned a few pages. "Look at this. '*Brísingamen is to Freyja much like Thor's hammer Mjolnir is to him. The torc represents her as a cultivator of war, possesses warrior strength, and embodies her powers of love, fertility, and healing.*' Do you think it could cure the ghosts?"

"Maybe, but we don't have it. Some of the stories claim that godly jewels and weapons have been combined to break spells, wards, and cures."

"That's good to know," she said.

Fleishman read from Ebony's book. *"'Like her brother Freyr, Freyja is a Vanir god.'"*

"Freyja created the Bewitching Forest by using *Brísingamen*," Ebony said. "That means the forest belongs to the Vanir gods. And if Njord's lineage is Vanir like you think, then Njord could have access to the forest."

"Sounds logical," Fleishman said.

Ebony kept reading. *"'Freyja is one of the hostages traded between the Aesir and Vanir gods during their peace treaty negotiations.'"*

"There's that peace agreement, again, and look." Fleishman tapped her page. "It's the symbol of the three triangles you saw. *'The Valknut is given to the slain warriors of Yggdrasil as a sign of respect and honor,'*" he read.

"Like the Purple Heart or Victoria Cross medal?" she asked.

"I guess," he said and turned her page. "The Valknut symbol first appeared on Draupnir, a ring belonging to the god Odin. Among other things, this ring can be used as a compass."

"Hold, please." Ebony pressed her hand over the page. "We can use it to find Lance."

"It's possible. Wait, forget it," he said and read, *"'Unfortunately, Draupnir was stolen some time ago and has yet to resurface.'"*

"Takes care of that idea." Ebony flopped back in her chair.

He fished though the piles of paper on the table. A study packet Ebony recognized as the rune alphabet Mentor Blu had given them topped one pile.

"Let me see your new marking," he said.

She pulled up her sleeve to expose her wrist. No glow, but the marking still looked jumbled. Fleishman covered some lines with two fingers. With his other hand, he hid more.

"I should have seen this before," he said. "This part of your new marking is the *Ansuz* rune. It can mean wisdom and truth." He looked up. "Ebony, this is Odin's rune."

"Uh, so?"

"It marks Odin's ring Draupnir, which has Valknut on it."

"And the grimoire showed me Valknut and Ansuz on something round." She inhaled. "Odin's ring. Why would the grimoire show me that if we can't get it? Maybe the grimoire gave me Valknut."

He shook his head. "I doubt it."

"Hey, I'm honorable and stuff."

He chuckled. "But you're not dead."

"Oh, that's true," she said.

"The grimoire showed you the ring and symbol for a reason." He hummed, "Why?"

"The more we find out the less we know." Ebony grumbled.

"Not necessarily." He covered the Ansuz rune to expose another rune alone. "Mentor Blu's packet says this one is *'Thur – i – saz.'*"

"That's what Erickson said," Ebony huffed. "I knew he had something to do with this."

"It says '. . . *translates to monster or giant.'*" Both took a breath. "*Associated with the color red and can mean magical power, the forces of evil, the undead—'*"

"Whoa . . ." Ebony interrupted. "The undead? Like Raw Bones and sick crows."

" '*Or chaos,'*" Fleishman read.

"Chaos as in Mist Gypsies, the soul eating stealers?" she said.

He continued reading. "*Represents an enchanted thorn cast with the power of sleep-poison to cause eternal sleep.'*"

"Sleeping Beauty?" she asked.

"I guess, but the people and animals in Sleeping Beauty fell asleep, didn't move or age. The sick crows hobbled around. Maybe this sleep poison keeps them in a comatose state, but let's them act out violently or deranged like a zombie and decay."

Ebony grimaced, and he sat back.

"You saw that crow before the Mist Gypsy tried to take the boy, right?" he asked.

She nodded her head. "It was pecking at a bush almost like on automatic."

"What if it was on automatic like in a trance or—"

"Asleep," she whispered, remembering the crow that pecked at Victoria in the boneyard.

"There are other oddities in nature that act this way," Fleishman said. "Like zombie ants . . . they feed off the veins of leaves to spread their disease."

"Eww, yuck."

"Zombie crows, wow." Fleishman spent the next few minutes rehashing what Ebony had seen in the grimoire and how her tattoo had decoded the writing.

"You're sure you saw Utangard?" he asked.

"Yes, on the lighthouse."

"That wouldn't point to Valhalla because it's in Asgard, which is inside the fence," he said. "I feel like I'm missing something."

"I saw it," Ebony blurted.

Fleishman gazed at her; his expression soft. He was such a good friend.

"Wizner's myth. The grimoire showed me a Mist Gypsy." She explained how that came about and finished by adding up the pieces from the protection spell.

"And pure chaos is the beginning of Yggdrasil when only dark elves existed." Fleishman whispered, "Daenir."

"See why I think this has to do with Lance."

"Chaos collectors," he stuttered the end.

Ebony exhaled. It felt good to tell him the whole truth.

"Whether they're working with Daenir we can't say yet." He stood and paced over to the reference station. "Xander, would you look up information on old spirits and myths?"

"Sure, let me pull up another screen." He tapped a few keys as a man pushing a dolly with large boxes on it walked backward into the Archive. "Oh, I have to get this, Will. Supplies and new artifacts, you know. Feel free to scroll through the article index I pulled up for you. I'll be a few minutes."

Xander ushered the man through a narrow side tunnel and vanished.

Fleishman strolled to the other side of the station to read through Xander's list. Ebony inched closer for a better look and stubbed her foot on a cast iron statue of wolves, nudging into Fleishman. His hand jutted sideways and downsized Xander's screen.

"What's that?" Ebony asked.

"We shouldn't see—" Fleishman moved the cursor to re-enlarge the tab but shrank it to the task bar instead. "Xander's working on an archive. It's a title page, The People of the North."

"Wait, Ethan told me about them," she said. "Something about the first berserker."

"You finally played Eons of Chaos with him." Fleishman smiled.

"So where's North?" she asked.

"Jotunheim."

"Of course, it's giants," she said and reached for the cursor. "The title is underlined. It's a link."

"Don't" Fleishman snatched her hand away. "There's a protection spell on the folder."

"Why would there be a protection spell on one file, and how do you know that?"

"Educated guess," he said. Seconds dragged on until he

swept his fingers over the keyboard, drawing symbols across the screen.

"Educated guess my boot." Ebony stomped her foot. "How do you know about luminary wards and spells?"

"I read more than what our mentors assign us in study."

Well, she wasn't doing that.

"My reverse ward won't last long." He didn't look at her but dragged the cursor over the symbol and clicked on it.

The file opened to a listing of Motley students by grade. Scrolling through the list, names they knew appeared until they came to the last entry. It wasn't a name, but a symbol.

"The grimoire showed me that ladder-looking symbol with the saggy rungs," she said. "And it's on Nesbitt's map. Click on it."

He did. And the name Lance McGyver filled the name line. The remainder of the form from next of kin, address, contact information, to past academic transcripts was empty.

"Why link to a blank student form for Lance?" she asked.

"It's not completely blank," he said. "For one thing, the file is dated."

"Yeah, but that date is only a month ago. If Motley knew Lance was one of the boys . . ." The revelation hit her square in the forehead.

"Ebony," he whispered, "what if he wasn't one of them, and Motley started this file when he showed up with us to fight Nidhogg in the gym."

"Which was about a month ago," she finished.

"I don't like saying this, but we might want to be careful around Lance until we know more." Fleishman cleared his throat.

Layers of quiet piled up between them until Ebony nodded in agreement. Fleishman restored Xander's screen and both scurried to gather their things.

twenty-three

Tactics II

Elli hid behind her cloak of shadows and crept along the path in the cemetery, not ready to be seen just yet. The idea of lowering her standards to interact with such measly creatures as humans was distasteful to say the least. Yet she followed the boy, Erickson, as he trailed the girl with the funky hair, her sidekick Fleishman, and his troublesome lizard into the cemetery. The lizard thrashed its tail against the bars of its cage, and the boy Fleishman soothed it with his voice. She paused her next step. No way that lizard could see her; she knew that. But the flare of florescent violet in its eyes said it sensed her.

She would have to do something about that reptile soon.

Erickson branched off from the duo, passing several crypts until he plopped down on a stone benched. His torso shrank and he dropped his face into his hands.

"Dad, I've tried to channel a ghost to reach you, but I can't do it," the boy whimpered. "I'm not good at it, like you said."

Aw, longing and a lack of self-confidence. This Elli could use. Brushing her fingertips down the sides of her body transformed the brown of her dress to the black of a mourner and her coin pouch into a small purse. Her shawl turned lacy veil. A wrinkled handkerchief squeezed in one fist was her finishing touch.

She stopped a few graves shy of Erickson to face a stone marking the eternal resting place of a young child. A simple sniffle and she had his attention.

"Are you okay?" Erickson asked.

"Oh, dear boy, one will never be right after the loss of a child." Elli waddled closer. "I am sorry for the death that brought you here."

"My father isn't dead." Erickson swiped at his cheeks.

"But you miss him." She pointed to the bench. "May I?"

Erickson scooted to one side. Elli sat and encouraged her bones to crack as an aged body would. Silence hovered over them.

"If death didn't take him away what did?" she asked.

Anger swamped his eyes. "People who think they're better."

Snobbery and betrayal, she understood. Her mind showed her hands bound behind her back, the others telling her not to fight, voices saying that being part of the trade for peace between the Vanir and the Aesir was an honor. And she remembered fingertips touching her face as she was dragged away.

"My father promised to make contact with me, but he hasn't?" The boy had been talking, but this was all that she caught. "I'm worried that he forgot."

"Contact?" She injected surprise into her voice. "Is your father Councilor Erickson?"

As expected, the boy's face beamed with light. "You know him?"

Elli hunched her shoulders to seem more mysterious. "I am the contact from your father. He wants you to know he's doing what is necessary to secure your future." This was kind of a joke, but Erickson had agreed of his own free will, which was all any god or goddess needed.

"What does he want me to do?" Erickson asked.

"To be ready," she said as something rustled behind nearby trees.

"I have to go." Erickson stood and ran down Ash Pathway.

Keeper Coffer emerged from the trees as Elli forced her silhouette to fade to invisible, using extra sigils to achieve it. This groundsman was the mage warding off and blessing the cemetery. He was becoming as meddlesome as that pet lizard.

twenty-four

Sweaty Armpits

If the last two weeks were about learning and memorizing, this week was about application.

Ebony plopped down next to Fleishman in Runestone Gymnasium. Her memory receded to the day one of Yggdrasil's magical doors appeared to her, right there at center court.

"I wonder why so many mentors are here," Glinda said, as she sat next to Ebony.

"With all the changes last week, I've given up asking questions," Dakota said to Quinn from the row in front of them.

Dakota had a point.

Mentors from different studies rolled in a virtual screen with the rune alphabet written across it in three columns of eight runes each. A corresponding letter from the English alphabet set to the left of each rune. They stopped next to a small table of items – a plant pot, a glass bowl, a desk clock, and a small metal piece that looked like a handle.

"My uncle uses runes all the time," Glinda whispered.

That could be useful.

Mentor Blu sauntered up to the bleachers, and all the boys shifted in their seats, quieting. Their reaction was no surprise. Even Fleishman stopped fidgeting. Ebony might have been a Motley student for only two months, but it was well-known that most of the boys thought Mentor Blu was pretty. Ebony supposed she was.

Her long dark hair snaked over one shoulder in a loose braid, and her bright green eyes sparkled from behind the black rimmed eyeglasses she wore. Flawless skin glowed from her cheeks down her exposed neckline in the softest salmon color. She looked younger than most mentors. The odd part was that her petite figure was dressed in yoga pants and a tank top. Ebony had never seen a mentor in anything other than dress clothes and a Motley robe. Except for recreational study Coach Rickman. And her father. Ebony swallowed the lump in her throat.

"*Helsingen,* everyone," Mentor Blu said in a soft voice.

Two football players on the front bleacher said, "God bless you."

Nervous laughter circled the gymnasium. Even Mentor Blu tittered.

"Translated from the language of the giants, we know this means . . ." she dragged out the final syllable until both foreign word and interpretation flashed on the virtual screen.

"Greetings," half the students answered.

"Correct," she said. "Remember, Jotunn is one of the oldest active languages of Yggdrasil, except for the *dökk álfa* – the dark elves."

Ebony felt Fleishman flinch beside her.

"Now that you're familiar with runes, it's time to learn how to use them," Mentor Blu said. "You'll find lots of information on the internet, at libraries, and on television that contain conflicting facts about the use of runes. Remember, as far as the rest of the world knows Yggdrasil is a figment of someone's elaborate imagination to create great fiction from a long-lost culture. But you now know differently. You are learning the real truth."

Real truth. Was that based on what information someone knew or did it have to contain all the facts? What if someone didn't have all the facts? Did it make what they knew the truth, their truth, or only half truth? And where did trust fit into that? Ebony held her sigh inside.

"Runes are an interpretation of thoughts, phrases, and combined descriptions. Like all things in creation, they are balanced, two-sided if you will. Each possess positive and negative energy, which one is applied depends on the user's intent," Mentor Blu said. "Take a baseball bat. It can be used positively to play a game or negatively to break a window. Technically, a baseball bat can have a positive or negative effect depending on what the user does with it."

Mentor Nesbitt stepped forward in his Cursed Rune T-shirt and shorts. "Rune stones are one-way luminaries and sensories can work toward a common goal."

Like Aunt Gertrude had said.

"And you'll have to work together during the Ullr games," Mentor Denarious joined the mentors up front. "If you want to win."

A gleeful roared rolled over the study body.

"I knew Denarious was a closet rebel." Dakota crunched knuckles with Quinn.

"Luminaries connect to their magick through nature sources – the moon, the alignment of the stars, herbs, or a simple bowl of water," Denarious said, pointing at the table.

"They draw on energy using rune stones, depending on what natural magick the rune represents and what interpretation the user uses. Runes can help you raise, direct, and release energy. I'll be using Berkana, a rune that can represent nature and birth, and Uruz, which stands for power or force. Concentrating on both will help me access the invisible energy the water in this bowl holds."

"I can't believe I missed that." Fleishman nudged Ebony's shoulder with his. "Accessing outside energy."

"Translation, please," Ebony said.

"That's what Wizner did in the boneyard. He collected nearby energy and used it to defend us," he said. "Poe and Asmund, too."

"Whoa . . ." Ebony said.

Mentor Denarious set the two rune stones on either side of the glass bowl and next to the plant pot. He began repeating a low-murmuring chant.

Water in the bowl vibrated softly. A weak wave formed. It grew stronger and seesawed between opposite sides of the bowl. Droplets crested the rim, sloshing over the sides. Translucent flickers wafted from the water's surface, colors of sky blue and silver like fog off a lake at dawn.

Ebony expected to see kids reacting to the colored energy, but no one flinched. Not even the other medium students. Warmth caressed her skin.

Wait, it was the energy off the water. She stared at her hands. Could she collect energy, too?

"You don't always need physical runes," Mentor Blu said.

Mentor Nesbitt raised his arms palms down in front of his chest. He drew patterns with his fingers, leaving the faintest shadow behind. And like in Ursula's study, Ebony could see the hint of green energy floating from his fingertips; it streamed to his overall aura.

The only thing cooler than this revelation would have

been a lifetime supply of Cheese Doodles.

The brass metal piece lifted off the small table. Students leaned forward on their bleachers.

Mentor Blu lowered her chin. "Sensories can call upon those patterns made by luminaries to manipulate an outcome."

A string of green energy from Nesbitt's work floated toward the young mentor. It melded with her pinkish aura. The elegant clock rocked on its base and lifted into the air. As it did, Denarious' plant pot wobbled. A handful of students gasped, but most remained silent.

"Individual runes can be used for protection, to bind . . . oh let's say an animal, or to invoke a spell or war." Nesbitt continued drawing the same invisible symbols in the air.

"Even to move an item," Mentor Blu added. "But to use them you must understand the meanings of each symbol. This can be tricky because each has multiple interpretations and holds special power when called upon." The rune chart on the virtual screen flickered to include meanings beneath each.

Her voice faded as Nesbitt's metal piece met the clock midair. Fitting together, it wound, changing the time on the face. The clock lowered to the table.

Groans of straining wood wafted from the plant pot. Lines formed on Mentor Denarious' forehead as a sprig of green rose from the soil. The perfumed scent of flowers filled the gym. The stem grew taller and thickened at the head until a red rose blossomed on top.

"Although both exercises were tame," Mentor Nesbitt said as he inched closer. "They are the same skills you'll use during battle magick."

twenty-five

Battle Magick

Of all mentors at Motley Junior High to teach battle magick, Ebony had to get Freeman. She'd already spent time with him in his newly titled Design and Enchantments Arts study and still smelled like chalky pastels and indelible marker to prove it.

Air pressure closed the rune ward surrounding their little training area of the gym floor, causing Freeman to clap his hands like a seal begging for more fish. Erasing that image of Freeman from Ebony's brain would have been harder if it hadn't been for Erickson staring at her. Along with Glinda, Dakota, and Quinn, she was being forced to work with her nemesis and his sidekick.

Burnt cheese whiz.

Fleishman waved at Ebony from his training group with Mentor Lyn. One thumbs-ups was all she had to offer, ticked off they'd been separated. She was glad he was coming over for dinner tonight. They needed to talk about all this.

"Luminary students, here are your runes to use." Freeman handed Dakota, Jed, Quinn, and Glinda each a small velvet bag.

"I can't do this!" Clare kicked at the rune stones, creating the protection ward around her group. The release of air made most students cover their ears. Clare raced from the gym, and Mentor Lyn followed her.

"Drama queens," Erickson snorted.

Mentor Freeman divided the six into two groups and set a piece of paper and scissors in front of Erickson, Jed, and Dakota.

"Levitate the paper and command the scissors to cut the sheet in half," he said. To Ebony, "You three must prevent them from accomplishing their goal."

Was he kidding? Giving scissors to kids learning how to control energy and magick wasn't the brightest idea. And why pit her against Erickson? Ebony glanced around for Bat-Face. She'd probably set this up.

Glinda and Quinn debated which runes to use. Ebony half-listened, more taken by Jed's interest in their discussion. Dakota elbowed Jed as he argued his reasons for using certain runes. Jed fished out a stone and dropped it back in the bag. Erickson leaned in, whispering, making Dakota's jaw tense. Jed didn't show any emotion, but the quiver of dark olive in his aura told Ebony he was unsure of himself.

Quinn and Glinda sat on the floor behind their chosen runes – *Inguz* (protection and work), *Nauthiz* (determination), and *Eihwaz* (defense and motivation). It wasn't until they'd finished that Jed committed to two stones.

Erickson threaded his fingers together and smirked up at the rafters. A soft chant vibrated from Ebony's teammates. Dakota crouched low, whispering, while Jed remained silent.

Sides drawn.

The duel had begun.

Faint energy grew visible around her three opponents, her teammates, and the water in each bowl. The lines framing Erickson warped; the others' lines barely waved. Erickson's energy seemed to be the strongest. An unfortunate truth for her.

She gaped at her team's bowl of water, wondering how to tap into the water's energy?

Trust. Ebony needed to trust them. Easier said than done.

Quinn's voice rose over Glinda's as they chanted.

Then again, they had to trust her, too. Maybe Ebony's problem was believing in their trust of her.

Jed's voice deepened and chanted out-of-sync with Dakota.

Ebony focused on the transparent energy floating above the water in her bowl. Her tattoos pulsated beneath her sleeve but held back their light. She imagined her energy reaching for the bowl. The layer of energy expanded. Threads of sky-blue weaved into the tapped energy. The pulse of her tattoos revved to a throb and she tried to ignore it. Frustrated, she lost her grip.

Moldy cheese.

She'd had it and would have kept it if she hadn't let her annoyance get to her. Wait, emotions played a part in her magick and skill. Aunt Gertrude had said her skills were connected.

Refocusing, she searched for the water's energy again, and this time she felt resistance.

The sheet of paper arched at the center, and Dakota

chanted louder. One corner waved and then the other.

"That's it," encouraged Mentor Freeman.

The scissors wobbled, but Ebony tugged at the energy in the air. Dakota tensed. He let out a groan, and the paper lifted off the floor.

Erickson pressed fingers to his temples. A transparent bubble of energy floated to connect with his energy. Scissors levitated, the paper at knee height. Jed and Dakota took turns tapping the rune stones. Glinda and Quinn drew symbols in the air, but Erickson's team was still winning. Ebony needed to get it together.

Energy off her opponent's water swept against her legs. Cool. Damp. Not in wetness but saturation. Heavy. The sensation wasn't like Aunt Gertrude had described.

Energy should feel natural, light and airy and part of you, her aunt had said.

Quinn tapped Ebony's boot. The corners of his mouth twitched. His long eyelashes fanned at her, pale blue irises sparkling beneath. Encouragement. And that wasn't a sensory or luminary thing. It was a friendship thing.

Time to muster some strength, and maybe a teeny bit of trust.

Her team's goal was to prevent Erickson's team from succeeding. Nothing more. And it didn't have to be pretty. Just accurate to break the string of energy from the water to Erickson.

Ebony clenched her teeth. Heat prickled her skin, and her tattoos itched. Her teammates sped up their chant. Jed and Dakota countered.

The gym spun. Acid stirred in Ebony's stomach. Waves of nausea crashed into her. If she didn't finish this she'd faint. Or worse. Puke.

Colorful spots dotted her vision. Her hearing waned, noise hollow. She stumbled off-balance, her boot edging into the Inguz rune stone which nudged into Nauthiz.

Energy sparks circled the two runes and darted at Ebony. Light slipped from beneath her sleeve, and she tucked it into her waist. Covered it with her other arm. But that hadn't been enough. Erickson's opened-mouth gawk verified he'd seen.

The scissors fell from midair and clanked to the gym floor. Glinda flinched. Quinn did, too. Dakota and Jed quieted. The sheet of paper drifted downward for Erickson to snatch.

"She cheated!" He lunged at Ebony.

Quinn scrambled to his feet, in front of Erickson, cutting him off.

"We win," Erickson said, bumping into Quinn's chest.

Mentor Freeman began, "There are no winners during—"

Erickson shot more accusations at Ebony, and mentor Freeman called for help. Jed yelled for Erickson to stop as Fleishman jogged into the group. Mentors Denarious and Blu rushed over with Nesbitt close behind.

"What happened?" Denarious asked.

Erickson's wide eyes speared Ebony. "She—"

"Bindrunes." Mentor Blu's voice cut in.

"Bind what?" Quinn asked.

"My grandfather has talked about those," Cermet said, wedging through the crowd of students.

Everyone quieted as Mentor Blu crouched low to touch two runes on the floor.

"We combine letters to create words," Mentor Blu explained as she stood. "But when two or more runes are joined power increases to create a new magical symbol – a bindrune. But unlike single runes, bindrunes only hold positive energy. They can't be used negatively."

Fleishman clasped his hand over Ebony's dual-rune tattoo. She glanced up at him. The grimoire had marked her with a bindrune. She'd used it to help Roger in the boneyard. What could that mean?

Cermet shifted beside them. Could he help? And Glinda? She'd kept the rune ward in place in Ursula's study.

The first bell chimed, sending kids to change in the locker rooms. Glinda walked beside Ebony with Fleishman and Cermet.

"Bindrunes could help find your friend's body," Cermet said.

Fleishman stopped walking. "What friend?"

"That Lance boy."

"You know about Lance?" Ebony asked.

Cermet snorted. "Everyone heard rumors that you brought spirits with you when you got back. Of course, most were talking all spooky stuff and joking. But I'm a medium, too. A horrible one, but I can see that kid. I can tell he's different."

Had the Cheerio Twins seen him, too? "Where?" Ebony asked.

"In school," Cermet said, "or outside, but only when you two are around."

That explained why the twins hadn't seen Lance. They steered clear of Ebony and Fleishman.

"And he's had an old lady with him, lately," Cermet added.

"What old lady?" Fleishman asked.

Ebony sighed. "He's been meeting other ghosts."

"And you knew this?" Fleishman said. "For how long?"

Ebony gave him a silent face and turned to her two friends before he could ask again.

"Would you help Fleish and me with something?" she asked.

"Sure," said Glinda.

"With what?" Cermet asked.

Ebony looked to Fleishman, and he nodded his head. She bared her wrist, revealing her new markings.

"My family grimoire marked me with this," she said.

"That's a bindrune." Their joint answer erased any doubt they'd back out.

twenty-six

Blueprint

ing went Ethan's fork against his spoon that wedged his butter knife under the rim of a plate.

He dipped his finger inside his glass. The ice cubes clinked against the sides as he raised the glass above his head, peering at it from the bottom. Ebony glanced at Fleishman, who looked as anxious as she felt waiting for Ethan to take a sip. But he swirled the glass, sloshing the cold liquid and ice against the sides. And he did it again and again.

She wanted to peg her half-eaten dinner roll at him, which caused sprigs of guilt to twitch in her stomach. The little squirt had been nice to her, lately. It wasn't his fault their mother insisted on quality time at another family meal.

Granted, she and Mom were getting along better since Njord Academy's resurrection, but her mother still wouldn't talk about Dad.

Aunt Gladys set a fresh pitcher of lemonade in front of her sister and settled into her chair. The two gabbed about the correct way to squeeze a lemon.

"So Ebony," Mom said and wiped her mouth with a napkin. "I never asked what you thought about Njord Academy and the Ullr games?"

Ebony didn't like it. She didn't trust them. "It's fine."

Her mother stared like she wanted to say more, but she picked up her fork. "Right."

What about the Raw Bone and the file on Lance? That twittering inside Ebony's stomach was back. It nudged her to ask the questions she had. But she'd have to trust in the answers she received. She didn't think she was ready to do that yet.

Ethan reached to set his water glass down but nicked his plate, tipping the glass over on himself. Fleishman pushed from the table, and Ethan leaped up from his chair. Water and ice cubes filled his plate, his lap wet.

"Ethan!" Mom tugged him to the foyer. "Upstairs to change."

The aunts went about sopping up the water, while Ebony and Fleishman sat quietly. With soggy paper towels in hand, Aunt Gertrude exited to the kitchen.

Aunt Gladys sat in her chair, her expression as if nothing had happened. "How has school been for the two of you?"

Fleishman's gawk pleaded with Ebony to tell them about the Mist Gypsy, Raw Bone, and how their grimoire had marked her. But her only reasoning for any of it was about finding that loser dark elf Daenir, putting Lance back together, and helping the boneyard residents, which would get her and Fleishman in trouble.

"It's school," Ebony said.

Fleishman sighed. Her regret for disappointing him, again, made her swing her legs beneath her chair and nudge her satchel. Bringing up Nesbitt's map might make Fleishman feel better. "Actually, do you know what location this map is showing?"

Aunt Gertrude ambled into the dining room and snatched the frayed piece of parchment from Ebony's hands before she could complete her pass to Gladys.

"How rude, sister," said Gladys.

"Never claimed to be otherwise," Gertrude said and winked at Fleishman; he blushed. "Goblin's breath, I haven't seen this in ages."

"You've seen it before?" Fleishman asked.

"A similar version, but this one is much older," Gertrude said. "Where's the rest of it?"

"That's all, Mentor Nesbitt had." Ebony's heart bounced in her chest. "He didn't know anything about it, so he said I could borrow it."

"One thing's for sure. This isn't a map." Gertrude held her skirt down to sit.

"Let me see," Gladys said.

Gertrude pointed. "That's a crypt and so is this one."

All Ebony saw was a couple warped upside-down letter Ys.

"What are you—" Gladys stopped as Gertrude tilted the paper. "Ah, good eye, sister. It is a map."

"Didn't she say it wasn't a map?" Fleishman asked.

Aunt Gertrude whirled the paper 180 degrees turning the upside-down Ys right-side up.

Fleishman leaned in closer. "That's a rune."

"Then why call them crypts?" Ebony looked at her aunts.

"Because the rune Algiz in its right state means life or man," Gertrude said. "Flip it upside-down and it represents death or the end. It's a symbol for crypts and tombstones."

"So," Ebony said.

"Little Herb, this map is a blueprint," Gertrude said.

"Of our cemetery behind the school," Gladys finished.

"How do you know it's Motley's cemetery?" Fleishman asked.

"I recognize it," Gertrude said. "Keeper Coffer showed me an updated version."

"You've talked to Keeper Coffer?" Ebony asked. No one talked to him. Ever.

Where Gertrude said nothing, Gladys was more than happy to fill in. She nodded at Ebony. "Denny, Keeper Coffer to you, and Gertrude are old friends."

"Yes, yes." Gertrude shifted in her chair. "Old friends."

Ew . . . Aunt Gertrude blushed, and Ebony lost her appetite. There should be an age limit on old people blushing, like after age twenty.

Aunt Gladys cackled, and Gertrude snorted in an odd sort of way. The two bantered through laughs and cutup words.

"What about this?" Fleishman pointed out the faded imprint of the ladder symbol, the one from Lance's file.

Gertrude plucked her eyeglasses from her skirt pocket and let them teeter at the end of her nose. "Looks like the web."

"The internet?" Ebony asked.

"No," they said together.

Talking to them was like pulling teeth.

"The web rune." Gladys spoke up. "It's the full rune alphabet's representation of the past, the present, and the future."

The 3Ms were Past, Present, and Future. That couldn't be a coincidence.

"Logical with the cemetery being the center of the center," Gertrude added.

"Because that makes sense," Ebony grumbled.

"Of course, it does," Gladys agreed. "See, Little Herb, Motley's cemetery was created as a direct link to Yggdrasil's trunk to preserve its magical elements: a time capsule of sorts. A few hundred years ago, all mystical traces through that link were wiped from human senses. With the reopening of the cemetery, a new connection has been established. Meaning energy, power, and nutrients can be harnessed from the three wells through the trunk." She tapped a finger on the table and counted off. "There's Urd, the well of fate, which you know."

"Thanks to *Nidhogg*," Gertrude interrupted.

"Mímisbrunnr," Gladys continued, "the spring of wisdom, and *Hvergelmir*, the well in Niflheim from which many rivers flow."

Hold the cheese. The Watchers were concerned about the wells. What would happen if dark elves got hold of all three wells? Could they feed chaos?

"Shouldn't I feel this energy with the boneyard reopened?" Ebony asked.

"According to the physics of Ebony's skills, she should," Fleishman offered.

The sisters shared a mysterious smirk.

Fleishman sat back in his chair. "Ebony, I think you have felt it. Increased energy would explain your trouble with calling on doors and how anxious you've felt lately."

"Energy has been redirecting since the cemetery reopened for spirit travel," Gladys said.

Maybe Nidhogg's visit hadn't been about draining the Urd well, but about redirecting its energy, which could explain the missing Yggdrasil elements Delia mentioned.

"Redirecting to where?" Ebony asked.

Both aunts looked down at their hands.

Gertrude finally said, "To the forbidden section of the cemetery."

"Where the jagged part of this map cuts off," Gladys finished.

Dead Alley. Had somebody torn that section of the map away on purpose? Could there have been a more sinister reason for her to stay out of Dead Alley?

"That place has been locked up for years, tighter than a caster's hex on an enemy's voodoo doll." Gertrude hooted.

"Locked up?" Ebony repeated.

"Wards," Gertrude winked.

That made sense. The weird vibe that flushed through her whenever she focused her attention on Dead Alley, and how she and Fleishman couldn't get in when they were younger.

"Why ward it, though?" she asked.

"The old Njord Academy closed," Gertrude said. "That section of the cemetery belonged to them."

twenty-seven

Silent Chaos

bony dragged the tip of her combat boot along the older section of Bjorn Trail where groomed land met a wall of overgrowth. "Dead Alley has to be here."

"This is a bad idea," Fleishman said.

Ebony pretended not to hear him and held her palms up. "These bushes are warded. You were right. I can feel it. Try what you did with Xander's computer."

"I'm a minimalist when it comes to wards." He fiddled with the strap of Nigel's cage.

She dropped her hands back at her sides. "If you did it once, you can do it again."

"These are too strong for me to break," he said.

"You know that *thing* you keep telling me I need to do?"

His face brightened, which told her he got that she was talking about trust.

"You kind of should take your own advice."

"You are not serious?" Fleishman said.

Red strands squirmed in his aura. The color fluctuated between dark and light like it couldn't make up its mind how it felt.

"Uh, I was."

Fleishman took a big breath. "Ebony, look. I'm supposed to help you be the Bearer of the Doors, right?"

Yup. He had been appointed her Norse advisor.

"Not to mention keeping you out of trouble."

What? Wait, he was right.

"And that takes a lot of trusting in you, which gives you some control over the situation and how things will turn out," he finished.

Ooh . . .

Balmy air waft around them. Ebony watched parts of his aura darken to burgundy, in other areas lighten to tangerine. She'd been so distracted by how she felt that she'd ignored what was right in front of her. Their new responsibility had affected Fleishman as much as it had her. Normally, he was mentally stronger than she was. He saw a problem, stuffed his face in a book to work out answers, and took care of it. She was making it harder for him.

"Sorry, Fleish." She truly was.

"Aw, it's okay." He was such a good guy.

Ebony fiddled with her apprentice medallion. "Ignoring this would be giving up, right?"

"I guess."

Silenced drifted between them, each in deep thought.

"I can't do that to the Boneyard residents," she said.

A bright smile spread across his face. "I knew you wouldn't."

Ebony's stomach did a gentle flip. The kind that felt good. "Okay, then maybe Glinda and Cermet can help us with the wards here, too."

"Why would they do that?"

"So we can get in," she said.

Pebbles shot ahead of them as he skidded to a stop. "We are not going in there."

"We'll discuss it." She kept walking. "Geesh, you need to exercise that give up control thing."

He jogged back in line with her. "Was that making fun of me?"

"Maybe." She smirked.

They crossed a row of graves to where Bjorn Trail forked onto Ash Pathway. Fleishman plucked his re-creation of Ebony's sketch from his backpack, while she searched for the residents to check on their illness.

"Dead Alley belongs to Njord Academy," she began, "and Njord Academy is Vanir. That means the Vanir could be responsible for the collapse of old man Pottle's crypt and the attempt at a vortex or black hole, not Daenir. And there's something weird about Seronious Bile, so he could be working with the gods to do something during the Ullr games."

"I know you don't like Dean Bile, but he wants his school to get ahead of Motley, not turn the world into a chaotic mess," Fleishman said. "Plus, it would take someone stronger to pull this off, like a Vanir god."

"Or maybe an enemy of the Vanir," she said. "You know, to make them look bad."

"It could be both." Fleishman tapped the stick figure part of the drawing. "Mentor Nesbitt said the nature goddess was Vanir and part of the trade during the gods' peace treaty. She was cast out with the Mist Gypsies," he said and continued walking up the pathway. "It fits with the image of that woman and storms."

"How does Valknut fit in with my new rune tattoo?"

"Since it was given to chosen warriors as an entrance pass to Valhalla, maybe it serves the same purpose for you," he said.

"For me to get into Valhalla?"

"Maybe or maybe someplace else," he said.

Twigs cracked, and a shadowy figure stalked along a row of graves parallel to them.

Keeper Coffer carried a dirty shovel over one wide shoulder. A toolbox dangled from the fingers of his other hand. The man paused as he noticed them. He tugged the brim of his straw hat down to shade half his thin face. Ebony tiptoed forward.

"Hey," Fleishman whispered.

"Relax, I'm seeing if he knows about the map." She raised her voice. "Hi, Mr. Keeper."

"It's Mr. Coffer," Fleishman said.

"What?" she volleyed back.

"His last name is Coffer, so it should be Mr. Coffer."

"Are you correcting me, right now?"

"I'm being accurate," Fleishman mumbled.

"Hi, Mr. Keeper Coffer," Ebony said to be safe and received zero response from the man. "Um, do you have a map of the boneyard, I mean . . . the cemetery with crypts or gravestones? Maybe runes?"

Keeper Coffer didn't crack a smile. Didn't say a word, only strode onto Ash Pathway, making his way to Bjorn Trail.

"Maybe your aunt was joking about knowing him," Fleishman said.

"She sounded serious." Ebony shrugged. "Aunt Gladys agreed, and that rarely happens."

The man stopped a few yards away.

Had he heard her? She hadn't meant to sound rude talking about her aunts.

Keeper faced them, gravel crunching beneath his feet. Ebony knew old people stuck together when it came to respect, so maybe he was going to defend Aunt Gladys. He gestured with his hands, but he was too far away and in the shadow of a Weeping Willow for Ebony to tell what he was doing. He returned to his business, striding until the rubble and overgrowth nearer Dead Alley swallowed him up.

A crow crossed Ash Pathway. Two more waddled over a grave marker. A fourth hobbled behind them, wings held unevenly as it spat out a caw, obviously annoyed with the others. Response caws batted back and forth until they flew away.

"They're more ornery than usual," Fleishman said.

"Pesky vermin." Amphylis shooed the crows, crabby about their left-behind poop.

"So is Amphylis." Ebony gripped hold of Fleishman's arm and the two stared, accessing their ghostly family.

Miss Prim scurried by Amphylis, her hand held beneath her dainty nose. Miss Proper's stuttered steps were close behind. Her dead stare locked onto Ebony. Dark circles rimmed her large eyes, and her prominent cheekbones were more pronounced, face thinner and skin an opaque pale; the bluish spots darker.

Hargraves crossed Ebony's view with Victoria clinging to his arm. He moved slower than usual, his steps labored, heavy. The young couple tipped their heads at her. All went silent.

Ebony's heart skipped a beat at the strange vibe she sensed. Roger's crow feathers felt more like that omen Fleishman mentioned.

Amphylis stopped dusting, handkerchief at her mouth to catch her cough. Old Man Pottle's spirit rippled enough where Ebony could see a stone planter behind him and . . . A door blurred into view.

Air crackled as the familiar Door to the Hall of Souls

thickened and opened. Delia spilled out. Ebony stepped around Pottle, tugging Fleishman with her.

"I have an update on the boy." Delia lowered her goggles to dangle around her neck. "He's fallen into a deep sleep and his coloring is off. His," she paused, "ghostly flesh is decaying."

Ebony cupped her hands over her mouth.

"Any idea what that means?" Fleishman kicked into problem-solving mode.

Delia slid her goggles back over her eyes. "Only that it's not good."

With that, she was gone.

The two stood in silence. Ebony wanted to fix it, but she couldn't do it alone.

"Fleish, I need you to tell me what to do," she said.

"No, you don't." He peered down at Nigel in his cage. "We need to work this out together."

His assurance bullied its way to her heart, and she let it.

A loud croak echoed.

"Why are the strange noises always behind us?" Fleishman asked.

"Should we look?" she asked.

He sighed, and the two pivoted around.

Wings fluttered from an oversized tombstone shaped like a cross. Crows of graying feathers perched on all sides and at least a dozen on the ground beneath; marbleized eyes bored lifeless gazes into their faces.

Fleishman whispered, "When did they get here?"

"No idea, but it wouldn't surprise me if they sprouted green bolts from the sides of their necks and held their wings straight in front of them, end feathers limp," she said. "They have the Frankenstein waddle down pat."

At that, caws and croaks exploded into the air and chased them out of the boneyard.

twenty-eight

The Seven Disciplines

Walking to the back lawn of Motley in two distinct lines of sensories and luminaries felt more like a death march than a field trip outside. All Bat-Face needed was a drumbeat.

"This is not a field trip." Charity pouted, and her sister snorted in agreement.

"Speak for yourself." Jed elbowed Erickson whose only response was to peg his chewed gum at a pair of crows, making them fly from their picnic table perch.

Meanie.

Ebony let her attention drift to where the back lawn blended into the natural field. Wild flowers of columbine and lupines swayed gingerly in the light breeze. Both were indigenous to Maine. Ebony really liked them. Her eyes caught something beyond the wildflowers.

"Psst." Ebony signaled to Fleishman, who stood farther back in line. "Come here."

His face contorted with *You want me to cut the line?*

Yes, the grimace on her face said.

His shoulders drooped, and he cut the line.

"Ouch." A boy stumbled back.

"Oops, sorry," Fleishman said, fumbling over the boy's foot to stand behind Ebony. To Ebony, "I feel guilty."

"You'll survive," she said and noticed Cermet lean out of line behind them. He raised his hand to wave, but dropped it to his side, his cheeks flushing.

Ebony spun to see the tail end of Glinda's return wave. Had he blushed because of Glinda. Did he like her? Or like-like her? Ebony still wasn't sure what the difference between like and like-like was, only that some of the seventh-grade girls used it sometime.

"Find any goddess info?" she whispered as the line moved ahead.

"I had a hard time concentrating after we outran those crows, last night."

She knew the feeling.

Movement flittered near the boneyard. Ebony skidded to a stop, causing Fleishman to bump into her and the next kid in line to nudge into him.

"By the archway," she said. "It's Keeper Coffer."

Crows circled above the boneyard. A few were bigger than the others, so Ebony decided those were ravens. She dropped her view to outside the fence, where a figure tugged the hood of its sweatshirt so far over its head. She almost couldn't make out who it was. Almost.

"That's Lance," she said. "And Keeper is looking in his direction."

"Do you think Keeper can see him?" he asked.

"He's not a medium."

"Are we sure?"

Now that he mentioned it. "No."

"What if Keeper Coffer has something to do with you-know-what?" Fleishman asked.

More crows joined the birds among the clouds.

Bat-Face clapped her hands and stopped, causing students to bump into each other. "Wait right here," she said and walked over to a group of mentors waiting among a few study pods. They greeted the Headmistress. After a brief discussion, mentors approached the two lines of students and divided them into smaller groups.

Of course, Ebony and Fleishman got separated. Again. She was starting to think splitting them up was a conspiracy.

Each smaller group was assigned to a specific pod.

Mentor Ursula stepped forward. "Students, you can see we've moved seven pods from inside the school to the back lawn. For our purposes here, we're going to refer to them as stations. Each station is marked by a rune that represents one of our Seven Disciplines." She paused to allow the chatter of the birds to quiet down. "Each station contains a quiz on its note screen that will test your qualifications for that particular discipline. Keep answering questions until the program within the note screen either determines you qualify for that discipline or tells you to move on."

"Once you have been assigned a discipline, come join me over here," yelled Mentor Nesbitt, who sat on the grass closer to the school building.

Mentor Blu stepped forward and fingered her eyeglasses at the brim of her nose. "The rune you see at each station has been chosen for its range of possible meanings. Writing in runes is not an exact science because of their multiple interpretations, but you won't need that for the Ullr games. We'll address that in study later on."

Ebony's mind drifted away from Mentor Blu's voice to

scan all the stations. Each discipline was marked by a rune painted in red with its name scripted above and a category written beneath. Uruz was the first rune she looked at; the word Physical ran under it for its category. Ansuz was next with the word Mental for its category.

There was Algiz with Spiritual – where Ebony stood – Hagalaz with Elemental, Sowulo with Apothecary, Kenaz with Ascetical, and Dagaz was the last rune with Centurion splayed along the bottom.

It only took a few minutes for two fellow sixth graders and three seventh graders to finish their first station and trudge to sit with Mentor Nesbitt by the school.

Ebony returned her attention to the digital screen in the Algiz pod: What color do you see the sky? Blue was logical, because . . . yeah, the sky was blue. But with Ebony's newly flourishing empathic abilities, she could see a rainbow of emotional energy up there. She chose endless. The next two questions were much the same, but she paused at the fourth one. What two ingredients must one possess to make an informed decision?

Crows gravitated to the area over where Dead Alley was said to be; they flew in a circle.

Refocusing on her question, one of the multiple-choice answers struck Ebony more than the others – *facts and an open mind*. She searched for Fleishman and found him over at the Ansuz station. He'd be proud to know she valued facts. But having an open mind gave the ability to see all possibilities that could affect a decision.

She tapped the screen to fill the tiny circle black. That choice sent her to the Kenaz pod. And from there to every other pod station until she arrived at Ansuz, leaving Dagaz the only other discipline she hadn't tested for. She'd been so busy taking the quizzes she hadn't noticed that Fleishman had already finished his testing and sat on the lawn near Mentor Nesbitt. Only five students besides herself remained at stations: Magdalen – the eighth-grade girl from Ursula's study (which was inspiring) and Aiden – the seventh-grade psychic shield (which was okay), Dakota (which was cool), Cheesehead Dwayne (which was unbelievable), and Erickson (which was awful).

She passed the first three questions of the Ansuz's test and moved on to a fourth. From the corner of her eye, she noticed Cheesehead Dwayne being sent to sit with Mentor Nesbitt. Shortly after, Dakota and Aiden followed him. Before she could answer the next question, her screen fuzzed over.

Bat-Face ambled forward. "Our little query is having trouble designating a discipline for those remaining. To remedy this, we've developed a write-in question, which Mentor Ursula will read out loud."

Erickson, Magdalen, and Ebony each picked up a small portable note screen.

Ursula said, "Your question: *You're in a burning building with two other people and only enough time to save one of them – your best friend or your worst enemy. One decision will bring you peace and one will bring you pain. Who will you allow to perish?*"

Magdalen tapped her teeth with her stylist, while Erickson stared down at his screen. Ebony chewed on her bottom lip, pondering an answer, but stopped as tingling spread over her new tattoo.

Sharp conversation between birds drifted over the student body from above Dead Alley. Prickles skittered across Ebony's wrist. The skin of her new tattoo swelled.

No glow. No glow. Please no glow. Ebony refocused on the question. It felt important. *In everything there is a lesson to learn, Ebony. You must look for it.* Aunt Gertrude, she thought.

Everyone would save their best friend, right? Then again, letting her worst enemy – Erickson, in case anyone wondered – perish wouldn't bring her peace, even though he was mean and kind of deserved it. Not saving Fleishman would be too painful. There was only one answer to avoid both emotions: send her best friend out of the building and let her worst enemy take her place. In that decision, she'd feel no pain, only peace for saving two people.

Good thing this was hypothetical because she wasn't sure she could live up to her answer.

Light flashed from Erickson's note screen, and he gave it to Ursula. Ebony finalized her answer and handed the note screen to Mentor Ursula. Magdalen did the same. Light mumbling exchanged between students.

"Erickson, Magdalen, and Ebony, you have achieved the same discipline. Dagaz, making you centurions, which means you possess abilities that, with the proper training, will enable you to utilize all seven disciplines," Ursula said.

Comments of *Sounds like a lot of work to me* and *Glad I didn't get that* whirled through the crowd. Ebony felt her tattoos flare with a sting.

A blanket of feathers rolled across the morning sky from Dead Alley, wings flapping, directing the flock to the field. The cluster elongated and thinned to a narrow point; not all birds in a line, but close. One mentor yelled for students to head inside and herded them up the embankment and out of sight. Another told some to take cover. The Cheerio Twins ran toward the school, screaming gibberish.

Jed had taken off, but he stopped to yell for Erickson, who wasn't moving; his attention glued to Ebony. If there hadn't been so much chaos, she'd ask him . . . Ebony stopped.

Chaos.

The birds soared with more procession and speed than Ebony thought possible, so fast the convention of hollow bones and beaks meshed into one blob, moving in sync from one fluent turn or twist to the next. A few kids raced past her and crawled under a picnic table. Most had made it back to the school.

"Ebony!" Fleishman waved his arms in the air.

But someone rammed into her body, and she hit the ground, landing hard on her back. The last thing she heard was a collection of blood-curdling caws.

twenty-nine

A Riddle of Stones

Leaves rustled to the sound of giggles transforming into shrills.

Elli hobbled to peek beyond a break in the tree line. Lifeless patches lay waste in her wake.

Being so old she shouldn't feel this giddy; then again, age had no effect on her. A pool of youth lined a field, boys and girls brimming in wild energy. The pores of her spotted skin opened like Lake of Fire guppies quenching their thirst. Her flesh inhaled the youthful blend.

It seemed those protecting Motley were attempting to teach these young ones' skills that required a higher level of study. She doubted a few students, if any at all were ready for that. What fun she could have tossing a little confusion at her prey. She'd choose two from the crowd. And she'd be gentle as to camouflage her naughty deed a bit longer because surely once it came to light these mentors would recognize her work. It was time to use a bishop in this game of chess. Or a knight. Maybe both.

The ruby stone cresting her ring flared with a bright flame. Round and round a wrinkled finger from her opposite hand circled the ruby. Off her lips swept a maiden's lullaby.

Toil to slumber the fellowship from me.
From troubles that double to create a new key.
To gain the next trinket,
Nine moons shall decay,
Unless debt be paid and Thee be saved.

With that a gemstone protruded from the ruby stone of the ring, one stone then two and three, until nine new stones dribbled into her palm; the original stone was left unscathed.

She tossed a new gem into the air, and it disintegrated into colorful mist. Red and violet streams cascaded downward until they hovered at chest height and swirled together. The more the streams rotated the more blurred the space became.

Elli plunged her hand inside. Slurping tongues and dripping water poured out as she tugged backward, and in her hand floated the mirage of a stained-glass bottle.

"Oh, how I can't wait to get my hands on you again, my pretty." Her voice had grown youthful. What mysteries whirled inside only she knew, and as it was foretold, it was only for her to know.

thirty

Bittersweet Petals

Y ou think you're better than everybody else!" Erickson yelled. The stench of sour milk and toothpaste still on his morning breath bounced off Ebony's face.

She rammed her hands against his chest. "Get off me!"

"Crows!" Fleishman's voice smashed through the loud booms of the wind.

Ebony pressed her head harder into the ground to tip her chin up at the sky and the birds diving at them. Dark shadows threaded between newly forming clouds. She sucked in a breath. Those weren't shadows. They were chaos collectors. "Erickson . . ."

"It's begun," he said, voice dull and breath now of tart apples. "You can't stop it."

Students abandoned their hiding spots. Jed and Fleishman jogged passed two students frozen in place, arms dangling at their sides and their skin paling gray. Black lines veined exposed skin like sludge oozing through tributaries.

Ebony struggled. "Erickson, we have to move."

"Fimbulvetr." The syllables fumbled off his lips.

Sunlight dimmed, despite being morning, and the temperature plummeted ten, possibly twenty degrees. Birds swirled overhead. Snow sprinkled out the center of their bird funnel. Their concerto of squawks deafened all other sounds.

Jed and Fleishman dropped to their knees, palms rammed against their ears. The dazed students collapsed, and Erickson's body shook with the bitter scent of rotting leaves.

"Go through the center. Follow the web runes beyond Garmr," he said in a voice not his own. "Tell him I'm sorry."

His body convulsed like separate forces fought inside him. He tipped sideways, enough for Ebony to push him off. She rolled to her knees and looked back at the boneyard. No Keeper. No Lance. But a female silhouette stood beneath the archway. Crows scurried at her feet, and ghosts crowded around her; with white skin and hollow eyes, these weren't boneyard ghosts.

The woman flipped a scraggly shawl to cover her head and bent to pluck a crow off the ground – literally staked the bird through its torso with something in her hand. Orange petals floated downward and seeped into the soil. The bird dropped to the ground; it waddled in a circle, and the woman's silhouette faded, vanishing.

Ghosts turned their heads as one to face the students, limbs rigid. One unhinged its jaw wider than naturally possible and released a shriek. Like the Raw Bone.

Jed jerked Erickson to his feet and toward the school, passing mentors Lyn and Nesbitt on their way back outside.

Nesbitt knelt next to the collapsed students. Vibrant yellow and orange energy rippled from nearby trees as he worked symbols in front of them; the energy linked to Nesbitt's aura. Flesh tones flushed the kids' skin. Life returned to their eyes. Nesbitt directed them to the school.

The flurry of snowflakes thickened. Shrills echoed across the field, and Fleishman crawled to Ebony. They rose to their feet.

Two chaos collectors swept over the field. Orange poppy petals floated in their wake. The wind batted at the petals, dissolving them into a tangerine mist as they soaked into the ground.

A flash of lightening dropped two Goths from midair. Asmund snatched a collector out of midair as he crashed to the ground. Three stiff punches from Asmund put that collector out of commission. Deep blue mist shot from Poe's wrists, catching another collector by a limb. The creature squealed. Metallic steam permeated the air.

More snow whirled; ice pellets bounced off every surface. Fleishman gripped hold of Ebony's arm.

Soil and grass bloated, a force rolling from beneath. The earth burst upward in small volcanos of gravel. A crow poked out one hole and another followed. A small army of waddling birds pressed in on Ebony and Fleishman.

"Gray feathers!" Fleishman squealed.

Ebony held her arms out to fend off the birds. Her new tattoo flared to life, and a crow marched into a stream of its light. The bird croaked garbled sounds. Murky steam rose from where its feathers had caught fire.

The flames spread to the grass and threatened nearby shrubs.

"*Du er i ferd med å være kålkake!*" bellowed Mentor Lyn. With one whack and then another, Mentor Lyn condemned the sickly crows to death, pummeling them beyond recognition. Normally Ebony would be grossed out, but there was nothing normal about this.

Mentor Nesbitt skidded in behind her, his hands drawing symbols in the air. The flames blotted out.

The remaining collectors surrounded the four, while crows stalked them from the sky.

Mentor Nesbitt tossed rune stones into the center of the circle. One collector jerked, body jolting as it flew off. He chanted and drew more symbols. Another dispersed. Asmund and Poe captured two more in a net of vapor, and with a crackle and a pop vanished with the collectors.

Ebony wished she knew how the two Goths disappeared like that.

Silence filled the next seconds. No wind. Every trace of snow, orange petal, gray crow, and chaos collector was gone. The only evidence left behind were speckles of white covering the field.

"What is that?" Ebony asked.

"Poop." Mentor Lyn pushed off her bent knees to stand. "Nothing like the ills of Yggdrasil leaving gobs of bird poop in its wake."

"But it was snow," Ebony insisted.

Mentor Lyn and Mentor Nesbitt exchanged a somber look.

"Now let me tell you," Bat-Face's words stuttered as she trampled defenseless wildflowers down the embankment. "This is unacceptable."

Mom jogged past Bat-Face. Ebony hadn't seen her mother once during this outdoor field trip slash exercise slash what-a-stinking-cheese-of-a-mess. She pulled Ebony into a hug.

"Are you all right?" she panted. Ebony murmured yes, enjoying her mom hug more than she had in a long time.

Bat-Face protested, but Mom cut her off, suggesting they head inside.

"This feels familiar." Fleishman eyed the long wood-paneled corridor that led to Headmistress Regina's office. Neither would forget the last time they waited outside her door, when Ebony accidentally spewed paint all over Mentor Freeman's precious fern plants.

"Erickson channeled a spirit out there," Ebony said.

Fleishman raised an eyebrow. "Are you sure?"

"He used a female voice and said he was sorry."

"Yup, totally not Erickson," Fleishman agreed.

"He also said to go through the center and cross grammar."

"Cross grammar?" He hesitated. "Wait, you think through the center means—"

"To break into Dead Alley," she beamed, and he moaned. "I also saw an old woman near the boneyard. Believe it or not, she stabbed a crow."

"An old woman killed a crow?" he asked.

She shook her head. "It didn't die. It waddled away like the crows during the night of the boneyard attack."

Bat-Face's mahogany door opened, hinges squealing for effect. Mom exited into the hallway, and she wasn't alone. "You remember Dean Bile."

Ebony didn't like this man standing close to her mother. So much had changed since her father vanished. Was seeing this a glimpse into Ebony's future? Was this what happened when one parent was no longer with us? Or when moms and dads broke up? "We remember."

Her mother frowned. "Come in. We'd like to speak with you both."

Ebony stood, but Fleishman darted in front of her. His protectiveness warmed her heart.

Bat-Face's office was pretty much how Ebony remembered. Every wall lined in molding, the strange mural of men and woman in flowing garments, one with horses battling serpents. The regal fireplace was there, but the image of an elegant tree with leaves of tourmaline gemstones hung above it. Ebony nudged into Fleishman.

"The Bewitching Forest." Dean Bile walked to the painting. "These trees are supposedly nourished directly from the goddess Freyja's most treasured necklace?"

"Brísingamen," Fleishman said.

"You know of the torc," Dean Bile said. "Impressive."

"I heard that the copper leaves can be used for potions and cures," Fleishman said.

"That is true," Dean Bile said.

Maybe Ebony liked him a little.

"Alas, the forest was mystically whisked away during the gods' peace treaty." He folded back the cuff of his dress shirt to look at his watch. "No one's been able to locate it since."

Nope. She still didn't like him.

"History lesson is over." Bat-Face pointed out the window. "We cannot have outbursts like that."

"Ebony did the right thing," Mom said.

"She could have burned students alive," Bat-Face challenged.

Letting the crows infect her fellow students was a better option? Doing the right thing was messy and unsupported, at times. But that didn't make the right thing any less necessary.

"She did the best she could." Mom smiled at Ebony. "That's all I ask for."

Tension drained from Ebony's body.

"My daughter's actions were a huge part of Nidhogg

returning to Yggdrasil," Mom said to the adults. To Ebony, "She and Fleishman have studied and trained tirelessly over the past weeks. They have a special bond with our cemetery and, it seems, the cemetery with them. Whatever that was, not only threatened Motley, but the cemetery itself. These two would never allow harm to come to it."

Ebony's heart nearly burst in her chest. This was Mom love. She hadn't let herself feel it in so long.

"But they know the boneyard is off limits for a little while," Mom said.

Some of that new Mom love drained away, replaced by an invisible cringe.

"All we ask is that you let us know if anything strange occurs," Mom finished.

"Actually . . ." Fleishman paused.

Oh no! Not in front of Bile. "Got it." Ebony tugged on Fleishman and headed out the door.

thirty-one

Cryptic Wards

bony steered the group around the bend at the end of Bjorn Trail that led to Dead Alley.

"Can't believe Mist Gypsies were here." That was the third time Glinda said that.

"I'm still wrapping my head around the stuff Fleishman told us," Cermet said.

Fleishman smirked at Cermet, the two intellects finding a middle ground.

Ebony slowed her pace, so Fleishman did, too.

"Ghosts?" Cermet asked.

"Yeah, but they're always following us when we're here," she said. "This is different."

Stray leaves littered the tops of tombstones; bunches

collected in the nooks and crannies of crypts. More bird poop stained the grave markers than a paintball game had paint.

"Did Amphylis finally give up cleaning?" Fleishman asked.

Ebony reached to touch his shoulder, giving him sight. "I don't think so."

Amphylis hunched over a tombstone. Her wipe-down grew more frantic with each jerk of her wrist. Victoria and Hargraves sat stoic on a bench, while George stared up at the sky. Miss Prim and Miss Proper sniffled in a huddle behind him their voices whimpers. Ghostly fingers touched each other's cheeks; the spots on their skin held a deeper blue.

"They look worse," Ebony said.

Old man Pottle hobbled behind the girls and stumbled near an octogen monument. Ebony and Cermet rushed to him, but Tanner helped him to his feet. Poor Glinda looked puzzled at a disadvantage unable to see ghosts.

Ebony stepped up to where the gravel path met ungroomed land. "This is it."

Heads tipped up at the natural barrier.

"Are you sure?" Cermet asked. "Looks more like a dead end than an alley."

Ebony pressed her palm against the invisible barrier. "I'm sure. I feel its wards."

"Hush, children. No more talk of it." Amphylis swiped at stray feathers. "Filthy. I've been cleaning this mess since those confounded crows arrived."

"Crows were always here," Fleishman said.

"Of course, Master Fleishman. Only not ones that attack like the night with the toddler boy." Amphylis lowered her voice. "Those come from in there."

Fleishman leaned into Ebony. "Crows, poppy petals, and Wizner's myth showed up that night."

"Well," Cermet started, "crows circled over this area during our field study."

"And chaos collectors dropped petals on the field," Ebony said.

"Delia was right," Fleishman reasoned. "Their illness is linked to the petals."

"Still believe we shouldn't break in there?" Ebony said.

This time, Fleishman didn't say a word.

"I've been looking for you guys," a new voice said.

"Lance!" Ebony said. Despite his possible involvement, avoiding him had been a dumb idea.

Fleishman seemed to agree as he waved an elbow. "Hey, Lance."

Ebony offered her other hand to Glinda, and Cermet nodded at Lance balancing on top of a crypt.

"Where are we breaking into?" Lance sat and dangled his legs over the edge. "I'm here to help."

Anxiety gnawed at Ebony's stomach. She hadn't told Lance anything, yet. Had she been trying to protect him or herself? "Dead Alley," she said.

Lance dropped to the ground. His silhouette seemed denser, limbs thicker, jawbone sharper the closer to Dead Alley he walked. Shadows danced across his face, and a rough sheen pitted the skin of his cheeks. If Ebony didn't know he was twelve years old, she'd think he was a lot older. He took another step and shook his head.

"Something wrong?" Ebony said.

"N-no." He backed up a few yards and covered his head with the hood of the sweatshirt he wore. He tugged the cuff of his sleeves over his hands. The tips of his fingers peeked out the bottom.

Fleishman's forehead creased, and Cermet tapped his finger against his chin. No doubt these two were quantifying possibilities. But Ebony wasn't about to wait until they finished.

"We need to break these wards," she said.

"To do that, we'd need to know what runes were used and what the intention for each was." Cermet faced Glinda.

"I might be able to tell," Glinda said.

She tipped the small velvet bag she carried to let some rune stones tumble into her palm. She set two on the ground, aligning them with the imaginary boundary of Dead Alley. A light chant swayed off her lips. The stones vibrated. Her flawless cheeks flushed soft pink, and she clenched her jaw. Her diaphragm expelled the breath she'd been holding.

"They're too strong," she panted.

Fleishman tugged Ebony backward. "We should tell Mentor Wizner what we know."

"I'm sure he knows most of it," she said. "Remember, he wouldn't fess up about his myth. And my mom keeps telling me the school is working on things." She edged up to Dead Alley. "The games are tomorrow, and things keep getting worse. We have to make sure nothing bad happens."

Or maybe Njord wanted something bad to happen.

Ebony turned to Lance. He inched closer, face downcast with each step pressing softly, carefully as though he were treading on lake ice that had cracked. One corner of his lip twitched, his shoulders tense. He shook his head beneath his hood.

"Are you all right?" Ebony asked.

Lance tipped his chin up, his expression hard. "We should break the wards."

Ebony watched him. He was acting strange. Then again, everyone was on edge. And with all that was going on, it was no surprise.

She flipped open her satchel. Air released from her lungs, and she slid her aunt's hefty grimoire out. Fleishman dropped his arms to his sides. She stopped him before he could protest.

"Ethan helped me with the grimoire before we had our talk," she said.

"You involved your little brother?" Fleishman's face reddened.

"We were playing Eons of Chaos, and Ethan masked an—"

"Item," he interrupted.

"Yeah . . . that," she said. "He wanted to show me that he'd learned how to do it in real life, so he used one of Aunt Gladys' herbal magazines and set it where the grimoire should be. You should have seen how excited he was."

She crouched down over the grimoire but stopped short of pressing her hand on its cover. *We're in this together*, was what Fleishman had said. "Hey, Fleish?" she said.

Fleishman stared at her.

"I want to ask the book for help, but I won't do it if you don't think I should," she said.

His face softened. He laid his hand on her shoulder to take in Lance and the other ghosts. "Sometimes our needs outweigh the risks."

The cover cooled her skin. She didn't remember feeling that last time, but she'd been so shocked it was no surprise. A glow illuminated the cover as the embers of her tattoos ignited. She giggled, and the threads strapping the top untied, freeing the pages between.

Victoria Givens applauded, and Hargraves nodded his head at Ebony's skill. Despite Amphylis' exhaustion, she gave Ebony a big smile.

Opening the cover, Ebony said, "Please show me the wards."

Pages waved, gaining momentum until they shuffled like old man Pottle handled his deck of cards. They rested at the back of the book where the rune alphabet lay strewn over two pages. One rune sparked with a reddish hue and then another and another.

Weight shifted near Ebony. Lance stood taller, fingers wiggly at his sides, his eyes transfixed on the pulsating runes. Ebony stretched to touch Fleishman so he could see Lance again.

"Lance," she said.

He shifted to one hip, before tearing his eyes off the glowing runes. "Keep going."

Something was off with him, but she didn't know what. Worry tensed her forehead and the back of her neck prickled with unease. "Fleish," she whispered, "should I?"

Fleishman nodded his head, but never took his eyes off Lance.

Ebony exhaled to refocused on the pages. She brushed her tattoos over the text. At first, it seemed to have no effect.

"Ebony, look." Fleishman pointed at the forest wall before them.

Runes glowed in different patterns on the invisible magical wall. The grimoire pulsed with light until every cryptic ward formula was exposed. At that, the book slammed its cover and retied its twine.

A discussion broke out about possible ways to break the wards.

Fleishman threw up his hands. "These are bindrunes. They're too complex."

"I agree." Cermet sat on a step of the octagon monument.

"What about your MM, Fleish," Ebony asked.

"Matter manipulation won't break wards," Fleishman said.

"Why not?" she persisted. "Wards are magical energy and energy is matter."

"Of course." Cermet stood. "You don't have to break the wards, alter them enough for us to fit through."

Fleishman set Nigel's cage down and tugged a small towel from the pouch clipped to it. He paused, glanced at Ebony and walked to a nearby spigot to douse the towel with water. He faced Dead Alley. The muscles of his jaw tightened. Droplets dripped from the drenched towel.

A rune at the center of one ward flickered. Three more dimmed from a different ward, and parts of other wards flashed like Aunt Gertrude's old TV screen during a storm.

"He's searching for connected energy," Cermet said.

Loose dirt vibrated at Fleishman's feet. He rung the towel in his hands. The tendons of his neck strained like Ebony remembered them doing when he'd successfully used his skill to manipulate the paint in Mentor Freeman's art study.

Fleishman's cheeks deepened with crimson as runes from one ward faded, eventually shrinking to the size of a dime. The faint point of light swirled, edges webbing out, clawing to fill more space. The alternating colors ate up space, leaving a wormhole to the other side of Dead Alley.

"I can see inside!" cried Glinda.

The wormhole began to shrink.

"I can't hold it," Fleishman grunted.

A low, murmured growl shook them from behind. Lance's wiggly fingers flexed and curled into his palms. His pupils dilated. The irises of his eyes lightened to florescent green. The last time Ebony had seen eyes do that was on Asmund the Goth. Lance's chest swelled. Muscles clenched beneath his sweatshirt.

Without a word, he swept passed Fleishman and gripped both sides of the wormhole. Ebony watched in shock as Lance stretched the diameter of the hole. When had he learned to give weight to his physical touch as a ghost? The last time they tried to slap hands only the sensation of touch was there.

"Go through," Lance grunted.

Fleishman stumbled to snatch up Nigel's cage. Glinda crawled through the narrow tunnel gate first with Cermet close behind. Ebony turned to the boneyard residents and nodded. Her hand brushed against Lance's as she stepped into the wormhole, and he shoved into her, hurdling both through the opening before it swirled closed behind them.

thirty-two

Time Capsule

ebony landed with a thud.

She rubbed her shoulder and gawked at Lance, who was too busy scanning their new surroundings to notice her.

Columns of stone lined the earthy path beneath their feet. Tree roots slinking above the soil slowed to a pause and then resumed. Stringy mildew clung to every surface.

"Are you seeing this?" Cermet gulped.

Ebony clenched hold of Fleishman and Glinda. "Be careful where you walk."

Bare bushes peppered the landscape of granite and concrete, but in an odd, chaotic way. Their branches sprouted in unnatural directions – fractured bones that had healed wrong; tips sharp as claws, joints skeletal and stiff. An ominous aura of grays and deep purple circled them.

"Ebony, let go for a second," Fleishman said. "Strange. Some branches of those bushes fade when you let go, leaving others that I can still see."

"That's okay by me because there's enough of them," Cermet said. "It's like a ginormous tree exploded, spewing its innards everywhere."

Withered poppy petals dangled from wrinkled vines that arched over the scene creating a dome. No sound could be heard. Even the chatter from the murder of crows silenced.

"It's too quiet, here," Glinda whispered.

"I agree." Fleishman flipped Ebony's wrist over to show her bindrune tattoo. "We should hurry."

The never-ending theme of Ebony's life, lately.

"See," Fleishman continued, "this part of her new tattoo. It's the Ansuz rune, and this part is Thurisaz, which represents a thorn and—"

"Sleep-poisoned," Cermet said. Of course, he knew that. He studied like Fleishman. "That could make sense why ghosts are sick. It can mean the force of evil or the undead."

"And," Fleishman released a huge sigh, "it's officially zombies."

"I thought being without my body was bad enough." Lance's voice surprised everyone.

His face was unreadable, his hoodie still shadowing his features. Ebony wanted to ask him if he was all right, but by what he'd just done she knew he wasn't. How could he be? It seemed he was starting to believe he'd be in ghost form forever or worse. And if Ebony were truthful, she had her own doubts about this turning out well. "Lance, how did you—"

"Grip onto invisible energy and bend it?" he finished for her. "I don't know. I want to figure this out soon."

"We're getting closer, Lance," Fleishman said. "We now know that the grimoire was giving us the cause of the undead crows and the sick ghosts. Someone used the Thurisaz rune to create the sleep-poison spell Delia talked about."

"Turning it into a bindrune with the Ansuz rune must have to do with how we reverse it, because Mentor Blu said bindrunes can only be used for good," Cermet added.

The group wandered down the path. Ebony thought about how she'd used her tattoo to help Roger. She wasn't sure what she'd done, but it had worked. Could she do it again?

Fleishman stopped. "Ebony, are you sure Erickson said grammar earlier?"

"Why?"

"Because that's Garmr," he said.

Ebony tipped her gaze up a concrete block to a huge canine cast in black onyx. The beast stood tall on muscular legs and paws the size of riding lawnmowers. Its eyes were fierce. Its jaw strong.

"As much as I don't want to say it, Garmr makes more sense," she said.

"Look here. It's the web rune your aunts talked about." Fleishman traced his finger over the rune engraved in a granite pillar. "And there's another over there."

"And farther down, too." Glinda pointed.

"Didn't you say that Erickson said to follow the web rune?" Fleishman reminded her.

Ebony ambled up to the next web rune. "It can't be that easy."

The group dodged crows and sidled between and around numerous bushes to follow Ebony as she searched for the next web rune along the path; Lance trailed a few feet behind them, quiet, distant. Ebony was thankful he was with them and not alone. Friends should be there for each other.

Need to reunite Lance with his body squeezed her heart. His body would make him whole again, and she'd do whatever it took to make that happen. She dragged her heels to pause at one oversized web rune.

Tombs and open-ended crypts filled with artifacts lined both sides of them.

"Delia was right," said Fleishman. "Someone is stock-piling Yggdrasil in Dead Alley."

"Looks like our garage when my grandfather gets ready for a yard sale," Glinda said.

Shelves upon shelves held golden chalices and trinkets. Books with bindings that read *The Trembling Path* and *Gilding Meadow*. Some looked like medical journals with an hourglass or seeing eye on the end. Hefty axes shone in black and bronze metals, handles of pure Ash wood engraved in runes. Tapestries of stories like found in the caves of the Incas or Aztec peoples hung in rows. There were jars of water and wooden boxes of soil labeled *Vimur River* or the *Island of Lyngvi*.

Fleishman focused on a timber cube carved in warriors and magicians, shields in their hands and fire balls hovering above their palms. "I've seen this sequence of runes before. It's Vanir."

Glinda pointed out a nearby atrium. "Those are images of herbs and charms on the altar. They followed luminary practices."

"Makes sense because the Vanir used those same practices," Cermet added.

"Fleish," Ebony said, "those leaves in that glass jar look like the healing leaves from the trees of the Bewitching Forest. Dean Bile said no one has seen the forest in a long time. He lied."

"I don't think he lied, Ebony." Cermet scrunched up one side of his nose. "The leaves are old and dead. They're not healing anything."

"Cermet's right," Fleishman agreed.

"I'd like to take a look, anyway," Ebony said.

Fleishman bowed his head. "Go ahead."

Ebony tiptoed over one of those strange bushes tucked against a crypt. Sweeping her fingertips across the clear glass stirred a glow from inside the jar. She pulled her fingers away, leaving streaks of light in their absence.

"You pulled residual energy from the leaves." Fleishman's face brightened.

Ebony's cheeks heated with excitement – for using a newly developing skill, and for choosing to seek Fleishman's advice and trust him. Working together didn't secure a specific outcome, but it shared the weight of the risk.

She curved her fingers around the glass, and her tattoos flared with a lavender glow. Life brightened within each leaf as she guided the jar into her grip. She inched over the bush and made her way toward the others.

"Uh, Ebony," Cermet's voice echoed.

The bush she'd passed flinched. It shook violently, tearing its few leaves from their branches. Snapping and popping echoed around them. Fleishman gripped onto Ebony's arm and Glinda huddled close to them.

"All the bushes are moving," he said.

Awkward branch angles straightened. Popping grew denser, and the snapping changed to the crackle of a hot fire. The stink of rotting seaweed choked the air.

Cermet coughed. "Should we be breathing this?"

Some branches clawed for the sky, sprouting tinier twigs from their tips, while others softened and slithered among themselves, knotting and coiling and draining of woodland color. Ovals and sharp angles thickened. Thinner branches congealed to form translucent bone, hair follicles, and even fabric. Before Ebony could digest what was happening, a small army of ghosts surrounded them. Whether sitting, lying, or standing, all ghosts had their eyes closed, all movement halted.

"Is it over?" Glinda asked.

"No idea," Cermet said, "but they look asleep."

"After that transformation, something tells me they won't stay that way," Ebony said.

As if her words had been a command, a female ghost propped against the crypt sat up, eyelids fluttering.

Glinda and Cermet gasped. Fleishman hugged Nigel's cage to his chest as the four huddled closer, even Lance.

Creases of dirt lined the worn fabric of the ghost's dress, and her hair matted to one side of her face.

Ebony stared at the leaves in the jar. "Did I . . . did this wake her up?"

"I don't think she's awake," said Cermet.

"More like activated," Fleishman added.

"Is that good or bad?" Glinda asked.

Cermet and Fleishman shared a long, drawn-out glance.

"Your silent conversations are getting annoying." Ebony tucked the jar against her chest. "Share, please."

Fleishman sighed, "You should call on Delia and try these leaves on the toddler first."

"You want me to use him as a test subject?" she asked.

"Better on him than these deadheads, and have it backfire," Fleishman said.

Cermet whispered, "I don't want to get eaten or whatever a ghost zombie can do."

"Ghost zombie?" Ebony asked.

"Officially, it's *Draugur Uppvakninga, Vakn* for short," Cermet said. "Yes, ghosts can be zombies, too. Like the physically undead, only in ghost form."

Fleishman puffed out his bottom lip. "I didn't know this."

Apparently, even smart kids had stuff to learn. And Ebony had yet another ghost type to memorize. She tucked the jar inside her satchel. "Fine, but let's keep it simple and stick with ghost zombie."

The group retraced their steps until they came upon two ghosts standing in the path. Ebony's bindrune tattoo ignited, and the glow inside the jar leaked out the stitched seams of her satchel.

"They affect the leaves somehow," Fleishman noted. "We should get that jar out of here."

More ghosts pushed off the ground. Some clawed up a crypt or nearby tree to stand. Skins pale with decay. Limbs stiff, and hoarse voices garbled. Still crows wobbled like they had been turned on by the flip of a switch.

"Like now!" Fleishman nudged Ebony, and she sidestepped the ghosts. The others scurried behind her.

More ghosts filtered into the pathway, blocking Ebony's line of sight. She tried to deviate between crypts and stone, but it was taking too long. Lance appeared in front of her, and she gave him the lead. Dormant ghosts activated as she passed by with the jar in her satchel, but once distance grew between them, they fell back into sleep. The wall of greenery came into view.

"Fleishman, you'll need to create another wormhole so we can get out," Lance yelled back as the four raced by the statue of Garmr.

The huge dog's chest fractured causing the kids to stop. The onyx encasing his legs fell away. Jagged claws elongated, and the stone sheathing the dog's head vibrated until it exploded.

Ebony toppled over a grave marker, and the others collapsed into a clump. The flap of Ebony's satchel fell open and the jar tumbled to the ground. It clanked at her feet, cover popping open, two leaves spilling out. The jar rolled away, and the glow from the leaves inside faded as did the light of her tattoos. Ebony grabbed the two freed leaves, one with each hand. She stuffed her right hand into her pocket, disposing of one leaf, but stopped short of hiding the second leaf at the sound of a deep growl.

Garmr crouched on his stone perch. Eyes of emerald pulsed. Black fur bristled along the strong ridge of his spine. He swept his fleshy tongue across his dark lips and lowered his snout.

"Why is it always ginormous animals?" Fleishman said.

An elderly woman Ebony recognized as the one who stabbed the crow during the field exercise stepped from the shadows. The hem of her ragged dress bunched in her spotted hand. Her image rippled. Aged skin and hair transformed to a young woman in sky-blue garments. The air shimmered like freshly cut diamonds in her wake as she strolled to Garmr. Crows flocked around her. One landed on her shoulder. She brushed her golden tresses to her other shoulder before petting the beast's paw. A glimmer sparkled on her finger, and Ebony's tattoos flared in irritation.

The kids linked arms and crept backward, Ebony still clasping the second leaf in her fist.

"It can't be a good sign when creepy ghosts look creepier," Cermet said.

"Even a worse sign when a stone dog lights up," Fleishman whimpered.

Silver sparkled from the woman's hand, a thick-banned ring on her finger. Gears shifted to elongate over two knuckles. Slender metal protruded from the tip, and after a few mumbled words from the woman, stones dribbled out the center gemstone, multiplying and turning to poppy petals; each spilled out her palm and glided down absorbed into the soil.

"Hold your breath, in case," Fleishman said.

Ebony's bindrune tattoo flamed red, and dogs of lesser size stalked out of vacant spaces, claws raking the ground. Divots of soil erupted in pockets and in numerous places. Lifeless crows towed their hollow bones to the surface.

"Borga skuldin skuldaði mér," said the woman.

She thrust the needle of her ring into Garmr's paw. A

deadened sheen rolled over his face, and his body went rigid. He tipped his head back to howl.

"Oh em gee!" cried Cermet, who broke link with the others and sped off.

Ebony and Fleishman spun to follow Cermet, but Glinda stumbled over a marker. She landed hard against a tombstone, dowsing the hem of her dress with puddle water.

"Keep going!" Ebony yelled after the boys and turned to Glinda.

A female ghost in a tattered dress hobbled forward; she was missing a shoe. Her auburn hair set flat on one side of her head, absent from the other side. Shadows waved across her face, but not enough to hide her eyes that were focused on Glinda.

Glinda dug her heels into the soil, pressing her back harder into the tombstone. Another ghost in similar condition inched in behind the first ghost, only this ghost had both feet bare.

The two staggered closer, and Glinda moaned out Ebony's name.

"Hey, you!" Ebony said, drawing the ghosts' attention.

Glinda pushed off the tombstone and raced for the boys.

The first ghost tipped her head at Ebony. A moment later, her body followed, her movements more robotic than human. Being so near, Ebony could see what the shadows had hidden. Patches of skin had peeled from the ghost's face, leaving voids of muscle. Even bone.

The ghost lunged at Ebony, and she thrust her arm in front of her in a jerk reaction of protection. Her hand pierced the chest of the ghost, sinking in halfway; it felt more solid than expected. Light flashed from the ghost's chest, illuminating the leaf that had been in Ebony's hand. The leaf sank into the ghost's figure and with it the glow slowly faded until gone.

Healthy eyelashes batted. A bright smile lifted the ghost's lips. Her complexion brightened. It smoothed out the dark patches on her face.

The ghost patted her cheeks with her hands and tipped her chin to give Ebony a thankful gaze. Ebony smiled back. It seemed the ghost was cured.

But Ebony had forgotten about the second undead ghost, the one that had inched in behind the healthy ghost. The sick ghost gripped onto the healthy ghost and plunged its hand into her silhouette. It tore a huge hole in her chest and pulled out a glowing orb.

"No!" Ebony screamed, understanding the orb was the healthy ghost's shade.

It was as if the healthy ghost had been hit by an invisible ray of heat. Welts erupted over the ghost's skin. A shrill of pain and sorrow belted from its mouth.

Two undead crows lowered their beaks and shook feathers from their torsos. They stretched and strained, growing limbs, heads rounding to form humanlike skulls. Slivered ligaments and sinew dangled off the skeletal figures – Raw Bones. They shrilled and charged at the once healthy ghost, clawing at it until it was no more.

The beautiful woman plucked the glowing orb from the undead ghost's hand. She offered it to the Raw Bones that tore it in two and gobbled up their portion.

A bolt of lightning cracked against the ground. The blast scattered ghosts and dogs over graves and shook Ebony to her core.

Keeper Coffer jerked Ebony by the shoulders and signed the letters R.U.N. in sign language and the word church. He pointed in the opposite direction of Dead Alley's entrance. Obviously, she had a lot to learn about Keeper. She had no idea where he'd come from or that he knew sign language, but if he was willing to help, she'd take it.

"Guys, this way," she said.

Pivoting, Keeper drew symbols and runes in the air like Mentor Nesbitt had done, only with his shovel. That was now on fire!

If she got out of this alive, someone was teaching her how to do that.

She leaped over boney shrubs – for most everything else still looked asleep or dead – and dodged sickly ghosts reaching for her. Cermet let out a yelp farther behind. She swept along a crumbling crypt until she spotted creepy gargoyles cresting the roof of a stone building that looked exactly like the boneyard's chapel, only smaller. She reached the stone steps to find Lance already there.

Fleishman and the others jogged in next to them, panting and leaning over their knees. Garbled moans edged the far corner of the pathway, as did a deep howl.

"They're coming," said Cermet.

Ebony touched Fleishman's shoulder. "Manipulate a tree or make those gargoyles come to life or something!"

"I can't MM now!" he bellowed. "I'm freaking out."

Glinda snatched runes from her bag. "I'll buy us some time."

Unlike with their battle magick exercise, Glinda tossed a few rune stones in front of her and chanted. Ebony concentrated on nearby energy until dull vibes began to float. Soon, she collected denser energy. The approaching ghosts shivered.

Keeper bowled through the ghosts. It would have been great to see him, if it hadn't been for Garmr gnashing at his heels. The groundsman gripped the handle of his shovel to wipe out a band of mad dogs. Without missing a beat, he slid the shovel through the leather strap across his back and raced up the steps, vanishing into the chapel. Ebony barged through the doors behind him. Fleishman arrived at her right with Glinda and Cermet; Lance drifted to her left.

"What are we doing here?" she asked.

Keeper clasped Ebony's hands and signed a message to her.

"He wants us to use our skills as best we can to stir up energy." Ebony looked to Fleishman. "And he told me to call on a door to Jotunheim."

Mortar crumbled from one wall of the chapel as the ground shook. Mad dogs barked from somewhere nearby, and Garmr couldn't be far behind.

Keeper drew runes in the air. Violet and gold energy streamed from the runes. Glinda tore a strip of wet fabric from her dress and handed it to Fleishman. He swallowed hard and concentrated on melding the doors together, while Ebony slowed her breathing to sense a door.

"They're almost here!" shouted Cermet from his lookout of a glassless window.

The initial tap of energy felt familiar, a little abrupt. But like outside the chapel, as Ebony relaxed to receive it, the sensation eased and flowed.

She whirled, looking for the door, but found nothing, until she looked down at the wooden floor beneath her feet.

A door wavered between this world and the next, blurring in and out of focus. Ebony let go more, and six-panel pines blotted to the surface of the wooden floor. The doorknob a knocker of wrought iron in the shape of Jörmungandr, the world serpent surrounding Midgard (Man's World). With Keeper's help, Ebony yanked on the knob. The door panel slammed open against the floor, and Keeper waved the kids to exit Dead Alley.

He didn't have to ask twice.

thirty-three

Keeper's Keys

mixture of grass and snow speckled the landscape of Jotunheim.

Dense forests strained toward the foggy sky; their edges melded into the shadowed wilderness, where danger and uncertainty prowled. Tentacles of rocky terrain splintered out in all directions. The hush of ocean waves weighed down by ice and snow whispered off in the distance, and winter's grip clung to the mountain peaks standing high above it all. Everything felt bigger here, which didn't surprise Ebony. This was the home of the giants, after all.

"Where are we?" Glinda asked.

Cermet tipped his head up. "That's the Mountain of the Mist, so we're in Jotunheim."

Ebony and Keeper joined the others already sitting on two large boulders; Lance leaned on a tree off to the side.

Ebony looked to Keeper. "You know my aunts."

Keeper chuckled and signed I suppose you're curious about a few things.

"Like the fact that you sign, for one," Ebony said.

I'm deaf. I can read lips, too.

Oh, wow. That explained a lot. "What are we doing in Jotunheim?" Ebony asked, signing the words.

He signed in response.

"He says . . ." Ebony paused to translate his message the best she could. "That he created an unveiling spell, hoping to lead to whoever created the initial ward spells locking up Dead Alley. Instead, it pointed him to a place here in Jotunheim. He was on his way to tell the Council of Mentors when we broke in."

Keeper signed, again.

"He wants us to follow him," she said.

Fleishman adjusted the strap of Nigel's cage on his shoulder, and the group trekked across a field dense with prickly blades of grass and unruly weeds. Keeper swept his shovel at the rebel greenery, using it as a sickle to clear their way. Ebony craned her neck to see Lance at the back of their pack, his hands clenched and his jaw tight. She wondered if she should talk to him but decided to give him space.

"Who was that woman in Dead Alley, Keeper?" Ebony asked and signed, pausing to let him answer. "He says she's a nature goddess of Yggdrasil. Her name is Elli."

"Wonder if she's the one Nesbitt mentioned," Fleishman said.

"He knows her because he's a master mage of the Watchers." Ebony remembered when Delia introduced her and Fleishman to some Watchers in Nilfheim.

"Wow. A master," Cermet said. "I've only read about those."

"The hawk," Fleishman said to no one in particular. "That's why it was always around. He was looking through its eyes."

Keeper's stubbled cheeks rose in a smile as he signed.

"It was him," Ebony said. "He says the boneyard was created as a capsule of rebirth long before man lived in Midgard."

"Ragnarok?" Cermet asked.

Keeper nodded, and Ebony translated. "Man has had many rebirths throughout its history. Noah's Ark, for example. Magical traces stored in the boneyard from Yggdrasil could be tapped to restart man."

"That matches what your aunts said," Fleishman said.

Ebony continued. "But as man matured, he became more reliant on himself than nature and what the gods offered. So a few hundred years ago, a spell was cast to hide those elements of Yggdrasil. Generations of Keeper's family have been Watchers over this link and the spell.

"He says a few years ago, energy shifted, and some of the hidden elements vanished," Ebony said and waited for him to sign more before she continued. "Whoa . . . the elements hadn't disappeared. They transferred to Dead Alley and were warded off. He's been unable to break those wards until the kids were returned from Yggdrasil."

"And the boneyard reopened to the Underworld," Fleishman concluded.

She slipped Nesbitt's partial map from her satchel. "Do you recognize this?"

Keeper held the paper in front of him like Aunt Gertrude did when she wasn't wearing her eyeglasses. He nodded and signed I do, and I think I'll have more answers for you when we arrive at our destination. Follow me.

The field blended into a trail that abutted a smaller range of hills. Jagged rock diced the side of the range. Cermet began to complain about his aching feet, and Glinda offered to carry Nigel for a bit. Fleishman handed the cage off to her and mentioned that they should find water to drink. Keeper assured him there was some up ahead. Ebony periodically checked on Lance. He never left them but traveled farther behind, scaling the rock wall or dodging between nearby trees. She didn't know what she could say to make him feel better.

Keeper stopped in front of a flat slice of rock and signed.

"We're here," Ebony translated.

"Really?" Cermet plopped down on a rock to rub his feet. "This looks like another dead end instead of alley to me."

Keeper withdrew a small pouch and bottle of oil and water from his pack that housed his shovel. He poured a small amount of both liquids on the soil forming a circle. Snatching a pinch of dry herbs between his fingers, he sprinkled the area around the circle.

Glinda inched up next to Ebony. "Smells like Blessed Thistle."

Ebony smiled at her. She hadn't known what the herb was called, but she'd recognized the scent from her aunts using it.

Keeper rubbed his hands together, gentle at first, then more aggressively. His lips spoke silent words. A flame burst out of the air above his palm, and he lowered it to the liquids and herbs; both ignited. Crinkling and snapping quickened as the mixture of earth and water and magick heated. The flame traced the heat and raced to complete the circle. As the two ends met, the rock wall opened to expose a hidden area.

Fleishman frowned and Cermet stared at him, but they followed Glinda and Keeper inside.

"You coming?" Ebony asked Lance, as she paused at the opening.

He didn't answer. She still couldn't see his face well. His

hoodie was starting to give her the creeps. What was wrong? Was it more than his fear of losing his body forever? Her heart pounded in her chest.

Lance ambled with her over the threshold, but he remained just inside where the opening of the wall crumbled and rock built itself back into a solid barrier to the outside.

A cot abutted the far wall of the cavernous room. Supplies from food and water to blankets piled up on wooden shelves. Extra clothes and first aid supplies were stuffed in a tall glass cabinet next to a round table with chairs circling it. And in the center of the table sat a large ring.

Keeper dropped a scroll he'd taken from an old desk onto the table and picked up the ring. Heat steamed Ebony's every pore from the inside out. She knew what she was looking at.

"Dad's ring." Her voice shook as Keeper handed it to her.

I knew I sensed your father's mystical fingerprint, Keeper signed.

A teeny giggle escaped Ebony's lips. Ethan was all she could think as she laced her father's ring onto her chain to let it dangle alongside her apprentice medium medallion.

Keeper unrolled the large sheet of parchment and pressed it flat against the table.

"This area is the boneyard as you know it," Ebony translated, and Keeper circled one hand over a large section of the map. "These lines represent tunnels, shafts, and canals that run beneath. Many species from the nine worlds can access these."

"Of course, they can," Fleishman said, dully.

Keeper tapped the faded web rune then signed.

"He says the web rune was placed in the boneyard by the high Norns to fortify the link with Yggdrasil," Ebony said. "Wait. He asked if we know details about the gods' peace treaty."

"Story goes—" Fleishman looked to Cermet. "You tell it."

Cermet smiled. "The gods got tired of fighting, so they called for peace by swapping some members." He lifted his head to Fleishman.

"The Vanir felt short-changed in the deal and killed Mimir, one of the traded gods of the Aesir," Fleishman finished.

"Why'd they kill him?" Ebony asked.

"Something about him not being as smart as they thought," Fleishman said.

"How unfair," Glinda said.

Ebony continued to translate. "History says after Mimir's death, the gods calmed and found peace. But on many occasions since, relations between them have been strained. The closing of the original Njord Academy and Dead Alley, for example. He says we must remember that bloodlines were crossed during the god trades, so there is a mixture of both lines at Njord and at Motley."

That could complicate things.

"What does this have to do with Elli?" Fleishman asked.

Keeper reached for a small leather-bound book he'd left on the desk. The book binding creaked as he opened the cover and flipped to where a dried daisy bookmarked a story. He motioned for everyone to take a seat and handed Fleishman the book.

Fleishman stared at everyone.

"He wants you to read out loud," Ebony whispered and silently thanked the cheese gods for her not having to read out loud.

"Oh, okay." Fleishman glanced at the page and read, "Elli, also known as Mother Mist, being a charge under the goddess Freyja is the common thread that links natural elements to the gods. At the beginning, as gods and beings were chosen to represent elements, winds, and seas, one was also needed to be the face of old age."

"She's old age?" Ebony asked.

Keeper nodded once.

"Yuck," Glinda whispered to Nigel in his cage at her feet.

Fleishman read, "As old age works in tandem with death, she is known in the Underworld. Ancient seas to the storms that have ravaged the nine worlds also know her. She's in every season and time, for each end. All except one – love."

"Why do these things have to get mushy?" Cermet squirmed in his chair.

"Shush," Glinda said. "This is getting good."

"Elli's heart longed for Balder, son of Odin, though he believed them good friends." Fleishman traced his fingertip under the next sentence. "Knowing Odin was desperate to find a god to take on this job and wanting to catch Balder's attention, she gave up her youthful verve and appearance to take on the task in exchange for a gift – the gift of his son.

"Odin, believing his son reciprocated Elli's feelings, assured her of his son's devotion. But he should have consulted Balder first, for Balder did love Elli, but his true affection was for the one he romantically loved, Nanna."

Ah, the difference between like and like-like. "Why didn't he tell her he didn't like her that way?" Ebony asked.

"He probably didn't want to hurt her feelings," Glinda said.

"The whole boyfriend-girlfriend thing is too weird for me," Cermet added.

Keeper smirked, which Ebony found strange.

"Odin bought time by offering Elli a gift of her choosing." Fleishman turned the page. "As Freyja was mesmerized by jewels, Elli was with nature. She chose the ability to gather splices of nature to admire at her leisure. But Nature herself is vast, and no boundaries were put into place, giving Elli free rein to collect from any area of nature including the evil, wretched, and vile parts.

"Time passed without Balder declaring himself to Elli, and because of Mimir's death another trade was needed, which forced Odin's hand. She became a casualty of the gods' treaty, banished to the Mist Valley in the foothills of Jotunheim near the Mountain of the Mist to rid the Aesir's of the problem."

"But she tried to kill Balder, right," Ebony said.

Keeper's next signed sentence punched Ebony in the chest.

"What is it?" Fleishman asked.

"Nesbitt was wrong. They lied about her. She never tried to kill anyone," Ebony said. She trusted them, and they betrayed her.

"No wonder she's so mad," Glinda said.

Fleishman read the next line. "The foothills are better known as the People of the North."

Ebony darted a gawk at Fleishman. That was the connection – the title of Lance's file on Xander's computer, the berserker in Ethan's game, and the translation Roger blurted out.

"Eons ago," Ebony picked up where Keeper signed, "the People of the North, who are mages with a specialty in guiding nature, worked in harmony with the Watchers. But they turned from Asgard shortly after Elli was banished. He'll tell that story another day.

"What he wants us to know is that the elements of nature Elli had been collecting were imprisoned in a secret vessel made for her by a dwarf and enemy of Balder. The storms from within the vessel were used by the People of the North to create the first berserker."

Keeper tapped the book for Fleishman to keep reading.

Fleishman read. "The vessel became so dangerous that Elli had it guarded by the People of the North, who sealed it with a complex ward. Later, believing the People of the North had lost their way, the Watchers stole the vessel from them to destroy it. That's when they realized the vessel also had been bound to the physical, a pawn they determined was the original berserker. But insanity had infected his mind, and he couldn't be reasoned with. This made it impossible to open the vessel to use, but also to extinguish the evils within.

"People with berserker traits scattered over the other worlds, masking their strengths. So, the Watchers hid the vessel inside a small crypt at the back of the cemetery."

"Pottle's crypt," Fleishman said. "Why hide it in Vanir territory?"

"What better place than right under their noses with Keeper guarding the place?" Ebony translated for Keeper. "He says the cemetery was breached through the underground tunnels, and the vessel became lost, the theft masked as an earthquake."

"Do we know who stole it?" Cermet asked.

Dark elves," Keeper signed with Ebony's translation.

"Daenir?" Ebony asked, and Keeper signed Y.E.S.

"He wasn't creating a vortex?" Fleishman asked.

Keeper signed the words not yet.

"Daenir has her vessel, but what good is it to him if he can't open it?" Cermet asked.

Keeper held up one finger and signed.

"The dwarf, Ebony translated, "also made Elli an enchanted finger ring, embodying her essence of old age, to rival Odin's mystical ring Draupnir."

Fleishman tucked the book under his arm. "Hold your

bindrune tattoo in front of you like you're looking at it."

"Why?" She pushed her sleeve up.

"Trust me," he said, and she did. "If I read the bindrune sitting in front of you it looks upside-right. But," he pushed from the table to stand behind her chair, "if I read it from your point-of-view, the Ansuz rune is upside-down and the Thurisaz rune is upside-right, giving different meanings."

Like the upside-down rune her aunts had found on Nesbitt's partial map, giving it a different meaning, too.

"Here Ansuz means the opposite or to reverse and Thurisaz means to awaken. These rival the other meanings of thorn and the sleep-poison spell like Odin's ring rivals Elli's enchanted finger ring."

"But how do I use it?" Ebony asked.

"The bindrune activated things in Dead Alley," Cermet said.

"That was with the healing leaf, and nothing stayed awake, anyway," Ebony said.

"Because you didn't have enough energy to draw from to go against all that Elli has collected," Cermet said.

"And what better way to have a ton of energy in one place than at the Ullr Games?" Fleishman said.

"Wait, so now Elli doesn't need this pawn?" Cermet argued.

Keeper signed, again.

"No, she does." Ebony translated. "Elli needs to create a new one, which she's been doing by using the chaos her ring has stirred. Keeper says she's been waiting for the perfect pawn to recreate the original berserker. He believes Daenir's theft of Lance's body opened that doorway."

Fleishman stiffened. "She wants to use Lance."

Lance, who hadn't spoken, stood taller shadowed by his hood.

"Not being dead," Ebony translated Keeper's next message, "but separated from his body, has left Lance's soul attached as spirit and ghost, making him unique and open to tampering. Elli couldn't have asked for a more perfect target to give the gifts that created the first berserker." Ebony pushed from her chair to stand. "No. We'll keep Lance away from her."

Keeper signed.

"What did he say?" Fleishman asked.

"That we might not have a choice if Lance wants to reunite with his body."

"What's the plan if she shows up?" Cermet asked.

"Too bad we don't have the leaf jar," Glinda said.

"I totally forgot!" Ebony lifted out the leaf she'd stashed away in her pocket.

"This is good." Fleishman smiled and picked up Nigel's cage. "We can multiply from this leaf, but that means we have to steal the ring off her finger."

"That's not going to be easy," Cermet said.

"No, but if we're right and she's planning to create lots of chaos, Ebony can draw from that and use her bindrune tattoo to activate as many ghost zombies as she can," Fleishman said.

"But we'll have to cure them fast because I'm sure the chaos collectors will be waiting for them," Cermet said.

"And the Raw Bones," Glinda added.

"Don't forget the crows," Cermet said.

"What about the boneyard residents?" Ebony asked. "I can't protect them, too."

Keeper signed.

"He says not to worry. He'll create protective wards and look after the boneyard," Ebony said. "He might need help, so he wants me to tell my mother."

"Telling your mom everything is a good idea," Fleishman agreed.

thirty-four

Mountain of the Mist

the expected door to take them home rippled in blurry waves of milky gray. It wavered, fading in and out, and the outline of a second door flickered behind it.

Ebony grumbled. "It's like more than one door wants to come through."

"Try again," Fleishman encouraged.

She relaxed her focus to picture the boneyard in her mind, the residents, and the landscape of crypts and tombstones. Both blurry doors warped and faded into a different yet familiar door. It swung open, and Delia spilled out through the portal to the Hall of Souls. Her light blue hair bunched at her ears as she lifted her metal goggles to her forehead.

"I've been looking for you. I finally picked up your activity when you called on a door." Delia exhaled. "I have news on the toddler ghost."

Ebony felt Keeper step in closer.

Delia scanned the small group. "He didn't make it."

"No!" Ebony cried.

Cermet and Glinda gasped, while Fleishman inched closer to Ebony.

"The decay spread over his tiny ghost form. At that point, his eyes opened, but he wasn't awake." She lifted her chin. "He'd turned Hrár Bein."

Could that be Elli's final goal? An army of ghost zombies?

"The spell quickened the normal stages of ghostly deterioration so fast it exposed his shade," Delia said. "It's like nothing we've ever seen. I am sorry, but I must return."

Ebony stared blankly, but Fleishman gave Delia an affirmative nod. She ambled back through the door, which faded until gone.

"Ebony," Lance said, finally talking. "What toddler?"

Ebony reached back to hold Fleishman's hand. She swallowed a wad of guilt lodged in her throat. "A little boy I tried to crossover."

"What happened?" Lance inched closer.

If only she'd told him everything earlier.

"What. Happened?" Lance asked, again.

Deep burgundy exploded in his aura. His apprehension and anger – no, rage – washed over her.

Fleishman whispered, "You have to tell him."

"Tell me what?" Lance asked, less than a foot in front of her. The rim of his hood shaded his face. She wished he'd take it off.

Ebony stuttered an inhale. "That Mist Gypsies are ancient soul eaters and that they attacked us and the toddler when the sick crows first showed up."

"They were here before Roger barfed up feathers?" he asked.

"I told you I had a rough training session with Wizner."

"That's more than just rough," he said. "You left out the important part."

Her stomach tightened with more guilt.

"Like when your mom kept part of the truth about your abilities from you," he said. "You told me how upset that made you."

Yes, it had.

"And that you didn't know if you could trust her anymore." He leaned forward.

Oh no! Her lack of honesty had ruined Lance's trust in her. "I'm sorry," she said.

"Not sorry enough." At that, he tugged one hand from his pocket to flip his hood off his head.

Ebony wished he'd kept it on.

Blue dots peppered Lance's face. They raced across his cheeks, along his neck, and spilled down his arms that he exposed by pushing up the sleeves of his sweatshirt. They showed much worse than the boneyard residents. Decay gorged out the center of each spot, and a chalky sheen glazed his skin.

"You've been changing clothes to hide your illness," Ebony said. "You left out the important part, too. You told me that another ghost was training you how to change clothes for fun, so you lied."

"You left out information that affected me, and I lied about why I was learning to change clothes." His voice grew gruffer. "What's the difference?"

The two locked in a dead stare.

Good question. What was the difference, Ebony thought? Keeping part of the truth hidden or lying about the truth seemed to gain the same result. They'd hurt each other even though their intentions were for good. It was clear that telling the whole truth was important.

"Lance, we both—"

"Doesn't matter," Lance growled and held his arms in front of him. "Damage is done. Looks like your crazy goddess has her pawn after all."

"Don't say that." Ebony reached out to touch him and gasped. "Why do you feel solid?"

He peered down at her. "Because I am."

Red blotted the whites of his eyes like ground water bleeding through cracked pavement. A transparent silhouette expanded beyond his ghostly figure. Hair lengthened. Muscles bloated. Fur sprouted on his shoulders and on his legs. He held an axe in his thickening hand. The silhouette grew, destroying the decay and overtaking his normal self.

"I had no reason not to make ghost friends because you didn't tell me I was in more danger," he said.

"This is my fault," Ebony mumbled.

Lance growled in a manly voice and turned up the path.

Ebony didn't share Keeper's next sign, but she felt it stab her in the heart. *She got him. It's too late.*

She gripped hold of Fleishman, hoping he could see the silhouette overpowering Lance's normal figure.

"His premonition," Fleishman said.

She'd forgotten about that.

"He is the berserker Elli wants," Cermet whispered.

"Can we reverse it?" Fleishman asked.

Keeper signed.

"He says the only chance is while he's in this state, so we must keep him away from his body." Ebony's translation tapered off at the end. She covered her face with her hands. "A couple weeks ago, I promised Lance I'd put him back together."

"That binds it as a contract," Fleishman said.

"I know." Ebony lowered her head. "We'll have to keep him away from his body until we find a cure."

"But he's deteriorating," Fleishman said softly. "We're running out of time."

"We'll find another way. Ethan said berserkers forget, but if they remember they can do good. We'll make him remember when he gets his body back." Her heels dug into the soil as she spun around. "Lance! Wait."

Ebony sped after him, having no idea what to do when she caught up to him. She pictured the boneyard residents in her head, the terror marring their faces at word of this news. It sliced her heart. But the disappointment they'd surely feel would make it bleed. They would doubt her, whether she could keep them safe or not. And she wouldn't blame them one bit.

"Ebony!" yelled Fleishman.

She slowed to a jog, thinking he wanted her to wait for him, but he ran past her much faster than she'd ever seen him run. A guttural snarl echoed from behind. Ebony craned her view over her shoulder to see a shadow lurking along the path behind Cermet, Glinda, and Keeper, who were racing toward her.

Taller than any normal man, the figure flexed its wide shoulders, bare and full of bulky muscles. Tattered cloth tied knots at both his biceps, while intricate tattoos danced along his forearms. Legs of thick fur, it seemed to have human feet, but Ebony couldn't be sure. A large axe dangled from his left hand.

Her boots slammed against the dirt path as she joined the others in a fast sprint. "Why does that thing look like the berserker poster in Ethan's room?"

"I don't know, but it's not your average berserker because it's missing it's head!" Cermet screamed.

The berserker howled into the air.

"How is it yelling without a head?" Glinda asked.

Keeper signed, telling Ebony to call on a door.

"I can't leave without Lance!" She looked to Fleishman,

and he clenched her hand in his to keep running in the direction Lance disappeared.

Teal fog plumed in tinier clouds as the mulisha cut through the path. They took a sharp turn up an adjacent path, where they almost crashed into another berserker – this one wearing full-berserker gear and his head. Skidding to change directions, they crashed into Cermet, Glinda, and Keeper.

"Go, go!" Ebony wasn't sure who yelled that.

The group shifted, too many people scurrying in different directions. They turned and twisted until eventually colliding on the original path, mere yards in front of the headless berserker. Ebony spun toward a crossroad, only to find another full-headed berserker, so she kept on the path.

Soon the air filled with mist and the scent of the sea. The weight pressed upon Ebony's chest, making it hard to breath. Webs of passing time and stillness strung from trees where gangly moss squeezed most tree trunks. The path widened to a vast coastline and the Mountain of Mist looming over it all.

The ground rumbled. Soil and clay rooting trees tore away to their left. Snow flaked down as the mass of land lifted into the air. Chunky fingers gripped knotty knees to reveal a giant standing tall. Another rose beside the first.

A frigid breeze swept over them. More giants stomped from their right. Blades of ice stiffened the hair crowning their heads. Icicles of all lengthens clinked and clanked at their waists, down their legs. Cold blue coated their eyes. Thick condensation hovered around the spears held in their hands, their armor crusted in shards of ice strapping their chests. A handful of berserkers marched in next to the giants. The headless berserker was nowhere to be seen.

The tiny mulisha backed into a circle. Keeper banged his shovel on the ground. Flames ignited and scurried to cover the shaft. Glinda squeezed the rune stones in her hands, and Fleishman tightened Nigel's cage at his shoulder.

"We're trapped," said Cermet.

The giants and berserkers closed in. The air shifted, and a wave of fog rolled off the water. A narrow path of land led out into the sea and vanished behind a corner of the rocky shoreline.

"There!" Glinda said.

Keeper signed *I'll hold them back* and pierced the ground with his shovel. The soil shifted and lifted, creating a fissure. His arms shook from the force. Ebony tugged Fleishman backward, Nigel's cage bouncing against his hip, and Glinda and Cermet stumbled toward Keeper.

"Go!" Cermet yelled.

"We'll help Keeper," Glinda added.

Ebony and Fleishman raced toward the bend in the shore and around the corner, where a lighthouse emerged off the coast. Next to it stood six pillars, sea water raging against its foundation of rock. Ebony slowed as a wintery scene flashed off to her left. A barnlike structure roofed in shields of armor and snow came into view. A mixture of runes and icicles decorated the wood on one side. Two huge doors provided an entrance, hinges iced over, and condensation wafted from the seal. Two overbearing statues of gargoyles guarded the ornate facade. The image faded and disappeared.

"Ebony!" yelled Fleishman.

"Coming." She sped up, again.

The narrow path of land thinned the farther they traced it around twists and curves. Pebbles flattened to soil that transformed to white granite speckled in grains of black and gray. The soles of Ebony's boots slapped the cold surface, and she and Fleishman slid to a stop. Excitement heated her entire body, for there in the center of the ornate pillars on a thick slab hovered Lance's body – real and in stasis.

"We found it!" She fed Fleishman a huge smile.

"This is too easy, Ebony," he said. "It's like Daenir left his body here for us to take."

"Oh please," a new voice said. "That lame elf deserves no credit for this."

The woman in gold, the one who'd fired up Garmr in Dead Alley, strolled into view. Nigel let out a chatter from inside his cage. His eyes flared a deep violet.

Ebony tried to swallow the lack of confidence lodged in her throat, but it wouldn't go down. "Elli."

"My name proceeds me," Elli said. "Good."

Her hair brightened to golden tresses that lengthened to cascade over her shoulders, her face the definition of female beauty. The scent of blooming gardenias and ripened apples permeated from her in sweet swirls. And trailing her was Lance.

Ebony felt her confidence take another punch. "Lance, I'm sorry I didn't tell you."

Lance lifted his chin at Ebony. The maelstrom of emotions swimming in his eyes struck her, but not like she expected. They all weren't directed at her. Many sources were responsible for his confusion, fear, and anger. Maybe he'd find a way to forgive her and let it go – like she needed to do with her mother.

"I told you I would help you." Elli swept her fingers across Lance's ghost cheek. "Your body is right there."

"Lance, don't," Fleishman said.

"It's yours to take back," Elli said.

"Lance, that pact of spit we made binds you to return to your body. I know that's what you want, but your infection might transfer to your body or you might become the berserker she wants. You have to fight this."

Nigel thrashed inside his cage. Even he agreed.

Lance's ghost chest swelled. Ebony could see the

wavering in his aura. Despite his anger at her, he wasn't ready to listen to Elli. Lance stepped away from Elli.

"Let me make this decision easier for you." Elli swept her hand in the air.

An image came into view. A rope dangled over the sea to the far side of the foundation. Serpents circled below. It took a moment for Ebony to trace her eyes down the rope to its end to find her father hanging upside-down, his eyes fluttering open. Green mist floated from the ties that bound his wrists and ankles, and most likely his powers, too.

"Dad!" Ebony screamed.

Fleishman struggled to hold Nigel's cage as the lizard scratched at the bars.

The tension on the rope loosened, dropping Dad a foot.

"Elli, don't." Ebony was surprised to hear Lance's voice.

"Once you reenter your body, you'll have the power to save this man." Elli darted her eyes at Ebony.

"And do whatever you want me to do," Lance said.

"A minor formality." Elli shrugged. "How much do you value this girl's friendship?"

"Lance . . ." Ebony couldn't lose her father, again. She felt smaller than she thought possible. How could she choose between saving her father or her friend? "You might not remember us."

Lance's ghost posture straightened, his voice scratchy and weak. "Fleishman, I'm counting on you to figure this out."

And with that, Lance dove for his body and sank into his skin. His torso trembled. A bluish glow leaked from his body's fingertips, his feet, and his forehead. His skin remained clear. His shoulders jerked, throwing his body off the granite slab. He writhed on the floor, his legs kicking, while his arms stiffened. Bulky muscle added weight to his limbs.

The rope securing Ebony's father loosened more,

sending him closer to the water and the restless serpents below. A herd of dragons flew toward them from the distance. Muffled cries staggered and echoed.

Lance stilled, eyelids fluttering open, eyes glowing torches of green. His body had grown into more than a mere man – a warrior, a solder. Not exactly a berserker . . . yet. Every muscle in Ebony's body tensed. She felt paralyzed as Lance stomped toward them. Fleishman lost his grip on Nigel's cage, and it crashed at their feet. The dragons broke into two groups, one speeding around the bend toward the giants, the other dashing straight for them, releasing fierce chatters.

Elli whirled two fingers in the air. Nigel threw his body against the sides of his cage. The rope and binds securing Dad's fate unraveled. He plunged toward the angry water.

Ebony held her breath for the next few seconds, but it felt more like an hour as Nigel burst from his cage and shot into the air. His torso contorted and paled to a snowy white. Jagged spikes of ice sprouted along his spine; the tips pulsed in blue and sizzled with electricity. Bones stretched the outer scales of his backside forming reptilian legs, digits, and double-daggered claws. Shorter legs thrust from his chest.

He shook his back to wring out a set of wings and swooped down to catch Dad. Turning, he fired icicles at Elli. The dragons above them roared, almost a cheer. Bigger Lance huddled over Elli, shielding her from the onslaught. She released a chant and, in an instant, the two vanished into a pliable portal that closed with a slosh.

Ebony exhaled a hearty breath, but also sorrow and guilt, fear and joy. She released Fleishman and tripped up the narrow path of land where Nigel landed, wings fanned into a tent shielding her father.

"Dad!" she bellowed and leaped into his arms. "I missed you so much."

"I missed you, too," he mumbled into her hair.

"Guys!" Glinda went around the bend in the path with Cermet and Keeper close by.

Fleishman jogged in front of them, pieces of Nigel's cage rattling in his hands. He dropped the metal near Ebony and her father to stare up at his pet. Nigel lowered his head and bumped his snout against Fleishman's chest. Fleishman reached out to touch him.

"Nigel's a dragon?" Ebony tipped her head back at the dragons circling above.

Fleishman shrugged one shoulder. "I guess so."

"Whoa . . ." Cermet stepped in next to them.

"He's so big." Glinda giggled.

Dad shook Keeper's hand and said, "Kids, see the markings on Nigel's wings. They tell me he's Verndari, meaning protector – a sacred herd of dragons pledged to protect Mankind. Each dragon must find his or her human person before they can mature to adulthood. The dragon and its person will be linked for life."

"Nigel really is more than a pet," Ebony said.

Fleishman brushed his hand along Nigel's front leg, petting him. Nigel curled his tail in behind Fleishman and tipped one wing to tug his human person into a hug.

One dragon roared and the others chattered off-sync. Nigel lifted a few feet off the soil. Dirt thinned to dust. Ebony's hair whipped at her cheeks, and her father tightened his hug on her. A rumble released from Nigel's belly.

"Good boy," said Fleishman. "I'll miss you."

Nigel flashed his eyes bright violet at Fleishman and then soared into the air, joining the herd of Verndari dragons.

thirty-five

Truce

bony set her satchel on the kitchen island, not yet having had a chance to switch her aunts' grimoire for the herbal magazine Ethan disguised. Her blueberry lip gloss spilled out the front pouch of her satchel. It *tinged* as it flipped end over cap onto the floor.

"Avoiding me?"

Ebony flinched at the voice. Her shoulders drooped from her silent sigh. Returning the grimoire to its rightful place would have to wait. She tucked her satchel under her arm to follow the voice. Her mother sat in the cushy living room chair she often did to read a book. But tonight, Mom held a familiar wooden box in her lap.

"Where's Dad?" Ebony asked.

"Sleeping," Mom said. "Having his skills bound weakened them. He's exhausted."

"Will they come back?" she asked.

"In time, with lots of rest," Mom said. "It was nice of you to get his ring for him."

"I'm glad we found him so I could give it back."

"You still worrying about Fleishman?" Mom asked.

Ebony exhaled. "I don't think he's ever been away from Nigel since he adopted him."

"He'll be okay," Mom said. "Change can be hard, though."

She wasn't kidding.

"I've been a grouch, haven't I?"

Should Ebony answer that? Staying quiet might look suspicious but answering truthfully could get her into trouble because Ebony's heart couldn't disagree with her mother. She fiddled with her apprentice medallion instead.

A halfhearted smile spread across her mother's lips.

You'll have to trust people again sometime, Fleishman's specter words repeated in her head. He hadn't been afraid to be truthful with her the other night even though the truth hurt.

"I remember how much I loved my celestial box when I was a little girl." Mom brushed her fingertips over the box. "I would collect smooth rocks from anywhere I could find and examine the patterns nature had created on each. Little did I know how useful this same exercise would become with the numerous plant leaves I would use as a healer."

Ebony sat on the love seat closest to her mother and set her satchel at her feet. How could she have forgotten? Her mother was a luminary, but also a healer like Freyja; not at god level, but still. Maybe Mom had insights into fixing this mess.

"Do you still use your box?" Ebony asked.

"No, once your father and I married our childhood

boxes were joined," Mom said. "As the years passed, images on the box have evolved like they do with all celestial boxes."

Images of predatory animals shifted on the cover as Ebony moved. An embossed moon melded in and out of its multiple phases. As she looked closer, a faint line blended the oak half of the box to the mahogany half.

"Like your father's eyes." Her mother traced a green gemstone in the shape of a rune.

Ebony wasn't sure what came over her, but she reached for her mother's hand. Words weren't needed to express the regret in their hearts and the joy of having Dad home. And even a bit of healing. Fleishman had been on to something about those crows. They could be a sign of some omen yet to come, but in this moment, they'd brought the change he'd talked about – change between Ebony and her mother. Maybe she could tell her mother how she felt.

"I'm scared our plan for tomorrow won't work." But she was glad that Dad, Mom, and Mentor Wizner were part of it.

"I'm scared, too."

"That doesn't help, Mom."

Her mother chuckled. "We knew this time would come. It's been centuries since a generation has been challenged to protect the Nine Worlds. That didn't mean those with evil intentions sat back doing nothing. Those who want to restructure Yggdrasil have been biding their time."

Ebony watched her mother speak those words, but finally heard what they really meant. Her mother had always been thinking of Ebony first – over Dad, over Motley, over everything – where Ebony had focused on what she wanted. Maybe Mom not wanting to talk about Dad wasn't her being selfish, but because once it was said out loud it became real and it would have been one more thing to think about.

"You know how we talked earlier with Dad and Mentor Wizner about Njord Academy, Dead Alley, and the boneyard residents being sick?" Ebony said.

Her mother answered, "Yes."

"You're a healer," Ebony said then paused. "That's why you've been so busy. You've been trying to figure out a cure."

A lonely smile lifted one corner of her mother's mouth. "For endless hours. But it's a complex spell. And though I don't believe Dean Bile cares about Motley, he does see ghost zombies and undead crows as a threat to both schools."

"You can't trust him. I saw him with Erickson in the boneyard," Ebony said.

"It's not what you think." Mom brushed her fingers along Ebony's cheek. "Seronious Bile has been keeping an eye on Erickson to protect him."

"From what?"

"From the woman Erickson believes will take him to his father," Mom said.

Ebony scooted to the edge of her couch cushion. "Elli?"

Mom nodded. "She's been talking with him to collect him as a debt paid to her."

"A debt?"

Mom looked away. "His father, Councilor Erickson, owes Elli and Daenir for helping him escape in Yggdrasil as Nidhogg attacked in the gymnasium."

"Mom," Ebony said in a whisper. Though Ebony hadn't liked it, her mother's betrayal had been to protect her. What Erickson's father had done to him was downright cruel.

"But protecting Erickson," Ebony paused. "How can we trust him?"

"It's not about trusting Erickson, but about doing the right thing," Mom said. "You are not responsible for how someone reacts to or receives your message as long as it's delivered with good intentions. We're only responsible for our actions. Erickson might make poor choices like his father, but we have no control over that."

Choices and trust. Ebony wished they'd had this

conversation before she'd messed up so badly. Heat flushed her cheeks, and she wiggled her nose as it filled with mucus.

"Hey." Mom pressed her palms on either side of Ebony's face.

"A ghost I tried to cross over was the first one to get sick." A lone tear spilled over her bottom lid. "He died, Mom. I didn't know that could happen. I couldn't save him."

Her mother opened her arms, and Ebony slipped off the love seat to her knees as she fell against Mom's chest.

"I'm sorry, Ebony," Mom said into the top of Ebony's head.

"Is he really . . . gone?" Ebony asked.

"I like to think there's a lot we don't know," Mom said. "So, I remain hopeful."

Ebony sniffled into her mother's shirt.

"This is not your fault," Mom said.

"But not telling Lance about my suspicions is. I wanted to protect him, but that ended up hurting him."

"Well," Mom tipped back to look at Ebony. "That sounds familiar."

"How could I do that to him, when I didn't like it done to me?" she asked.

"Because you care about him. Your heart was in the right place."

"Sorry I was mean to you." What Mom had done didn't feel so bad now.

"I understand," Mom said. "Protecting you was worth your anger."

"He hates me."

"No, he doesn't." Mom nudged Ebony's chin up. "We all make mistakes. Decisions like these are always risky. It takes practice to weigh the pros and the cons of both sides, and in some situations, there isn't a win no matter how we act on it. It's all about learning and growing."

Ebony still wasn't sure what was right and wrong in

these situations. Maybe that was the point, to look at each with a good heart and then decide. She remembered her father's favorite quote.

"A mistake is never a mistake unless you don't learn from it," she said.

"No truer words ever spoken." Mom tucked a tangle behind Ebony's ear. "You've had a lot thrown at you in a short period of time. Mentor Wizner told me how wonderful your training has been going. Your father and I are proud of you."

Somehow Ebony felt a little older. "Thanks, Mom."

Her mother stood and walked to the staircase with Ebony snatching up her satchel and following. "We both need to get some rest. Tomorrow will be a big day for all."

"Will Dad be there?"

"He will," Mom said. "I told him he needs to rest, but I lost that argument."

Ebony grinned. It felt good to have her family back. She stopped on the third step. "Thank you for trusting me with this plan, Mom."

Mom reached for Ebony's shoulders. "I won't tell you that I'm not worried, but I know you play a big role as bearer of the doors to Yggdrasil and caretaker of the ghosts in the boneyard."

"I wouldn't be able to do it without Fleishman."

"I'm glad you have him, but," Mom tapped Ebony's satchel, "you need to put the grimoire back."

"You knew?"

"Your brother is getting better at masking items, but not that good yet." Mom winked.

Ebony reached to switch off her reading lamp and caught sight of her celestial box on the padded bench pressed against her footboard. It had been there since she returned home after Nigel defeated Nidhogg in the gym.

She crawled over her comforter and reached for the box. The familiar scent of rosewood swirled around her head as she scooted back on her mattress; only the box smelled a little used, which brought a smile to her face.

As with the family celestial album, Ebony's box was a visual evolution of her life. It wasn't long ago it was basically bare. Now the familiar symbol of a door and her first rune tattoo representing peace recorded her recent accomplishments. She traced her finger over a shape that hadn't been there before, but that she recognized – the web rune. And there, in between the weaving perched a squirrel. There was no mistaking that image.

thirty-six

Awakening Slumber

ebony tipped her head to rest on the middle pane of her window. She peered through her reflection to the narrow canopy of trees marking the trail into the woodlot. The rising sun rolled its horizon up the wall of tree trunks.

She hardly remembered life before Yggdrasil, when her only care was exploring her woodsy backyard and the boneyard with Fleishman. Despite having Fleishman all these years, she realized she'd done things mostly on her own. Asking him for advice was more for show; she never really listened to him. Honestly, she hadn't realized she'd been doing that. But things were different now. She was ready to trust, be a part of something bigger, and give up some control. And she had two new friends in Glinda and Cermet.

"Ebony," Aunt Gladys said with a soft knock on her bedroom door.

"May we come in?" asked Aunt Gertrude.

"Sure," Ebony said.

She dangled her legs off the cushions of her window seat as her aunts entered.

Aunt Gladys stretched out her arm to reveal a pile of runes resting in her palm. "Protection for you and your friends."

Ebony pushed off her cushion. "Runes?"

"Blessing charms of sorts," said Aunt Gladys. "A rune of magick to aid you during the games. Fehu is the rune of fulfillment. No matter what battle you encounter, think about what would bring you contentment and peace, and it shall be yours."

"What your aunt is trying to say is wear these during the games, today, and you're good." Gertrude clamped the metal loop of the rune to Ebony's apprentice medallion like one would on a charm bracelet. "She's also saying that you get out of things what effort you put into them."

Gladys snorted. "Toe-may-toe, toe-mah-toe."

"Sister, did you make a funny?" Gertrude beamed.

"These are for your friends." Gladys set the other blessing charms on Ebony's bed.

Ebony clamped her hand around her medallion and over the rune. The etched out Fehu symbol pressed into her palm. She knew what she had to do.

Elli freed the train of her golden gown from between two grave markers and circled the backside of an onyx crypt. She patted the undead crow perched on her forearm. With her other arm, she welcomed the boy Lance.

No, he was no longer a boy or a mere shadow of himself, but a maelstrom of muscle and strength, brawn and glory. He would win back her rightful place in the hierarchy of the gods. Ragged breath exhaled from his mouth, nostrils flaring.

"Shh . . ." she soothed him.

"I do . . . don't want to do this," he growled.

"You'll get over it," Elli said and thought *Because you won't remember them.* She tittered. Again, she was having too much fun.

She whirled her finger in the air. Her enchanted ring flared to life, gemstone aglow as she drew on energy from the dead. Ghosts nearest her stirred. Ghostly palms pushed against the earth and laden feet scuffed the ground to stand. A gathering of ghost zombies surrounded them.

Elli reached for a wooden bowl and dipped her fingers inside. "This is why you shall be made more unique than your ancestor. My one-man army of the dead and the flesh, needing to rely on no one. You will shift pawns on the board like the whirl of my favorite hurricane."

At that, the wind whistled, and dense clouds swirled into a twister above Dead Alley.

"*Vertu sterkur vindur, sviksemi, og hefnd, Folket Fra Nord!*" she shouted the spell above the wind and looped a necklace ordained in bones, fur, and elk antlers over Lance's head.

He tipped his head back. Tendons in his neck strained. He rolled his shoulders, head shaking his lengthening hair as he stepped away.

The boy resisted her. Had she underestimated her strength and the dense energy from the undead? Or the bond of his wavering friendship with the two misfits? She needed more energy but drawing on too much energy from the dead would alert Hela in the Underworld. Elli had made that mistake a few times and was still shocked Hela hadn't figured out it was her.

The circle closed around Lance. It was time to share his truth. Were there risks? Sure, but this game had been played for eons of chaos and energy was energy with no end, only redistribution. Death, birth. Death, birth. Or was it birth and then death? She could never remember.

Chapter

thirty-seven

Ullr Games

Refreshment tables abutted the field at the back of the school; the right side sported a large obstacle course, while the left looked like a patchwork-quilt of earthy squares. A crow waddled on top of a fountain centered inside a flower garden. Two more cawed from a nearby tree.

Fleishman reached to shift the strap of Nigel's cage on his shoulder that wasn't there for the millionth time. He sighed.

"Nigel will be okay," Ebony said.

"I know, it's just weird being without him."

Although Dad was back, the time she'd spent without him had taught her that. "You'll see him, again."

Fleishman nodded. "Anyway, are we ready for this?"

Ebony tapped the healing petal inside the pouch of her satchel. "I trust you."

Fleishman's face warmed with a smile.

Njord and Motley students shuffled across metal bleachers. Erickson starred up at Ebony from two rows down. Dark half-moons crested his cheeks and his shoulders slouched. He didn't look so good. With more important things on her mind, like stopping Elli, she decided to save that observation for later.

Ebony trailed Fleishman to the next bleacher. She quickly realized there was no more room for her in this row. Mentor Blu motioned for Ebony to start down the next bleacher, moving her to the opposite end of where Fleishman was sitting.

Fried cheese curds.

Headmistress Regina wobbled across a raised platform, where she met Dad. Although he still looked tired, it was good to see him up there and in charge, again. She wasn't sure why Dean Bile still had to be there. He was just Njord's headmaster. Who cared?

Unlike the six robe-wearing Motley mentors and Njord elders seated on the platform, Dean Bile wore a stuffy black suit. A crystal dangled from a thin leather strap that hung around his neck and over his button-up shirt. He casually tucked his hand in the front pocket of his dress pants. Ebony chewed her bottom lip, tasting her blueberry lip gloss.

"Welcome, everyone." Bat-Face held out her arms. "Firstly, as you can all see, Overseer Charmed has returned from his trip abroad."

"Some trip," Cermet tipped backward from the other end of the bleachers to mouth to Ebony.

She brushed him off. No one was supposed to suspect her father had taken anything other than a trip.

"Today," Bat-Face continued, "Motley and Njord Academy celebrate the first joint Raidho-Tiwaz, a challenge of honor, justice, leadership, and evolution, named in honor of a great bowman, warrior, and above all, athlete – Ullr of the Aesir gods," she said as Seronious Bile lifted a beautiful wooden bow into the air.

More crows drifted to land on picnic tables. Bat-Face swung her square head toward Dad, then toward Seronious. What was it with people and their silent conversations, lately?

"And the winning school will keep possession of the bow until the next games," Bat-Face finished. "Now, if our combined member panel would select the obstacle course participants, we can begin the games."

The first names were called, but Ebony was distracted by a vacant space rippling near the right side of the platform; it didn't look like a door. She kept her attention on the form until it vanished among a tall row of shrubs. The final two students were chosen. Not Ebony.

Thanks be to cheese.

Simple tasks were scattered throughout the course. Participants were instructed to physically alter the object or use a skill from their luminary or sensory bag to complete the task. Their battle magick training made sense, especially because the Njord kids relied on magick far more than physical manipulation.

The rippled form reappeared and softened into a silhouette. Darkness seeped from its outline, filling limbs and bleeding to its center.

"Fleish," Ebony spat a whisper to the other end of the bleachers.

"Quiet please," Mentor Denarious said from somewhere next to the bleachers.

She mentally growled and waited for him to move along. "Fleish!" she said and mouthed *There's something by the trees* when he glanced over his shoulder.

Bat-Face hobbled down the platform steps to stand in

front of the braided rope sectioning off the center of the field. The long pendant she wore bounced against her chest. A crystal. All the mentors, elders, and even her father wore identical crystals. Maybe her aunts made these.

The headmistress paused as a murder of crows flew overhead. They circled above them for what felt like forever, eventually settling on the fountain.

"Mentors and elders," Bat-face continued, "it's time to choose your field challenge four-member teams."

Njord chose their team first. Ebony recognized Aurelia from the dance and Marcus, the boy at the drink table. She didn't know the other two students, but they were taller, so she figured they were eighth graders.

Motley began with Magdalen Priest, which Ebony thought was a fabulous choice. Kids found her strange, but she knew tons about ghosting and stuff; plus, strange was cool. Clint was next. Mentor Lyn approached the bleachers and smirked.

"Ebony Charmed," she said.

Bat-Face questioned Lyn's choice, saying a more physically apt student might prove better; Ebony couldn't argue that point. She looked to Dad for advice, but Mom beat him to it, interrupting and ending the discussion. Ebony's heart squished more for her mother as she stepped off the last bleacher. Mom kept her word to trust in Ebony. She hoped she never pushed Mom love away again. At the sound of Cermet's name, Ebony stepped sideways to let him join Motley's team.

Squares representing wood, gravel, water, slate, and patches of sod were arranged in multiple shapes, sizes, and patterns across the field. A cross between a giant chessboard and the game *Sorry!* Some squares had the rune of a discipline, while others were blank. Mentors and elders lined the borders of the field-board, acting as referees, while the two teams of students gathered at opposite ends.

"The rules are simple," Dean Bile said. "Teams will battle for squares on the board using their skills and knowledge of magick and runes. Win a square, and it lights up with your team color. You may overturn a lit square or a row of squares by bordering them as well. First team to light up a continuous row, column, or diagonal line of squares across the board wins."

Clint and Aurelia were chosen to spar energy for first turn. They faced each other, palms held up. Clint tipped his chin down at their hands. Aurelia chanted. Within ten seconds a tiny orange flame flickered over Aurelia's palm. Njord won first turn.

A Njord boy rolled a big lop-sided dice. It landed on a square with the air symbol, showing celestial objects. He pressed his hands together and pulled them apart to create a teeny wind tunnel; it collapsed instantly. The crowd clapped as his square lit up Njord green, winning a Hagalaz rune.

Clint stepped up to take his turn. Instead of rolling the block, he tapped his fingers at his temples, choosing a square on his own. He stared intently at a square representing gravel two rows from Njord's lit square. The square exploded with soil and rocks, lighting up Motley blue. A physical Uruz rune win was announced. Motley students cheered.

Two crows landed next to the bleachers. Mentor Blu shooed them away.

The next few turns resulted in two Njord and Motley gains each and one Njord steal. Aurelia from Njord rolled the block, and it landed on a square with foliage. The square aligned with a weather square already won by Njord. Hands in front of her, Aurelia vogued with her fingers. Specks of light flashed from the tips. She pushed her palms away from her body, guiding them over her rolled square. An incantation spilled from her mouth, and fog bloomed over the specks; they fell to the Hagalaz rune square as it lit up Njord green.

Ebony's lips parted. The specks turned umber, bronze, burnt-orange and floated weightlessly. Orange and weightless – flower petals.

Aurelia flipped her hands over, her face full of surprise, even fear. Ebony didn't know much about this girl, but from meeting her at Njord's dance she was sure Aurelia didn't scare easily. Had she conjured the floating petals? Ebony scanned the crowd. Or had someone else?

"It's your turn, Miss Charmed." Bat-Face's voice boomed.

Ebony shuffled the dice between her hands. The Algiz square aligned with five Njord occupied squares and one blank in between. Winning that square put the Njord and blank squares between two Motley squares. The Njord squares would have to turn over to Motley, which would light the field-board for Motley from one side to the other.

Crows squawked from the boneyard. Spiritual energy amped up like she'd felt in Dead Alley. Ebony didn't see Elli yet but couldn't imagine her not showing up.

She rubbed at her rune tattoos and lifted her chin to get a better look at the floating petals. They lifted higher in response to her movement, and Njord's green light flickered. The crowd gasped.

"Uh." Cermet leaned into Ebony. "I see Lance."

Ebony snapped her head to the side, breaking her connection with Njord's squares.

Lance stood at the opposite end of the field-board. The muscles and manly statue present after he astral projected back into his body were gone, his hair back to its wavy russet color. A jean jacket replaced his sweatshirt, only torn like he'd been in a fight. Multi-colored bruises shadowed one eye; the other left no doubt he was staring at her. His jaw clenched; fingers twitchy at his sides. And a necklace dangled mid-chest. Had he AP'd out of his body or was this a trick?

"We don't have all day," Bat-Face said.

Ebony raised her hands, drawing on energy from nearby trees. It swathed over her tattoos; the itch instantly unbearable. Green light from the Njord squares sputtered.

"Ebony," Cermet said softly.

"I'm concentrating."

"But, Ebony—" He tugged on her.

She pivoted to find Lance a foot from her, and Mentor Wizner walking toward her.

Lance mouthed voiceless words. His ghost skin glistened in sweat.

"How did you get away from Elli?" Ebony asked, barely clinging to her connection with the energy.

Lance's face contorted in pain, and his image blinked in and out. He gripped onto Ebony's hands and slammed them down in front of her like she slapped a tabletop. The petals smashed against the square, exploding. The Njord squares cleared, all squares lighting up Motley blue. Lance vanished.

The Motley crowd roared, and students from both schools spilled from the bleachers. A breeze stirred the treetops inside Dead Alley. Plumes of black mist shot up between them.

"Look!" Cermet whispered, as a dark silhouette congealed into an aged woman with ashen hair – Elli. "Do you see her ring?" Cermet asked.

"Not yet, but I'm sure she has it," she said. "Do you have any idea where Lance could have gone?"

Thunder rumbled beneath their feet, preventing Cermet's answer. Small sink holes scattered across the field. Crows burst up from the holes and into the air, sprinkling soil down.

Fleishman jumped off his bleacher and reached up to help Glinda. Ebony's mother was guiding Dad off the platform.

Erickson stood near the tables, his face red with rage, as he watched Elli transform into her youthful self.

A hefty man strutted to her side, face and body thinning as he did. His sinister grin ignited his charcoal-colored eyes; they flared a violent blue. His skin scrunched up on his now-slender cheekbones. The suit jacket he wore faded, replaced by his vintage gray vest; a gold chain dangled from his breast pocket as did his brass goggles from his belt. Short, dark tangles lengthened to tap his shoulders, framing his pale face. And his signature derby cap rolled off his head.

"Wait, that was George from the cemetery," Cermet said. "Who's it now?"

"Daenir." The name felt dirty on Ebony's tongue.

At Ebony saying his name, Daenir changed form, again. She and Cermet watched his human skin flake away. Ivory cords of tendons and muscle coiled his limbs. A sheen of armor locked onto his torso, shins, and feet, all while a sheet of darkness sprouted from his back to form a ragged cape.

"You mean—"

"Yes." Ebony snipped Cermet's words. "The dark elf that took Lance's body."

Motley had looked everywhere for him, and he'd been under their noses all this time. He'd invaded the boneyard. Her boneyard. Fear and insecure trust melted away leaving righteous anger in its wake.

Daenir handed Elli a bottle. Stained in blues, greens, and purples, the bottle held an aura all its own; the edges pulsed, inhaling and exhaling. A living vessel of Nature's atrocities.

She tucked it beneath her gold breastplate at the waist and stretched her arms in front of her, fingers flicking once. Soil at her feet percolated. Pebbles and dirt bubbled to a boil until it erupted, pulling a girl from beneath the ground. Knotted tree roots loosened from the girl's torso, arms. They crumbled to her feet and seeped back below. Dirt blew off her cheeks as she ambled bare-footed to Lance, who'd reappeared.

He flinched at the girl's touch. Changing expressions marred his face – a struggle with something Ebony couldn't see. He rolled his shoulders and angled his face in Ebony's direction, his eyes flaming yellow. Was he trying to tell her something?

"*Vertu farin!*" Elli directed toward a group of Motley mentors, exploding the crystal pendants they wore to dust.

Elli slinked up to Lance's other side and combed her fingers through his hair. His body twitched; his ghostly silhouette bloated. Ebony backed up, matching her steps with Elli's forward ones.

"Borga skuldin skuldaði mér!" Elli chanted to the rising wind, and Lance's ghost jerked and thrust high through the air, landing somewhere in Dead Alley.

A torrential downpour of orange petals showered the area. No longer simple flower petals, but windows of a nightmare, portals showing Yggdrasil creatures at all stages of ghostdom dripping in rotting flesh all zombie-eyed.

Daenir spun away from them, his focus on Erickson, who didn't notice Daenir marching at him. Ebony tensed. Something was wrong, especially that she felt Erickson needed her protection.

The breastplate of gold shifted at Elli's waistline as she walked. It brushed against her pants, rumpling the fabric. Netted cloth flowed over her arms to her wrists; those were circled in bracelets dangling in bracteates. She picked up one of the crows sidling along the thick rim of the fountain. Ebony froze in place as she spotted Elli's ring on her finger. It ignited. The needle protruded from the ring, and Elli plunged it through the torso of the crow.

Mist Gypsies dove from the sky, plucking students off the ground.

CHAPTER

THIRTY-EIGHT

Frankenstein Crows

All chaos broke loose.

Elli set the crow down. Hollow bones hardened, and feathers faded to gray. The infected crow pecked at two black crows that in turn pecked at others. The first crow hobbled into the crowd of stampeding students; it got trampled.

A volcano of blackness collected over Dead Alley. The mass shifted. Crows darted toward the school, swerving in between Mist Gypsies. Those on the large fountain lifted in the dying light of the day. Still more crows scattered over the field and obstacle course, pecking at anything that moved. Kids shrieked as jagged beaks pierced skin.

A Mist Gypsy dropped two boys to the ground and reached for a girl. Dark mist slithered out the arm of its robe.

Metal fingers clicking with gadgets gripped the girl's skinny neck. She batted at the grip, wriggled and wailed, but she couldn't break free. Tipping her face closer, the creature inhaled. Swirls of thick breath pulled from the girl's lungs until a glowing orb floated out between her lips. It disappeared beneath the creatures hooded robe.

Holy rotten cheese!

The girl's hoarse cry dwindled. A dull glaze rolled across her face.

"It took her shade," Cermet said.

One boy limped, dragging a leg behind him. The kid next to him bobbled his head like it was loose and about to fall off. Dazed and confused, their expressions the same as the girl's.

Mentor Nesbitt had said Mist Gypsies were soul eaters, but he'd left out where that didn't kill the person. It left them as zombified as ghost zombies.

Ebony spotted Erickson, feet dangling off the ground, the neck of his shirt held in Daenir's hands. Erickson was about as trustworthy as a fire giant with a match, but he needed help. In this case, Ebony didn't have to trust him, just herself. "Let's go," she said to Cermet, and they raced in his direction.

Mentor Denarious darted by Fleishman and Glinda, who were crouched next to the fountain, and lunged at Daenir. The dark elf dropped Erickson to avoid Denarious' energy punch, but he took a hard blow in the leg from Mentor Lyn and her club. Mom and Dad were ushering some students to safety.

Ebony and Cermet helped Fleishman and Glinda drag Erickson out of harm's way. His blond hair stuck to his sweaty face.

"Go away," he said weakly.

"You need help" she said.

He pushed up on his elbows, trying to stand. "What I

need is Abigail, the girl from the ground. She's a slave to the woman in exchange for protection of her father's bones. They were lost when Daenir breached Dead Alley and broke that bottle."

Pottle's bones. "How do you know this?" Ebony asked.

"Because I do." He tried to yell; his breathing labored. "I channeled her at school."

Ebony had been right.

A loud roar swept over the field as Elli's ring throbbed with colors, dribbling emerald gemstones into her other hand.

Lance bolted into view from the boneyard and toward the frenzied crowd. Dreadlocks of chestnut and charcoal swayed down his back of taut muscle. His tanned skin glistened in runes running along his arms, thighs, back, and chest. A fur pelt strapped around his waist, and he wore fur boots on his feet. They kind of reminded Ebony of the bulky boots she wore when Dad took her snowmobiling. Bone fragments threaded a chain around his neck.

"He's back with his body," Fleishman said.

"*Vera af eðli þínu!*" Elli shouted and blew greenish mist from the stones.

Berserker Lance howled and dropped low, punching both fists into the ground. Two fountains of earth exploded and spread debris. Sonic waves of green mist stalled in the air then shot like a bullet over the human crowd. The pandemonium of students slowed, movements lethargic, sleepy. Some crumbled to the ground. The four mulisha members fell to their knees next to Erickson.

The boneyard archway illuminated in runes and sigils, and a hard gust whisked over the field from Dead Alley. A stone wall at the back crumbled, creating an entrance where leaves, twigs, and grass swirled.

"A vortex!" Fleishman shouted.

And ghost zombies poured out.

"Did you activate them?" Glinda asked.

"No," Ebony said.

"It's Lance as berserker." Fleishman frowned, his freckles droopy. "It's always been the berserker."

Raspy snarls echoed across the field. Garmr and his wolf-dogs charged out of the hole in Dead Alley. Berserker Lance smashed the axe in his hand into a picnic table and ghost zombies gathered behind him. He stalked the five kids.

"Lance, it's Ebony and Fleishman," she said. "You have to remember."

Sleep-ridden students trudged for the school. A few immune kids rushed by; their parents probably made them wear protective runes, too.

"Look!" One pointed. "It's Yggdrasil."

The sky opened above the field. Serpents flew between constellations, nine moons, and gossamers of energy. Only the serpents looked strange. Their scales had paled to normal colors, and they breathed frigid ice instead of fire. None breached the opening; at least not yet, but the vortex forming above Dead Alley strengthened.

It rained orange petals and snowflake flurries.

"Fimbulvetr," Erickson whispered.

A ghost zombie barreled past Berserker Lance, mouth open in a shrill.

Ebony raised her arms over Erickson in protection. Light flared from her bindrune tattoo.

The ghost zombie's shrill turned tortured soul as it shook and melted into oblivion. Berserker Lance stopped dead in his tracks.

"You fried it," Cermet said.

"I didn't mean to!" she yelled.

Fleishman gripped her wrist. "Your bindrune doesn't activate them. It protects the living, unblemished, and independent spirit."

Of course, the grimoire.

Uneven thuds crashed down next to her. To Ebony's shock, Asmund's face of vapor and Poe's human-likeness stared at her.

"We've got this," Asmund said in his throaty voice and sped for Berserker Lance.

"Don't hurt him!" Ebony screamed.

"We'll do our best to contain him," Poe said. "But you must get that ring."

Ebony liked Goths, now.

Mentor Nesbitt and Wizner drew runes, writing wards and spells in the air; the light marking their sketches faded. Mom and Mentor Blu chanted, and Mentors Denarious and Lyn battled Daenir. Mentors who'd lost their crystals slowed or succumbed to the greenish mist, asleep. But the crystal-wearing Njord elders were busy herding their students away, more worried about themselves.

Poe lassoed a stream of his bright energy around Berserker Lance's axe. Asmund landed hefty kicks to the pack of wolf-dogs that joined the fight.

Flying horses with female warriors emptied out the sky portal to Yggdrasil.

"Valkyries!" Fleishman yelled.

Mist Gypsies scrambled to abduct more students.

Elli called on Garmr and uncorked her bottle. Clouds collected above the vortex, and winds roared, sweeping at her dress. The bangles of bracteates on her wrist chimed together. One broke free, tumbling down the fabric and rolling away. Abigail crept low and reached for the shiny piece. Elli flicked her wrist, tossing Abigail to the side.

Erickson wobbled, trying to stand. Ebony steadied him, but he jerked away and ran to Abigail.

Berserker Lance flexed his hands into fists of fury, and the ghost zombies bumped into each other. His glare fixed on Erickson and Abigail.

Loud grunts sounded from those downed by Mist Gypsies. Ebony and Fleishman faced the wall of fallen students, arms bent at strange angles pushing their bodies off the ground. Shoulders hung unevenly and eyes dead to thought. Exposed skin grayed, black squiggles surfacing like fat veins. They moved forward.

"We should go," Glinda said.

The zombified kids reached for them and shrieked.

"Like now!" Cermet linked an arm with Glinda.

The wind raged against all that wasn't tied down. The fountain shook. Pieces flecked off and tumbled into the vortex. Refreshments spilled onto the ground as two wolf-dogs slammed into the long tables. Plates and cups lifted into the revolving air. Erickson clung to a bleacher, reaching his hand out to Abigail.

Crows gathered into a blackish cloud above them. The mass compressed. Ebony spotted Berserker Lance shed Asmund off his back.

It was now or never. Ebony sprinted toward Elli.

Fleishman ran alongside her, but Glinda and Cermet tripped on sleeping bodies, slowing them down. Ebony skidded along a slope in the land and fell.

The first wave of crows reached her at top speed. She shrank, tucking her face into her knees. Their screeches clawed invisible scars down her limbs. Her torso shook from the wind the birds created. They spun too fast.

Ebony was frozen in place, waiting to get eaten by birds. Not a fire giant or a jagged-toothed dark elf. Not by the fiercest serpent in Yggdrasil, who would use her bones to file its seriated claws. Nothing monstrous or hero-worthy. Death would take her by a bunch of cockamamie birds.

The past few weeks flashed through her mind. Fleishman might have been terrified of pretty much everything, but he wouldn't give up on her. She trusted him.

Wings flapped as one section of crows moved into a

linear formation. Beaks pecked the air. Hollow-boned bodies twirled in a dance only they understood. One weaved in, while another threaded out. Ebony's name muffled through the tornado of birds. She felt Fleishman's arm lock with hers, and he tugged her to stand. Lifeless feathers landed at their feet.

The mass of feathers stretched like a body first waking in the morning. The birds were no longer single, but a true community woven into one body.

Twine of blackish oil coiled into a skeleton of chrome and onyx. A torso of wings tightened into a chest of muscle. Silky feathers twisted into a line of sinew from both sides of the torso. Each solidified at the ends and elongated into hands and chubby fingers, while two pillars of feathers exploded from its base, forming legs that slammed a pair of square feet against the hallowed ground. Empty eye sockets filled with a penetrating glow. A mouth gleaming with serrated teeth pulled together the last bones of a skull. A lightning bolt shot across one side of the dark forehead, etching an illuminated stitch of green.

Armor of metal and leather protruded from the inside of the creature, and a choker of bolts spun around the thick neck, making Ebony sure this was some sick Halloween joke where Frankenstein got the better of the townsfolk.

The Frankenstein of feathers and beaks bent its poultry knees and leaned toward Ebony. It growled, *"Borga skuldirnar,"* with the voice of something dark rising from its belly.

Fleishman yanked her so hard that she crashed into him, knocking them down. As Ebony pushed off his chest, Elli ambled beneath the Frankenstein beast to Berserker Lance.

"Like what I've done with my pawn? He's magnificent, isn't he?" A devilish smirk exploded on Elli's face, and she circled Ebony and Fleishman. "Too bad you won't fulfill your destinies because taking you will pay off many debts owed—"

"I know what they did to you," Ebony interrupted. "You never tried to hurt Balder."

Shock extinguished the tension in Elli's face replacing it with soft reflection and longing Ebony recognized from missing her father.

"I know what it's like to trust people and have them let you down," Ebony said, still on the ground. "I'm sorry they did that to you."

The nature goddess gazed down at her finger ring.

"It doesn't have to be this way," Ebony said. "You have a choice."

A hollow expression hardened Elli's posture. "And I choose to trust in myself alone." To the feathered beast, *Gera það.*

Feathers whooshed as the beast swept its huge hand beneath Ebony and Fleishman.

"Lance!" Ebony bellowed. "It's me. Please remember."

The Frankenstein creature closed its grip around the two. Ebony tried to expand her lungs, but the pressure was too much. A meek whimper slipped out between Fleishman's lips. Ebony coughed, each breath shorter than the last until the grip loosened.

Through fuzzy vision, Ebony watched Berserker Lance pry the feathery fingers open. Ebony and Fleishman rolled onto the ground.

Elli pressed her palms on Berserker Lance's cheeks, forcing him to face her. "Your friend is correct. You should remember. *Mundu.*" Her voice sang the last word.

Berserker Lance shook his head. His face flinched, jaw clenching, but recognition resonated in his eyes.

"Yes, my boy. It is true," Elli said. "Your memories do not lie, and neither do I. You've never been human. Not fully. Your birth father was of the Watchers, a loyal light elf.

Your mother a human, who sadly died giving birth to you. Your father's grief over her loss was enough to sway him to the dark side."

Dark side? That Njord kid with the bangs tipped blond said that to Marcus.

"He turned dark elf under Daenir," Elli continued. "We've prepared you for this."

Berserker Lance roared and punched a hole through the nearest tree. He tore limbs off its trunk. His skin sheened red like the wraiths Ebony had studied.

Elli raised one hand, and the Frankenstein creature lifted its mighty leg over Ebony and Fleishman. Ebony twisted toward Fleishman and locked onto the fear in his face, the towering giant behind her reflecting off his eyes.

"Lance!" Ebony yelled and spit into her palm – trusting, giving up control – and offered it to him. "Motley Mulisha members stick together." She flipped on her back, forearms crossing her forehead, the beast's feathery foot inches from her face. She shouted, "Leave here!"

Her original tattoo, the one she remembered meant peace, pulsed in sapphire light that speared the beast in the foot. It hobbled backward over Berserker Lance, who axed it in the knee. The creature bellowed a collective caw that seemed to go on forever.

"You remember," Ebony said, looking up at Berserker Lance.

"*Borga skuldirnar*," Elli commanded the beast. To Lance, "*Þú ert minn!*"

The necklace of bone around Lance's neck lit in a greenish hew. He backed away and clawed at it, and Ebony begged Elli to stop. The fur around his waist and legs bristled. Tendons strained in his neck, and tension gripped the muscles of his face. He roared.

"It's the bones in the necklace," Fleishman said. "Buy me time to MM it."

Ebony rolled off Fleishman, and he popped up on his knees.

The Frankenstein beast steadied itself, glowing eye sockets turned back to Ebony.

Fleishman pinched fingers of both his hands together and pulled them apart; energy collected between them. The bones separated.

The Frankenstein beast lunged at Ebony.

"I said leave!" she cried, thrusting her arms in front of her to draw on nearby energy.

The beast recoiled and shook its crow-ridden head. The bolts on its neck dimmed. Berserker Lance bumped into the platform. He wrenched at the necklace, spaces growing between the bones.

You get out of something what effort you put into it, Ebony remembered her aunt's words. She felt energy – natural, light, and airy – from the dead in the boneyard; she called on it.

A stronger bolt of her light pierced the midsection of the beast. It vibrated to a major tremor until it broke apart, returning to a flock of crows that flew into the sky and vanished. Berserker Lance's necklace exploded off his neck, fragments falling to the dirt; Abigail peeked out from her picnic table shelter and scurried to collect the broken bones. Berserker Lance was too busy with his sights set on Elli to notice.

Elli uncorked her bottle of keepsakes, calling upon a frigid storm. The vortex gained strength and snow fell. The scent of burning grass mingled with the freshness of wintery air.

Elli cackled, giving Berserker Lance his opening. He gripped hold of the Ullr bow, drew an arrow back, and released it. The arrow pierced the center of the bottle in her hand, shattering it into dust.

"No!" she shrieked.

The portal to Yggdrasil shrank, and her Mist Gypsies shrilled, dropping kids; some stopped mid-air and folded in on themselves until gone. Streaks of greenish mist were all they left behind.

Lance dropped the bow and wheezed as his physical body lost some mass, taking on a more teenage berserker appearance. Though no longer under Elli's control, he was still a berserker and all that came with it.

Ebony traced both runes that made up her bindrune tattoo, concentrating on their meanings.

"Reverse and awaken, reverse and awaken," she mumbled.

White light glistened from the ring on Elli's finger. Ebony chanted the words louder, and Fleishman, Mom, and other mentors joined in. Ghost zombies stilled and zombified kids woke – the decaying spots of flesh returning to both. Valkyries halted fighting and chanted, too.

Gears whined above the wind as the ring fired with life. The needle head glowed fire ember orange like melted iron ore before casting. Metal dripped, shrinking from the tip.

"What are you doing?" Fleishman broke from the chant. "You need the ring."

"But I don't," Ebony said and showed him the glowing parts of her bindrune tattoo.

"The grimoire hid Valknut within the bindrune." The surprise on Fleishman's face was all the payment Ebony would ever need. Though she appreciated his help, it was nice to have figured this one out on her own.

Elli screamed as the ring broke apart and fell off her finger. The force from the open vortex wrenched at her dress. Youth drained from her facade returning her to the personification of old age. She called on Daenir and slid on her feet to Dead Alley, dragged across the field by an unseen tether. Garmr and the wolf dogs lifted into the air, sucked into the vortex that closed with a slight blip. Daenir merely faded away.

"We lost him," Ebony growled.

One Valkyrie adorned in leather and armor stepped forward. "We were able to get a reading on their destination."

"Where?" Ebony asked.

"Valhalla."

Fleishman elbowed Ebony. "Guess that's where we're going next."

Chapter

thirty-nine

The Fallen

All the infected gathered around Ebony, even the boneyard residents. She was glad to see Keeper and his protective wards had kept them safe from any further harm.

Her bindrune tattoo glowed. The Valkyries bowed their heads. Ebony tugged the lone healing petal from her pocket and laid it on her forearm. Flakes of the petal seeped into the tattoo until it was gone.

"As the Valkyries are charged with choosing the fallen warriors and gifting them with Valknut, I choose each of you," she said and raised her arm to cast the glow over them.

Decayed flesh vanished, and shades returned to their owners, leaving all as it was before the nature goddess arrived. But Ebony was surprised to see Abigail hobbling forward.

"How are you still here?" Ebony asked.

"All I needed was this." Abigail raised her hand to reveal a braceleate between her fingers. "It's how I can break from Elli. I offer it to you, Ebony Charmed, as my next destination, and ask to stay with my father and Tanner." She opened her other hand. "These are remnants of my father's bones, the ones she strung around Lance's neck."

Old man Pottle ambled to his daughter. "Abigail," he said and wrapped his ghostly arms around her.

Ebony's throat tightened, and happiness filled her heart. She accepted the shiny coin, which she tossed to Asmund, who "poofed" with Poe into thin air. She scanned the field of Motley and Njord students cleaning up and spotted Fleishman who was listing a training regimen for Lance to learn control over his berserker side. Lance's shoulders widened, and he inched closer to Fleishman. Ebony jogged in to wedge herself between them.

"Fleishman, you're making him mad," she said. To Lance, "Relax. He's only trying to help."

Lance grumbled, the tendons of this throat tightening as he swallowed. "Sorry," he said gruffly. "I feel weird."

"That's understandable," a Valkyrie said. "You absorbed berserker traits. It will take time for you to adjust. With Ebony's advisor's guidance, we'll help train you to control your new traits."

Fleishman stood a little straighter, obviously proud this Valkyrie knew who he was.

"I can't believe you!" Erickson charged through the tiny group and shoved Ebony. "Elli was my only connection to my father." He spun from her and walked away.

Erickson didn't look any better. His father's promise to Elli was still valid like Abigail's would have been without a braceleate. The look on Fleishman's face said he'd already figured this out. Ebony upped on her toes and whispered in his ear.

"It might work," Fleishman said.

"Hey, Tanner," Ebony called. "I wonder if you'd help us with something."

"I reckon, after all you've done for us, Miss Ebony."

Ebony shared her idea with Tanner, and he agreed to help. She drew upon the life energy closest to her.

"Erickson!" she yelled.

As he turned to face her, she thrust the energy at him, stunning him still. Tanner slipped inside Erickson's body, and Erickson received him with a stuttered inhale.

"I'm inside," Tanner's voice said out of Erickson's mouth.

"Whoa . . ." Fleishman said.

Tanner raised Erickson's hands to examine them then padded them against his torso. "Dang."

Amphylis waddled nearer, confusion painting her face.

"Erickson's father made a deal with Elli and Daenir," Ebony explained. "We're hoping this will buy us time to figure out how to keep Erickson from being bound to that agreement."

Erickson's body twitched.

"I feel sad all of a sudden," Tanner said. "He didn't know about his dad, did he?"

One of the Valkyries approached Ebony. "I am Svaja. It seems that you have averted Fimbulvetr here, but I've received a report that parts of Yggdrasil have not been as fortunate."

"Fleishman, when we first got to the pillars where Lance's body was, I saw a door or portal trying to open up. Inside was a huge building with shields on the roof and tall gargoyles guarding the front. And now that I think about it, most of it was iced over."

Svaja conferred with another Valkyrie. "Sounds like

Valhalla, which is one of the places reportedly hit by a huge winter storm."

"The Hall of the Slain," Fleishman said.

"And what Fenrir said," Ebony added.

Svaja gripped the shaft of her sward. "You saw Fenrir?"

"In the boneyard," Fleishman answered.

"Then it is settled." Svaja whistled, and the Valkyries horses galloped up to them. "We will accompany you to Valhalla, where we'll meet many perils to reverse the Three Winters. Your mother will work out details of engagement with Njord Academy, while your father continues to recover."

"What'd she say?" Ebony leaned into Fleishman.

"We're going to Valhalla, it's probably going to be dangerous and cold, and your mom will duke it out here with Seronious Bile while your dad gets better," Fleishman said.

"Nicely translated, Advisor," Svaja said in her stately voice. She adjusted the sheath of her sword and mounted her horse, sweeping Fleishman up to ride with her. Fleishman released a girly cry that would have embarrassed even the Cheerio Twins. Ebony mounted a horse, joining another Valkyrie, and laughed as they galloped toward the school. Lance stomped in a light jog behind them, but not before he gave Ebony a grunt and a stiff smirk.

She smiled at the directness of Lance's actions and Fleishman's words – the plain 'ole truth of them. The whole truth freed a person to grow; Ebony knew that, now. Parts of the truth might not have been to her liking, but that didn't change that it was the truth. Leaving parts unsaid or hidden only prolonged having to deal with it. With a new sister school to live with and a wintery journey ahead of them, Ebony understood that full honesty between she, the boys, the Valkyries, and whoever would help them was a must. And she was okay with that.

But there was one truth she was still curious about –
how to master the flying horses.

She wondered if one of the Valkyries would show her.
That had to come in handy where they were going, right?

THE END

~ Yggdrasil Facts and Whatnot ~

The Nine Worlds

The Upper Worlds

Asgard – Land of the Aesir Gods
Vanaheim – Land of Vanir Gods
Midgard (Man) – Land of Man
***Bifrost** – *the bridge connecting Midgard to Asgard*

The Middle Worlds

Jotunheim – Land of the Giants
Alfheim – Land of Light Elves
Svartalfheim – Land of Dark Elves

The Lower Worlds

Nidavellier – Land of the Dwarfs
Niflheim – Land of Ice; Home of Ice Giants and Winter Dragons located to the north.
Muspelheim – Land of Fire, Home of Fire Giants and Solstice Demons located to the south.
***Helheim** – *Land of the Dead lies somewhere beneath the ground in Neflheim.*

Mythical Places

Forest of Ironwoods – a forest located east of Midgard (Earth), inhabited by troll women.

Gjallarbrua Bridge – the bridge which spans the river Gjöll in the underworld.

Healing Pond – a pond in Alfheim

Island of Lyngvi – where the wolf Fenrir was imprisoned

Lake Vänern – icy lake in Yggdrasil

Scarlet Poppy Fields – vast fields in Vanaheim

Shifting Hollow – a hidden cave somewhere in Valhalla

Three Wells of the Norse Worlds

- **Urd** – the well of fate
- **Mímisbrunnr** - the spring of wisdom
- **Hvergelmir** - the well in Niflheim from which many rivers flow

Vimur River – the greatest river in the world of Jotunheim

List of Mythical Creatures

The Ancients – Aesir and Vanir gods of Yggdrasil; numerous powers.

Berserker – ancient Norse warrior; excessive strength and anger

Dark Elves – potted skin in all shades, jagged teeth, eye color varies between black, red, and yellow; quick, agile, clever. Can appear human; pretty and handsome.

Fire Giants – large, can flame on and off, deep-throaty voice, immense strength.

Goths – part dwarf, part giant with mechanical parts; neutral party for the Afterlife

Ice Giants – similar to fire giants, except for the ice.

Light Elves – skin of ivory, olive, and tan tones; soft spoken, kind hearted, strong, intelligent.

Norns - the Graces and goddesses of Fate, who watch over and direct the fate of all the Ancients and man.

Rock Giants – extremely tall, strong, don't speak, and usually filthy.

Cast of Mythical Characters

Asmund – a Goth

Brísingamen – necklace of the Vanir goddess Freyja

Daenir – a dark elf

Delia – a light elf; friend of Ebony and Fleishman

Elli – a lesser god; old age personified

Fenrir – a god in wolf form and a son of the god Loki

Freyja – the Norse Vanir goddess of love, beauty, & war; seiðr.

Garmr – mythological dog

Hela – the Queen of the Dead; lives in Helheim and watches over the dead.

Keeper Coffer – the Boneyard's undertaker/grounds keeper

Lynheid – a dwarf; disguised as Mentor Lyn and protector of Ebony.

Nigel – Fleishman's legless lizard, which turns into an icy-armored dragon

Nidhogg – the fiercest of all the serpents of Yggdrasil.

Poe – a Goth

The Three Norns/Fates (*Ebony calls them the 3Ms):
- **Urdur** – The Past; played by Meandering.
- **Verdandi** – The Present; played by Mischief.
- **Skuld** – The Future; played by Mayhem.

Valkyrie – female warrior on a flying horse

<u>Boneyard Residents</u>

Abigail Pottle (lost daughter to Mr. Pottle)
Amphylis Margaret Moate
George Yates
Hargrave Synx
Mr. Pottle
Roger Sputtenickel
Tanner
Victoria Givens

~ Important Terms ~

Aesir – one of the two sets of gods in Norse Mythology; believed to be the younger sect.

Adjustors – create temporary fixes for physical disasters (Luminary)

Bindrunes – two runes joined together to utilize both their powers and influence

Bracteate – a gold coin in the Norse worlds

Cleaners – provide balance after a catastrophe; restore the realms to balance

Cloakers – mask nature or objects to hide something like damage. (Sensory)

Dispatchers – emergency fixers; make problems go away

Draugrs – flesh zombies

Hrár Beins, also known as **Raw Bones** – ghostly energy turned to pure chaos.

Innangard – inside the fence; civilized and ordered

Jötnar – Norse word for giants

Mist Gypsies – chaos collectors

Premonition – an event that hasn't happened yet but is seen by a person.

Regulators – negotiate between the worlds; police force

Seidr – one who guides spirits to their next destination; some foresee future

Shade – part of the soul that emanates emotions, empathy, concern

Thurisaz – a rune; sleep-poisoned

Utangard – outside the fence; uncivilized and chaos

Valknut - given to the slain warriors of Yggdrasil as a sign of respect and honor

Vanir – one of the two sets of gods in Norse Mythology; believed to be the older sect.

~GLOSSARY OF LANGUAGE~

Aftur niður – Back down

Borga skuldirnar – Pay the debt

Borga skuldin skuldaði mér – Pay the debt owed me

Dökk álfa – dark elves

Folket Fra Nord – the People of The North

Fólkvangr – A meadow, particularly the one some slain heroes go.

Etunaz – eat; to eat

Gera það – Do it!

Glundroða safnari – chaos collector

Kveðja - greetings

Leyfi henni – Leave her

Miðju miðstöðvar milli Yggdrasil og Midgard – the center of the center between Yggdrasil and Midgard

Mundu – remember

Þú ert minn – You are mine

Þú ert um það bil að verða krákubak – You're about to be crow pie!

Vaknaðu - Wake Up

Vera at elk line – be by your nature

Vertu far in – get going

Vertu hér – Stay here

Vertu kyrr – Be still

Vertu sterkur vindur, sviksemi, og hefnd, Folket Fra Nord – Be strong wind, deceit, and revenge, Folket Fra Nord

~ SChOOLS ~

Motley Junior High – original Asgard gods, who remained in Asgard to keep the peace and mingled with the "exchanged Vanir gods"

Njord Academy – original Vanir gods, who Asgard to live in Vanaheim to keep peace mingled with the "exchanged Asgard gods"

Motley Study & Mentors

Design & Enchantment Art Study – Mentor Freeman

Deadly Creatures & Relics study – Mentor Lyn (really Lynheid)

Language & Runes study – Mentor Blu

Planes & Mystical Beings study – Mentor Ursula Dufort

Ruins & Mystical Realms – Mentor Nesbitt

Recreational study – Mentor Rickman

Quantum study – Mentor Denarious

Warding Off & Readings study – Cornelia Spruce

Spirit Tracking study – Mentor Wizner

Xander Willington, Jr. – curator of the Archive; Man's counterpart to the Norns of Yggdrasil

S.A. Larsen

~ seven disciplines ~

SEVEN DISCIPLINES

DISCIPLINE	RUNE		MEANINGS *ONLY BRIEF DESCRIPTIONS
PHYSICAL	URUZ		pragmatic knowledge, manifestation, primal power, organic structuring
MENTAL	ANSUZ		mental stability, stregnth
SPIRITUAL	ALGIZ		divine plan, higher spiritual awareness; detect higher vibrations
ELEMENTAL	HAGALAZ		weather, damaging natural forces; disruption, interference, control
APOTHECARY	GEBO		all gifts a curse; cautious, sacrifice, balance
ASCETICAL	KENAZ		torch (stars), knowledge, intellect, skills and abilities; cunning
CENTURION	DAGAZ		enlightenment, unity, synthesis

Other Runes Students Use:

Inguz – protection & work
Nauthiz – determination
Eihwaz – defense motivation

~ Psychic & Celestial Skills ~

(USING NATURAL ENERGY)

SENSORY

Students with a range of psychic abilities

- **Astral Projection or AP** – can quiet body so deeply they can separate their spirit from their body for a period. *Caution: must return to body in a timely fashion.

- **Channeler** – can allow ghost/spirit to enter body and talk for them.

- **Clairvoyant** – can see the future; predict possible outcomes from what is seen, but there are many variables that play a factor so nothing is written in stone.

- **Clairaudience** – can hear or perceive sounds or words from outside sources in the spirit world.

- **Elementals (Air, Water, Fire, Wind)** – can shape and manipulate the four basic elements. Each element is an entity of its own.

- **Matter Manipulation** – can alter the state of physical matter, anything that has substance and mass. Ex: paint, break it down to water and powder; use both to create something else.

- **Medium** – can see, talk to, or touch ghosts/spirits.

- **Mind Control** – can control other's minds; make other's do things.

- **Psychic Shield** – meditations to defend spiritual

energy.

- **Pushing** – can implant thoughts into someone else's mind.
- **Telekinesis (Telekinetics)** – the ability to move and control objects with the mind.
- **Telepathy** – can read the thoughts of others; can communicate back.

LUMINARY

Students who track the stars, work with herbs, conjure potions, and draw energy from nature.

- **Auras** – life energy seen in colors swirling around a person or living entity.
- **Clairempathy** – can detect emotional resonances from other locations and times. They can also perceive emotions across species, as well as from the past, the future, the spirit world and (if strong enough) the realms of the divine.
- **Force Fields** – can harness energy from the cosmos to use as protection.
- **Clairsentience** – can sense the present, past, or future physical and emotional states of a person without using the normal five senses. Can retrieve information from houses, public buildings, outside areas, etc...All the "Clairs" are extra sensory perceptions (ESP) closely related to nature and natural energy; tapestry of life, things connected. Limitations.
- **Charmed** – can conjure spells to alter a person's reality, appearance, or nature such as the weather, foliage growth. Can also heal and guide into the spirit world – shaman.

- **Claircognizance** – is a clear knowing of something, yet one cannot prove it.
- **Clairalience** – can sense a person, entity, creature, not of this plane by sense of smell. Naturalist, as in one with nature; close.
- **Clair** – the ability to experience the taste of a substance formerly near or having a connection to a person/being/creature, but never actually touching the substance.
- **Empathic abilities** – sensitivity to others' emotions.
- **Enhanced Senses/Electromagnetism** – an altered "keenness" about cosmic energy.
- **Photokinesis** – can bend, shape, absorb, create light; shift light particles.
- **Stargazers** – track changes in the heavenly bodies

~ SPIRIT LEVELS
& RANKINGS ~

- **Unblemished** – a newly departed spirit.
- **Ghost/Spirit** – living in a cemetery close to their bones, choosing not to cross over.
- **Traveler (Reika)** – early stages of deterioration from separation from their bones: loss of memories, body slows down, seems disinterested at times, dazes. Silhouette fades briefly & faintly at times, but doesn't affect them. Returning to their bones will restore them. Wanders and can cross onto other hallow ground than where its bones are kept.
  - o Wanderers – stage 2 of Travelers: more confused, harder time to control bodily movements, more emotional. Still no outer signs of change other than fading once in a while.
  - o Shade – stage 3 of Traveler: stage 2 symptoms worsen; fading is more pronounced and doesn't return as quickly.
- **Fade** – later stages of deterioration from separation from their bones. Physical changes show. Hostile, fidgety, cross, sometimes arrogant, and forceful. Slowly changing into a Raw Bone.
  - o Next stage is distribution to numerous stages from Shades, poltergeists
- **Hrár Bein** – Raw Bones – no return, lost cause, basically waiting for (Mist Gypsies) Drifters to sweep them up and end them.

S.A. Larsen

~ bonus ~

Want to see which of the Seven Disciplines you belong to?

Take the quiz to see your assignment.

SEVEN DISCIPLINES

DISCIPLINE	RUNE		MEANINGS *ONLY BRIEF DESCRIPTIONS
PHYSICAL	URUZ	ᚢ	pragmatic knowledge, manifestation, primal power, organic structuring
MENTAL	ANSUZ	ᚨ	mental stability, stregnth
SPIRITUAL	ALGIZ	ᛉ	divine plan, higher spiritual awareness; detect higher vibrations
ELEMENTAL	HAGALAZ	ᚺ	weather, damaging natural forces; disruption, interference, control
APOTHECARY	GEBO	ᚷ	all gifts a curse; cautious, sacrifice, balance
ASCETICAL	KENAZ	ᚲ	torch (stars), knowledge, intellect, skills and abilities; cunning
CENTURION	DAGAZ	ᛞ	enlightenment, unity, synthesis

Dead Alley

Choose an answer that best fits you, but don't think about it too long. Have fun with it!

Gym is your next class. What do you do?

    1. Race to the gym. I love playing sports!

    2. Pause as my stomach drops, wondering if I have any gym clothes in my locker.

    3. Fake a headache and go see the school nurse.

My favorite kind of day is . . .

    1. Bright sunshine and lots of heat

    2. A thunderstorm

    3. Any day that doesn't include school or chores

If you were an animal, which would you be?

    1. A venomous snake

    2. A graceful gazelle

    3. A loafing buffalo

Do you look at your food as you eat it?

    1. Of course! I examine each and every bite. You never know when a fly is hovering around.

    2. Maybe before I start.

    3. Uh, nope. I gobble it up as fast as I can.

When someone in my house is sick, I . . .

    1. Help as much as I can

    2. Tell them I hope they feel better, but do my own thing

    3. Steer clear. I don't want whatever they have.

Family BBQ time. I . . .

    1. Eat fast so I can talk to everyone.

    2. Avoid pretty much everyone except a few cousins my age.

    3. I imagine aliens landing and wonder what we'd all do.

My favorite games to play are . . .

    1. Board games

    2. Video games

    3. Puzzles and word searches

Do you visit cemeteries?

    1. Sure, as long as I'm not alone.

    2. Absolutely. With all the names and dates, there are so many stories there.

    3. No, no, & NO!

You've been assigned your next test. You start studying . . .

    1. A week before

    2. A day before

    3. As I run to class, I listen to my best friend go over facts with me.

During class I . . .

    1. Take lots of notes.

    2. Listen and take notes in between my doodles.

    3. Wonder what would happen if the creepy monster poster hanging on my teacher's wall came to life.

Dead Alley

When something unexpected happens, I . . .
    1. Take a breath and figure it out
    2. Panic
    3. Run, hide, and hope it blows over.

Which Motley teacher do you like best?
    1. Mentor Nesbitt
    2. Mentor Blu
    3. Mentor Ursula

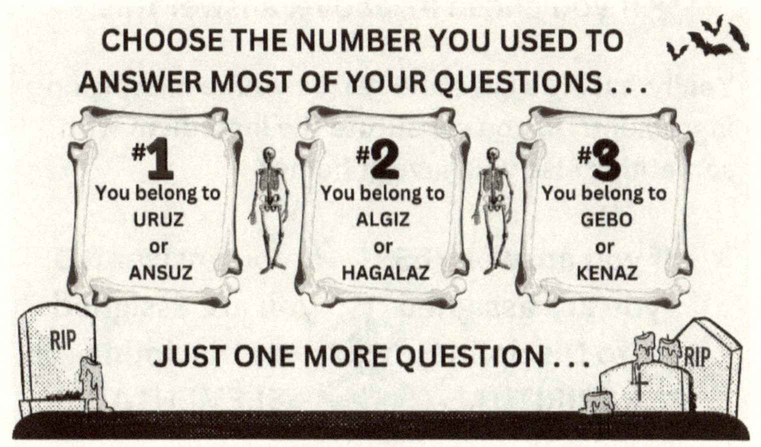

#1 If you chose #1 above, answer this:

If the gears on your bicycle stop shifting correctly, do you fix it yourself?

If you answer YES, you are assigned to Discipline PHYSICAL

If you answer NO, you are assigned to Discipline MENTAL

#2 If you chose #2 above, answer this:

You're baking a cake and realize you're missing one ingredient. Do you substitute the ingredient with something else you have at home?

If you answer YES, you are assigned to Discipline SPIRITUAL

If you answer NO, you are assigned to Discipline ELEMENTAL

#3 If you chose #3 above, answer this:

Would you stitch a deep cut on your leg by yourself at home?

If you answer YES, you are assigned to Discipline APOTHECARY

If you answer NO, you are assigned to Discipline ASCETICAL

*If you answered equally – 4 A answers, 4 B answers, 4 C answers) – then you are a rare CENTURION.
CONGRATULATIONS TO ALL!

acknowledgements

Well, you've come to the end of the book that almost never was . . .

Why, you ask?

I began writing this story about a year after *Motley Education* released and just after my YA novel, *Marked Beauty*, released – end of 2017. Fast forward eighteen months, and *Dead Alley* was in the hands of my previous MG publisher. The manuscript needed some rewrites, but before I could complete those my publisher closed its doors. Thus, the book died to future readers and in my heart.

But something miraculous happened. My YA publisher offered to publish *Motley* as a second edition and take on my recently departed manuscript sequel. My writer veins flowed with excitement as we worked on the continuation of Ebony and Fleishman's story. A release date of December 2020 was set, but with the pandemic and its effects in our personal lives, as a team we decided to postpone the book's release. This book has been doing the Deadman's crawl for some time. But it's finally here, and there are many who deserve my sincere gratitude . . .

To God, for His all-encompassing love and care of me and my family. My teeny heart belongs to Him.

My Publisher and the entire Ellysian Press team & author family, for always believing in Ebony and Fleishman's adventures and encouraging me to keep believing, too.

Writer friends Sharon Mayhew and Kristin Smith, my critique group of Abbi Cortez, Lisa Perron, Shell Jewell, and the entire #SpookyMG crew over at spookymiddlegrade.com, especially our original members Kim Ventrella, Samantha Clark, David Neilson, Lisa

Schmid, Sarah Cannon, Janet Fox, Victoria Piontex, Cynthia Reeg, & Jonathan Rosen (Former members: Patrick Moody & Lindsay Currie). Your talent, spooky humor, and friendship have been invaluable to me.

My hometown friends, who weathered the craziness of the pandemic with me in humor and lots of sunset cruises on the "Deathstar" on China Lake, your devotion to our friend family is refreshing and a blessing in this life. And to my special friend Tammey Quirion, our countless conversations bring joy to my heart.

All #KidLit Book Heroes out there who fight faithfully to get books into the hands of students and young readers, who support authors at book signings and virtual school visits, and who read and review our work, thank you!

To my family: my parents who continue their example of "finishing the good race," my children – Joshua, Jacob, Katelynn, and Caleb – your resilience, compassion, faith, integrity, and commitment to family are the building blocks that strengthen the foundation your father and I have built. And to my husband, Arthur, I wouldn't want to do this life thing with anyone else.

about the author

Photo by Kelly J. Smith Photography

S.A. Larsen is the award-winning author of young adult and middle grade books. She loves to explore the sojourn of life, faith, and becoming who we're meant to be through stories of adventure and mystery that challenge the mind, heart, and soul. She lives in the land of lobsters and snowy winters with her husband, four children, two German Shepherds, and a trio of cats.

Visit her cyber home at **www.salarsenbooks.com** where she stores all sorts of bookish goodies, and helpful links for teens/tweens and their parents or guardians. Feel free to leave her a friendly note. She'd love that!

She tweets from @SA_Larsen, shares on Instagram: @sa.larsen, and does most of her spookiness over at **www.spookymiddlegrade.com**, brewing up all sorts of creepy ideas with a group of #SpookyMG authors. Stop by for a visit . . . if you dare.

about ellysian press

Ellysian Press is dedicated to putting out quality books in the following genres:

Science Fiction

Fantasy

Paranormal

Horror

Paranormal Romance

Young Adult in all of the above genres

To find other Ellysian Press books, please visit our **website**:

http://www.ellysianpress.com/